MRS. HUDSON
INVESTIGATES

Seven stories by Susan Knight

Paperback ISBN 978-1-78705-484-4
ePub ISBN 978-1-78705-485-1
PDF ISBN 978-1-78705-486-8

Published in the UK by
MX Publishing
335 Princess Park Manor,
Royal Drive, London, N11
3GX
www.mxpublishing.com

Cover design by Brian Belanger

For Ann O'Kelly, loyal reader and encouraging friend

Contents

Mrs. Hudson and the Smiling Man

What was I supposed to do, the two gentlemen being away? The lady was in such a state and, besides, she refused point-blank to take no for an answer. I felt it incumbent on me under the circumstances to do my best and, if I say so myself, did not manage too badly in the end. Mr. H said not a word about it when he heard. Just asked for his smoking jacket and a pipe. The doctor, now, when I asked could he write up the case the way he did for Mr. H, just laughed and patted me on the shoulder.

So, there you are, I said to myself, Martha, you are on your own here. Either you do the penning of it or no one will and though I am not much of a one for fine words, I intend to try and set it down as it happened and hope for the best.

It was a foggy morning in November and, as I said, the two gentlemen were away out of the city, no doubt getting to the bottom of some new mystery. I was about my usual chores, mightily vexed, it has to be said with the new scullery maid, Phoebe, a gormless country girl of thirteen years, who like as not had never washed a plate in her life before, so many getting broke in the attempt that I had her polishing the silverware, more polish on her hands and nose and forehead and apron than ever on the spoons and forks.

Suddenly there was such a hammering and a banging on the front door as caused us to start even there down in the kitchen, Phoebe, dropping all the silverware on the floor in her agitation, added to the noise and confusion. I hurried to the door, leaving the foolish maid with a stern injunction to recover the spoons and forks and restore them to a sparkling condition, she sobbing betimes.

The impatient visitor turned out to be a young lady, but one in such a state as to have almost lost her ladylikeness (if such a word there be).

"I need to see Mr. Sherlock Holmes this very instant," said she, attempting to stride past me into the hall without so much as a by your leave.

"That, I am afraid, is an impossibility," quoth I, barring the way.

She flashed dark eyes at me then, and muttered something under her breath that sounded like "impertinent vixen," although I might have been mistaken, her voice being so low. I would then have shut the door in her face only that the young lady seemed truly distressed.

"Mr. Holmes and Dr. Watson are away from London at the moment," I explained further, "and I have not an inkling as to when they will be back."

My words, though a simple statement of fact, affected the young lady so hard that she sank in a swoon on the doorstep. I called to Clara, my housemaid, to assist me and together we raised up the visitor and brought her into my parlour, sitting her in my favourite chair by the fire. I then bade Clara fetch a weak concoction of brandy and water and meanwhile attended the young lady with my sal volatile. This soon revived her. She sat up straight, looked around at what I pride myself to be as neat a little room as one might wish for, and finally let those flashing dark eyes alight upon me.

"Away," she said, picking up on my last words to her. "They are away, you say. Alas, what am I to do?"

At that moment, Clara arrived with the brandy and water. The young lady swallowed it in a single draught and coughed not once, indicating to me that, lady or no, she was not completely unaccustomed to strong spirits. She sat up straighter then and addressed me as follows.

"Forgive me, ma'am, for my impetuous assault on your charming abode but... what is your name..."

I told her.

"Mrs. Hudson," said she. "I am at my wit's end and if someone doesn't help me, I fear it may soon be all over for my poor grandfather."

"I see that you came here in a great hurry from home and from the railway station too," said I.

"Yes, indeed," she replied. Then looked at me closely. "How can you tell?"

I have not been Mr. H's landlady for so long without picking up a little on his powers of observation.

"Your hat is askew upon your head. Your hair looks barely fashioned. Your blouse is buttoned up all wrong. You are wearing odd stockings and you are still clutching a return ticket to... well, that I cannot tell you, though no doubt Mr. H would have deduced it from the nature of the mud on your shoes."

"Astounding," she said. "Yes indeed. After what happened over the past two days and the way it has affected my grandfather, I made all haste to catch the early train from N to Marylebone station and then ran all the way here without a thought for my appearance. I must beg your forgiveness."

Despite the untidiness of her dress, before me sat a young woman of considerable beauty. Indeed, the rush through the cold morning had brought a fine rosiness to the porcelain of her cheeks and a sparkle to her brown eyes. The chestnut curls falling around her face, though shocking in terms of etiquette, made a charming picture, and I hastened to reassure her that under the circumstances, a grandfather's welfare being in question, there was no need for apologies.

"But let me tell all," she said, "and then perhaps you can advise me further."

I shook my head at that but was flattered that she thought

7

me capable of assisting her.

"My name," she said, "is Beatrice Trueblood. My parents being deceased and me an only child, I dwell with my widowed grandfather in the village of N in Buckinghamshire. Oh, Mrs. Hudson," she added impetuously. "I owe everything to my dear grandfather who took me in when I had nothing and no one to turn to."

"But now your grandfather has fallen on hard times," I ventured and she looked at me again with those eyes.

"Only I see, my dear," I explained, "that your dress, though of quality fabric, is somewhat faded and not of the most current fashion, while your gloves are positively..." I was about to say "revolting" but amended it to the kinder "worse for the wear of them."

"Mrs. Hudson," said she with determination. "You have convinced me that if Mr. Holmes is unable to help me in this, I can only hope to throw myself on your mercy and further desire, nay insist, that you accompany me to Braxton Parvis forthwith."

To say I was astonished does no credit to the extremity of the emotion I was experiencing.

"My dear Miss Trueblood," I babbled. "I can assure you that I have no ability, no experience in solving mysteries. I leave that sort of thing to the gentlemen."

"But the gentlemen are not here, nor, as I understand it, likely to be so in time to halt what I fear is otherwise an inevitable catastrophe. My dear Mrs. Hudson, you have proved to me, through your few words, the perspicuity of your observation and judgment, and you would honour me by accompanying me home. I can explain further the details of the case on the train. I assure you, there is no time to be lost."

Well, there she was flattering me again. And to tell the truth I was tempted. I had not ventured out of London, nay barely out of Baker Street, for many a long year, not since the passing away of Henry, my dear spouse, and I craved to see the fields and lanes of my youth once more. For the village of N was not unknown to me. As a girl I had a favourite aunt who dwelt in the very place and as a child, with my sister and brother, I had visited her often.

Thus it was that before an hour had elapsed, I found myself on the train with Miss Trueblood, a small case packed with necessities, since the lateness of the morning meant that I should have occasion to stay the night away. I had left dear Clara in charge, instructed to be stern with young Phoebe and note any further breakages to be offset against her wages. I am not in general a harsh taskmistress but hold the firm opinion that only such extreme measures can teach the young to mend their ways.

It was on the train that Miss Trueblood fully opened her heart to me. She explained that it was only for the past few months that she had dwelt with her grandfather. Since the deaths of both beloved parents in the Asian flu epidemic of the early nineties, which took so many worthy lives, she had spent her youth, as she said, (she was now, I surmised, to be aged barely twenty) at boarding school, and her holidays, having as she thought no other living relatives, with her old nurse, Nancy.

Following the passing of this beloved individual and the ending of her schooling, her only recourse as a young woman utterly without means, would have been to take up a position as governess or lady's companion. However, it was at this moment that, quite unexpectedly, she received a letter from the grandfather she had never met, indicating that he was now returned to England and would be delighted for her to come and stay with him. This same grandfather, Arthur Bastable, the father of her mother, was by calling an anthropologist who had spent the largest part of his life in foreign parts until encroaching age and feebleness had earlier this very year caused him to retire to England. The aged gentleman had paused not a second, as she said, to offer succour to the homeless child that she was become and thus she came to live with him on his estate in

Buckinghamshire. Her grandfather being something of a recluse, it was a quiet life that she now enjoyed – for which I understood a lonely one – but secure from destitution.

I have to say in parenthesis that this was all of considerable interest to me, since I recalled how my aunt would talk in hushed tones of the queer folk who lived in the big house and, the same aunt being a most pious woman, of the unseemly and sacrilegious appurtenances of the place as reported back by various maids and manservants. These same appurtenances, as I now surmised, must have included the primitive objects Mr. Bastable had collected in foreign parts in the course of his life's work. At the time, my aunt, fearing who knew what devilish practices, abjured us young children to stay well away from the house and we generally obeyed her, although telling a child not to do something has often, as is well known to those of us who have had the rearing of them, the opposite effect. Indeed, my brother George did once, with some village lads, creep as far as the orchard to plunder some apples but they were chased off, as he told us, by a blackamoor, perhaps some individual brought to the country by Mr. Bastable himself as a younger man, this same exotic brandishing some sort of an outlandish weapon and calling out in a strange tongue.

Miss Trueblood having hesitated and seeming lost in thought, I coughed slightly and recalled her to the matter.

"I am of course most grateful to him for his kindness," she said, but in such a way as to make me wonder. Indeed, what sort of grandparent would he be not to take in the orphaned and friendless child of his daughter? However, I kept that thought to myself and Miss Trueblood continued her narrative.

It seemed that her grandfather had, over his working years, amassed a quantity of papers comprising a definitive study of some remote tribe of the Amazon of which Miss Trueblood, no more than I, had ever heard. Her grandfather desired to publish his findings in a book which, he told her, would be the last word on the matter and cause a great stir in the world of anthropology. Failing eyesight and a kind of tremor in his hand had however halted the sorting and writing- up of this until Miss Trueblood offered her services, having acquired at school some rudimentary training in secretarial practices. She now paused in her account and looked out of the window as the train sped past muddy wintry fields and trees sparsely decorated with a few remaining withered leaves. I had never visited N in winter and foresaw that it would have a very different appearance now from the sunny summer days of my recollections.

"At least," Miss Trueblood was saying, her voice quivering with emotion. "That was his habit until very lately."

She paused again. Apparently the account was painful to her. I patted her hand.

"If I am to be of assistance to you," I said, "you must tell all." She nodded and continued in firmer tones.

"I do not know," she said, "in what way my work fell short of my grandfather's expectations but suddenly, without consulting me, he took into his employ a young man to do the work which I had previously executed gladly and for free, even though this placed even tighter restraints on the household budget."

"Did you enquire into the reason for this?" I asked.

"I did, indeed I did. But my grandfather just muttered something inconsequential about sparing me so much trouble, and refused to discuss the matter further. You must understand," she added, catching at my hand, "he is the dearest man, Mrs. Hudson, but one with whom it is impossible to argue, once he has set his mind on a course of action." And she lowered her eyes, as if she could say more on the subject.

There was yet another pause which I waited for her to fill, but, since she stayed silent, I asked, "So who is this young man?"

"Oh, a pleasant enough fellow to be sure."

Did I mistake or did a pretty blush infuse the young lady's lily-white complexion?

"His name," she continued, "is Charles Devoy." "And does he reside with you in the house?"

"My grandfather insisted on it, since it is his habit to work at irregular hours. This was one reason why, as he said, he wished to spare me the inconvenience in future, although, as I assured him, it was no trouble. In any case, as you will see, it's a large house with many rooms, so accommodation is not the problem, even if heating the place is."

I could see that, since Miss Trueblood regarded her grandfather with such deep gratitude, his exclusion of her from his literary activities was a severe blow. However, I wondered too if the old man had fixed on a plan regarding his granddaughter's future.

Feeling himself failing, and poverty ensuring that she had little opportunity to go out into the world and meet marriageable young men, perhaps his employment of young Mr. Devoy was in the hope of providing her with a spouse. I kept this surmise to myself, however. I would soon see how the land lay when we reached our destination.

"But before we arrive," I said, "you must explain to me the events of the past day that have precipitated your attempt to contact Mr. Holmes."

"Indeed," she said. "It started on the eve before last. Dinner having concluded, Charles... Mr Devoy... as was his custom, withdrew to smoke his pipe, while my grandfather and I chatted in an inconsequential manner, he drinking a glass of port."

"Your grandfather doesn't smoke, then?"

She looked at me with puzzled eyes. "Why do you ask?"

"I am simply wondering why he didn't accompany Mr. Devoy, as in my experience gentlemen usually do."

"Ah no... I have never seen my grandfather smoke." "I

12

see. Go on."

"My grandfather was seated facing the window while I had my back to it. As I said, we were talking of nothing of any consequence when suddenly he leapt from his chair and clutched at his chest, the colour draining from his face betimes, his eyes staring. Mrs. Hudson, I thought he was having some of fit or even a stroke and I arose to minister to him if I could. But before I could reach him, he stretched a trembling finger and pointed to the window, as if something there had terrified him near to death."

"Pardon me, but were the curtains then undrawn?"

"Indeed. My grandfather has a strange quirk in that he likes to view darkness as it falls over the garden, despite the bitter draughts coming through the panes." Miss Trueblood gave a little laugh. "One of his many idiosyncrasies, Mrs. Hudson."

"And did you yourself not see what had so terrified him?"

"I did not. When I turned to look there was nothing there. But my grandfather, who by then had subsided into his chair, muttered what I finally understood to be "The smiling man. 'Tis the smiling man."

"Very strange," I said.

"Yes indeed. What can it mean?"

"No, what I find strange is that your grandfather did not instantly hasten to the window to see what was there. Would that not be the more natural reaction?"

"I suppose. But he is not a strong man, Mrs. Hudson. And he was overcome."

"I see."

"But what of his words. What can that mean? The smiling man?"

"Presumably your grandfather can answer that."

"He refused to discuss it. Once he had regained a modicum of

13

composure, he just shook his head and told me it was nothing, a mere fancy, a trick of the light, a reflection compounded by the flickering effect of the wind in the trees."

"And how do you know it was not?"

"At first, I believed this explanation. I myself have often seen how simple shadows can take on fearsome forms when one is susceptible. However, his manner changed from that moment, Mrs. Hudson. Although he tried to conceal it from me, I could tell that he was badly shaken. Before I retired and after he had betaken himself to an early bed for once, I took it upon myself to go into the garden with a lamp and examine the ground outside the window."

A very enterprising young lady. Mr. H would have been pleased with her.

"Imagine my shock," she continued, "when I tell you that the imprint of two enormous boots was clear upon the soil, consistent with a giant of a man having stood close up to the window peering through."

"A passing tramp, maybe, drawn by the light," said I, more to console the young lady, than to convince myself, for already there were elements to her tale which disturbed my composure.

"Most unlikely," said she. "When you see the disposition of the house and grounds, you will understand why. But I would not have come rushing to London today had I not become truly alarmed at the sudden change and decline in my grandfather following the apparition at the window. Mrs. Hudson, it was as if overnight he had changed from a man reasonably fit for his age and in control of his faculties, to the fearful, broken individual who could barely rise from his bed on the following day..."

"And did he rise?"

"In a shuffling, mumbling way he did and continued thus all day. But when I suggested that the curtains be drawn at dinner-time, he refused, as stubborn as ever, though his eyes were fixed on the window throughout the whole meal as if anticipating a return of the previous night's horror. Mrs. Hudson, there was madness in that stare."

The poor young lady trembled at the recollection. "And did the apparition return?"

"It did not. But that did not seem to reassure my grandfather in any way."

"And did you apprise Mr. Devoy of the events of the previous evening?"

A blush again suffused Miss Trueblood's features at the mention of the young man's name.

"I did. And in deference to my anxieties, he remained with us throughout the whole meal, for once foregoing his pipe, until my grandfather again stated his intention of retiring early to bed."

I could not help but wonder at the significance of this change in behaviour on the part of the young secretary. Was it out of concern for grandfather and granddaughter, or was there another reason? I would consider the possibilities when I met Mr. Devoy and meantime keep any suspicions to myself.

"My fear, Mrs. Hudson," Miss Trueblood stated, clutching at my sleeve, "is that some unknown person has designs upon my grandfather's sanity, if not upon his very life."

The train was slowing down and we were nearing our destination.

"There is one more thing," she resumed, "that I must impress upon you before we arrive."

She instructed me then that I was on no account to reveal my true identity but to present myself as her late father's godmother (do I really appear that elderly? I who am barely fifty! Although I have noticed that young people, on seeing grey hairs, imagine that they must indicate a very great age indeed). The said godmother, being a person of the name of Mrs. St. Claire, had, it seems, kept in touch with the young woman in a distant kind of a way over the years. Her grandfather had met the lady but once, many years previously, and had shown no inclination to renew the acquaintance.

"But he will surely allow me a visitor," she said. "In fact, I shall tell him that he approved the arrangement already. He may not remember that he did not."

All this appeared most unsatisfactory to me, and I wondered, had she apprised me of this plan in Baker Street, would I have ventured from my home under such false pretences? I understood that the young woman wished to spare her grandfather the consciousness that she was so seriously troubled regarding his well-being as to have sought advice from the premier detective in all of London and I puzzled how then she would have explained the presence of Mr. Sherlock Holmes and Dr. Watson, the doctor of course by nature of his profession being in possession of a more convincing reason to visit than the detective. But what, I asked, if I were to be questioned about her father of whom I knew nothing except that he had perished near enough ten years earlier?

"You have become confused and forgetful on the subject," said she airily enough, as the train drew to a halt.

However, I need not have worried on that score, from the grandfather at least. Mr. Bastable appeared to show no interest in me at all on that fateful evening, apart from being severely vexed at my intrusion (of which more anon), being preoccupied with other matters. But I am getting ahead of myself.

It appeared that my companion intended for us to walk from the station to the hall – no doubt to continue her tale, overheard only by the trees and the wind – and also possibly with the mundane intention of saving the few coins it would cost for a conveyance. Being however a woman somewhat past my prime (though by no means aged) and afflicted with the rheumatics besides, I prevailed upon Miss Trueblood to engage the services of a ginger-haired fellow hanging about at the station with a horse and wagonette. The young man, of a pleasing enough if rustic appearance, seemed well acquainted with Miss Trueblood, and enquired courteously regarding her health and that of her grandfather to which she replied that they were both good.

"I am most glad to hear it," quoth he, as he helped us clamber aboard the vehicle, myself somewhat squashed between himself and Miss Trueblood.

As he lightly whipped his horse into movement and we started to trundle down the track, he asked in an offhand kind of way, "I was wondering, Miss Beatrice, if you yet raised again with Mr. Bastable the matter of the copse."

"Not yet, Ned. But I will, I promise. Even though you know that he has set himself against the sale."

"You have told him my father will give him a good price, a fair price?"

"Indeed, I have."

This Ned then turned to me, to include me no doubt in the conversation, Miss Trueblood having introduced me as Mrs. St Claire. "The copse in question. ma'am, is on the edge of Mr. Bastable's estate where it adjoins our land and would provide a fine source of timber for us."

"I fear my grandfather won't hear of it, Ned."

"Even though it sits unused and neglected… Does that make sense to you, Mrs. St Claire?" The young man turned to me again.

I shook my head and tried to look wise but since I am long unacquainted with rural matters, could not contribute to the conversation which continued as we rattled down the rutted track, Ned cajoling, Miss Trueblood promising.

"If I or my father could but meet with Mr. Bastable and make our case…"

"My grandfather as you well know has withdrawn from society and meets with none but myself, Mr. Devoy and the household staff."

"Ah yes, Mr. Devoy, Mr. Devoy..." The sneer in the young man's voice was clear. Could it be that he saw the secretary as a rival for the affections of Miss Truebood? Surely he could not presume so much. Yet I could not help but feel that his manner was less one of deferential peasantry and more of a man confident of self and status and indeed of his masculinity, for his glances at my young companion as he drove along bordered, I considered, on the insolent.

The wagonette proved an uncomfortable and primitive enough conveyance but I was at least grateful not to be walking – especially now that a light rain was falling – and it served its purpose well enough, for within fifteen minutes we were in sight of Braxton Parvis, with me no further enlightened, Miss Trueblood being rightly unwilling to talk of the affair within the hearing of this Ned. Instead she warned me not to have raised expectations as to my comfort for the evening.

"It is a cold house," she said, "and our cook, though she apparently came with the highest of recommendations..." (driver Ned here giving an inexplicable and unseemly chortle) "Well... you will see for yourself."

Braxton Parvis turned out to be a looming, gloomy sort of a place, set far from the main highway over a rough and bumpy track, and I understood why my aunt had impressed upon us children the need to stay well away from it. At one time it must have been impressive in a formidable kind of way but in recent years had fallen into disrepair. Indeed, were it not for the dim lights visible from a single window (the day having already declined towards evening), a passer-by, if any such there be, might have taken the place for an abandoned ruin. However, I was reluctant yet to dismiss the notion of a tramp who wandered up to the place in expectation of a roof over his head for the night, only to be disappointed when, peering through the dining room window, he found it already inhabited. Although to be

18

sure, a tramp would have been bound then to make his way to the kitchen to beg for scraps from the dinner. The Baker Street Irregulars, as Mr. H is pleased to call the little ruffians he sometimes engages to assist him in his detecting, have no compunction about knocking on my door for that same purpose. Well, I would see what I would see, and interview the kitchen staff on the subject.

Miss Trueblood having dismissed our driver, who refused the coins she proffered with a careless dignity and broad smile – he was admittedly a most fine-looking lad, ruddy complexioned with a mop of reddish curls – she conducted me to the house.

Having been shown to a bedroom as cold and draughty as forewarned, I busied myself, no housemaid presenting herself, in setting a fire from the bucket of wood beside the grate. Luckily the wood was dry and caught quickly so that soon it was tolerably comfortable if you sat right beside the heat. However, the room being large, anywhere away from the fire was chill, and when I ran my hand between the sheets of the bed, I felt them not only to be cold but also damp. As a result and fearing the effect of this on my rheumatics, I stripped the bed of its sheets and hung these on the back of a chair which I positioned near the blaze. Then I prepared myself for dining as best I could, not having a change of dress. But my best shawl covers a multitude, and, on regarding myself in the long mirror of the wardrobe, I deemed myself presentable enough, and quite in the character of a godmother.

Descending the stairs, I was shocked to hear angry voices coming from one of the rooms which I subsequently understood to be the study. That is to say, one voice, that of a man I deemed to be the master of the house, expressed anger, shouting "You had no right to bring her here uninvited," (the which remonstration I feared related to myself). "You know how I abhor company." Miss Trueblood's softer tones interposed, but the man was not to be calmed and ranted on. I knew not what to do with myself. At that moment the housemaid entered the hallway, Phoebe's sister in competence if not in blood, from my first sharp look at the girl, a pale freckled creature with coppery hair caught up in an untidy bun beneath her cap. She had her arms full of tablecloth, as scrunched up as if she were on the way to the laundry. I found, however, that this same cloth was destined for our dinner table and, pleased to find something to do, followed her into the gloomy dining hall. There I could not desist from admonishing her and even helping her by smoothing the crumpled and stained thing as tidily as possible over the ill-polished wood.

Her name, it transpired was Elsie, a village girl whose first position this was. Now, I have to say I would never have employed such a one as housemaid. First she would have had to learn the ways of the household in the scullery. But scullery maid in this abode there was none and poor inexperienced Elsie had to do all. That she was a good and well-intentioned, if unintelligent girl I soon perceived, and spoke more kindly to her thereafter.

Of Miss Trueblood there was no sign, although all was peaceful now in the hallway, and Elsie, having let slip how cook was at sixes and sevens trying to get dinner ready, I accompanied the girl to the kitchen, which anyway served my purposes well. In this untidy and smoky space, I found an ill-favoured woman wrestling with pots and pans and saucepan lids. This Mrs. McAdam (Mrs., as she described herself, though I perceived she wore no wedding band) was a stringy yellow-skinned body of forty-odd years. I bethought myself of my mamma's words, "Never trust a thin cook," mamma herself being nicely embonpoint as the saying goes and myself built along similar lines. I introduced myself to the cook as Mrs. St Claire, a guest of Miss Trueblood's, and offered to help with the gravy.

A struggle deformed the woman's already twisted features but finally, with an ill-grace, she agreed. Lumps had formed in the said sauce but I was able to save it somewhat by straining it through a fine sieve. I also managed to brighten up the bland taste by adding some dried herbs I found pushed to the back of a dusty shelf, along with a dash of Worcestershire sauce. Amazed I was, meantime, to observe the woman's idea of cookery. All was chaos: meats nudging cheeses and pies and bacon, earth encrusted potatoes and turnips next to milk and cream and between all a cabbage boiling dry.

I mentioned Mrs. Beeton, and stated how I preferred Eliza Acton.

"Don't know 'er," was the churlish response. "Don't know either of 'em."

I was astonished: that this person who had come with the highest recommendations should not be aware of the two foremost cookery writers of the century!

When I then asked if a tramp had called to the house on any night recently, looking for food and shelter – perhaps a trifle too abrupt a query on my part – she paused in her attempt to gut the sorry grey-eyed trout on the slab in front of her, her knife raised in what some might even describe as a threatening manner, and enquired of me what business it was of mine, pray.

"Miss Trueblood mentioned a scare they had last night," I replied calmly, "and I was just wondering if it was simply some old tramp who had wandered here. If such a person had indeed called to the kitchen, I could put her mind at ease."

"I already told 'er there was no such to my best knowledge and nor to Elsie's."

The knife descended and she chopped the head off the fish, with little care or delicacy, then slit it down its belly and pulled out the bloody organs which she tossed on the floor. A mangy cat ran out from under a cupboard and ran off with the lot. I felt myself losing what was for me a usually healthy appetite.

When the party finally sat down to dinner, at a later time than I would usually dine – the which circumstance I attribute to the inadequacies of the cook rather than the habits of the house – a strange and uncomfortable atmosphere hung over us. This was hardly decreased by the character of the chamber in which we found ourselves, with its walls of sickly green, its heavy, dark old furnishings and hangings, all barely illuminated by dim and flickering gaslight. An odour of decay permeated the place, and chill it was certainly, despite the fire that burned in the grate, a meagre enough blaze it has to be said, and as Miss Trueblood had intimated, not made more cosy by the wind which whistled through the ill-fitting glass of the uncurtained window or the rain lashing at the panes. Outside thin branches of trees swayed in the gusts and blasts and even to me, who is of an unsuperstitious cast of mind, the effect was unnerving, as if troubled spirits were crying out for quiet and peace.

In this unpropitious atmosphere, only Miss Trueblood seemed to have any life in her. I much approved of the wine-red velvet gown she was wearing, though admittedly it had seen better days. Nonetheless, it contrasted most beautifully with her fair skin, dark hair and eyes. The two gentlemen of the company made no such positive impression, Mr. Devoy being a thin and bloodless young man with sparse blond hair, too ready to smile. Mr. Bastable, having entered the room with a handkerchief over his face, gave a harsh chuckle at the sight of me. The removal of the handkerchief then revealed a crabby old autocrat of maybe seventy years, with rheumy eyes, a sharp red nose and matching dewlap which gave him the appearance of a bad- tempered turkey cock. I could see nothing in him of the broken spirit of which Miss Trueblood had made mention but, of course, had nothing with which to compare his present state.

To me he was less than courteous, in accordance with the outburst I had overheard earlier. When introduced by his granddaughter, he merely gave her a look and me a curt nod.

Mr. Devoy on the other hand seemed almost overly

interested in my identity. In fact he started with considerable astonishment when learning of it, and began to interrogate me concerning my "godson" with questions I was unable to answer – I didn't even know the man's first name – but I burbled on like the senile old person I was supposed to be. He then enquired what it was like living in Brighton – a place he assured me with a baring of his teeth in another big and insincere smile that he would love to revisit and me never having visited it at all had to mutter that it was "very nice" and I wondered again why Miss Trueblood had placed me in such an invidious position.

The conversation soon shifted away from me, thank God, although occasionally throughout the soup course (a watery broth) I caught both Mr. Bastable and Mr. Devoy turning appraising eyes in my direction, which I countered with an appropriately vacant smile. Over the fish, of which I declined to partake, they started discussing the copse of wood on the estate which our driver had mentioned, Miss Trueblood duly reporting that Ned Tilling's father would be willing to offer an excellent price for it, whereupon Mr. Bastable grunted an objection.

"But grandfather, think how even a little extra money would ease our situation here."

"No, no, no," quoth he, bringing a fist down so heavily on the table that the very glassware trembled. "Not the copse. The estate must not be broken up. As to handing it to those poaching rascals, the Tillings…"

Miss Trueblood fixed eyes on the plate of fish in front of her, a dish which, wisely I felt, she had barely touched.

"You know nothing about it, Miss," the man raged on, uncaring that there were strangers present. "There's money coming. Lots of money. Soon, soon. So no more talk of copses, if you please."

Silence followed this outburst and I at least was most relieved when Elsie staggered through the door bearing the roast, even though it was as dried up a joint of mutton as ever I did see, all the joy drained out of it. However, I was secretly gratified when Mr. Bastable, now calmer, commented, "At least Cook seems at last to have mastered the gravy." Pouring half the jug over his meat.

The rice pudding that followed all, though more like nursery food, was the most successful dish of the evening. It is hard to go wrong with milk, sugar, rice and raisins baked in the oven, and although the skin on top was almost black, as the meal ended, I felt reasonably satisfied.

It was at this point that Mr. Devoy got to his feet, excusing himself from the company and making off to smoke his pipe. Miss Trueblood rose too and fetched a decanter of port from a sideboard, along with one glass. I wondered that she did not offer any to me – I being partial to a small measure after my dinner to assist my digestion – but it seemed that the thought had not occurred to her and I, as a guest, could hardly demand it.

"Do not forget your elixir, my dear," her grandfather said in softer tones and she poured herself a tiny measure from a brown bottle. "A healthy blend of herbs," he turned to me in a more friendly fashion than heretofore, "that I collected from a native tribe in the Amazon delta. Said to have a calming effect on the nerves of young women. And I think, my dear, you have found it so."

"Well maybe, grandfather," she replied, "though I could wish it tasted less bitter."

After this we each sat immersed in our own thoughts, her grandfather sipping at his glass, she with hers, me having no such recourse to refreshment.

Miss Trueblood appeared still upset by his recent rages and perhaps he noticed this, for after a while, he stated, "I regret, my dear, that I was intemperate awhile back. I know that you worry greatly about our circumstances here but I can assure you that…"

He did not finish his sentence, instead suddenly letting

out a yell of pure terror.

I turned immediately to the window, towards which his gaze was directed, and cried out myself at the sight, a horrid grinning face pressed up to the glass and staring in at us. Recovering quickly, I hastened to the window but the apparition disappeared as suddenly as it had materialised. I threw up the sash and stared out into the murk, but not a sign could I see, no movement except the skinny supplicating arms of the beech trees waving in the wind.

Meantime, Miss Trueblood was hanging over her grandfather, whose condition, it must be said, gave considerable cause for alarm. His customarily flushed complexion had turned grey and a heavy film of sweat sat on his brow, his breath coming in harsh gasps. I hastened to the sideboard and hunted out a measure of brandy from a dusty bottle I found there, mixing it with a little water from the jug on the table. I gave the concoction to Miss Trueblood, who held it to her grandfather's lips. He swallowed a small draught and coughed violently.

"We must send for the doctor," said Miss Trueblood, to which Mr. Bastable shook his head and muttered, "No need, no need."

She nodded meaningfully at me, however, which I understood to signify that I should pursue the matter, and I left the dining room forthwith, intent on finding Mr. Devoy. In fact I almost bumped into the same young man, who, claiming to have heard the scream of terror, was even now hurrying to find its cause. From the study across the hallway to the dining room was a matter of a few steps and I wondered that it had taken him so long to respond, full several minutes at least. However, I kept this question to myself and instead asked if he could fetch the doctor.

"Does Miss Beatrice really think it necessary?" he enquired. "On the last occasion, Mr. Bastable recovered speedily enough from his delirium, Mrs. St. Claire." (The last said with a kind of unpleasant sneer, whether directed at his employer or at me, I could not tell).

I assured him that it was no delirium and that I too had witnessed the apparition at the window, though I could not say if Miss Trueblood had done so. I asked further if he himself had seen or heard anything of the horror that had caused Mr. Bastable's fit while he was out of doors.

"What do you mean?" he asked sharply.

"I see, Mr. Devoy, that your hair is bespattered with rain drops and that your boots have fresh mud on them and so I presume that you went outside to smoke your pipe."

The young man laughed heartily. "You aren't such a brainless old biddy as you would like us to think, are you, Mrs. St. Claire. Yes indeed, I stepped outside for a few moments but can assure you it was on the far side of the house from the dining room, and I witnessed nothing but the wind in the trees."

Disregarding his rudeness to me, I persisted. "But you heard the cry."

"I was at that very moment returned and in the process of taking off my topcoat."

We stared at each other, each of us perhaps about to speak further, when the dining-room door opened and Miss Trueblood stepped out.

"How is he, Beatrice?" Mr. Devoy hastened to her side and took her hand in his, his voice suddenly turned soft as down from the breast of a turtle dove.

"I should like Dr. Mortimer to see him but I fear the hour is late."

"Not too late if you wish me to fetch him."

"Oh Charles..." She turned a look upon him so beseeching that it would melt the coldest heart.

"And perhaps the doctor needs to see you as well, my dear," he said, with a speaking intimacy. "You seem overcome."

Indeed, all colour had drained from the young lady's face

and she seemed to stagger. He supported her to a chair.

I speculated if further recourse to the brandy bottle would be required but she gathered herself swiftly together.

"A momentary weakness," she said.

"Of which you have had many recently, Beatrice," said he, again in familiar tones. I wondered was there then already an understanding between them. "Yes, I will fetch Dr. Mortimer on condition that you let him examine you as well."

"How can you make conditions under such circumstances, Charles?" she asked.

"I think," I said, breaking into the conversation, "it would be wise to concur with Mr. Devoy and have the doctor look in on you."

At that she nodded wearily and the young man, to his credit, responded with alacrity.

"I'll take the bicycle," he said. "It will be quicker." And with that he rushed out.

"But Mrs.... Mrs. St. Claire," she said, keeping up the pretence even though Devoy had now departed. "Please attend to my grandfather. He should not be left alone."

The old man was as I had last seen him, stretched back in his chair, but breathing more regularly now, his colour somewhat better. It irked me to sit by him when I had so many questions in my head that could be resolved only through precipitous action, and I was therefore pleased to see Elsie enter the room. She, if nothing else, could surely remain at the old man's side and call out if his condition changed.

The girl looked to be terrified but I tried to assure her that her master would be quite well if left to recover peacefully.

"Perhaps you can help me move him to the chaise longue," I said.

With eyes like saucers, she stared at me with incomprehension.

"Over there," I said, indicating the said piece of

furniture, strangely situated in a dining room but useful for the present circumstances.

The move effected with little visible distress to the old man, who however seemed still in a bewildered state, I settled the girl into a chair beside him.

"Do you sit here and watch the master," I said, "and call to myself or Miss Trueblood if he seems to get worse."

"Oh no," she babbled. "Don't leave me with him, please, ma'am. I can't stay alone. And Cook will be that vexed if I don't fetch back the dishes immediately."

"Now, now, nothing to fear. Just stay here for a moment. I will send in Miss Trueblood straight." And with that I left the silly goose, praying most forcefully that the old man should not depart this world under her watch.

The aforementioned young lady still appearing wan and dizzy no doubt from shock, I apprised her of Elsie's vigil. She stated her intention of returning to her grandfather's side forthwith, so I hurried to don my cape. Taking an oil-lamp for illumination, I made my way outside.

It was lucky that the rain had now stopped, both for my own convenience and to avoid the likelihood of any prints having been washed away. And, lo! as had Miss Trueblood before me, I found the imprint of the soles of two enormous boots pressed into the soil under the fateful window, proving, if proof were needed, that our unwelcome visitant was no apparition but had human form, despite the daemon face. From the size of the boots I surmised that their owner must surely be a big built man, bigger certainly than Mr. Devoy, who was slight and whose feet, as I had most particularly observed, were small and neat. And yet, peering in the window and seeing Miss Trueblood there leaning beside her grandfather, her demeanour that of extreme fatigue, while Elsie stood trembling beside her, I could not but wonder.

I made my way round the side of the house, along the gravelled path, to the kitchen entrance. A kind of a lobby stood

28

behind the back door, where hung all manner of topcoats and mackintoshes, one noticeably damp from recent exposure to the elements, while a tumble of galoshes and clogs stood on the floor beneath. I studied them carefully. None fitted the prints I had seen, so I stooped to have a closer look. My persistence was rewarded for, pushed back behind all, what should I discover but a huge pair of boots, the mud still sticky upon then. I removed this pair and walked back round to the dining room window, where I was able to fit them perfectly into the imprints. Then I returned, more thoughtful than ever.

Back at the kitchen door I found Elsie on her way out with a bucket of slops. My sudden appearance must have startled her, because she cried out, dropping the bucket so that slops ran all over the lobby floor. Mrs. McAdam appeared behind her, wrath etched on her features, directed first and foremost at the silly girl.

"Elsie Tilling," snapped she. "Can you not perform the simplest of tasks!"

And then she turned on me, "As for you," she said. "What are you doing dallying round the back door frightening my maid near out of her skin? And what the devil," she added, seeing what I was holding, "do you think you are doing with my boots?"

Now, I had not noticed that the woman had outstandingly large feet, and sure enough, on further observation, I could see that her feet were of normal size.

"Your boots!" I exclaimed.

"My late husband's boots," said she, grabbing them from me. "They serve well enough when I 'ave to traipse through the yard. If it's any of your business, madam, which it is not. Now, if you please, leave this poor idiot be to clear up the mess she made."

With which she swept back into the kitchen, boots and all.

Most puzzling and yet it had given me the inkling of an explanation.

Meanwhile the little maid had returned with a broom and was attempting to sweep the slops out the back door. Her face was downturned and I could tell she was in some extreme distress.

"Don't mind her, Elsie," I said. "Accidents will happen and it was my fault for affrighting you, coming out of the dark like that."

"Oh, ma'am," said Elsie. "I meant no harm, truly I didn't." And then she burst into tears and rushed into the kitchen.

I had no wish to confront the formidable Mrs. McAdam once again and therefore made my way along the path to the front of the house. My arrival there coincided with that of the doctor, who had come post haste in a horse and carriage. No sign of Mr. Devoy who presumably was pedalling back on his bicycle.

I followed the doctor into the dining room and was relieved to see that both grandfather and granddaughter seemed revived, although the old man remained feeble enough.

"Well now, Bastable. What's this I hear?" The doctor was a bluff country type, stout and tweeded, with fine black whiskers, a man in his middle years. "Frightening yourself near to death with shadows, are you."

He took the old man's arm and felt his pulse. "Hmm," was all he said.

"It was real enough," Mr. Bastable said querulously. "As real as you, Mortimer. I swear to God."

"Hmm," the doctor said again and laid a hand on the other's forehead.

"I can attest to the truth of that," I remarked. "It was horrible.

A ghastly sight but no dream."

The doctor looked at me for the first time.

"This is Mrs. St. Claire," Miss Trueblood put in. "A visitor." "A visitor?" said the doctor smiling. "Good gracious, Bastable. What! Are you becoming hospitable in your dotage?" Doctor or no, Mortimer seemed to me a very rude man.

"And you also saw... what exactly, ma'am?" he asked, addressing me.

"A face pressed to the window. A horrid grinning mask of a face."

"You see," said Mr. Bastable. "You see, Mortimer. I am not mad."

"Hmm," said the doctor yet again, looking sceptical. He no doubt took me for some brainless old biddy – as Mr. Devoy had been pleased to describe me – easily subject to fancies.

"The footprints still stand under the window," said I, "and the muddy boots that made them are in the kitchen. They belong to Mrs. McAdam."

A most gratifying silence fell at this revelation. All stared at me in amazement, including Mr. Devoy, who had just arrived.

"Are you suggesting, ma'am," the doctor finally asked, "that the cook put on her boots and stood outside the dining room window making faces at those within?" And he laughed heartily at the thought.

"Not necessarily," I replied, a tartness in my voice. "They are enormous boots and not originally belonging to the cook. Anyone not in the dining room at the time might have taken them from the kitchen lobby. Anyone." And I looked meaningfully across at Mr. Devoy.

"Not me," he countered. "Why should I?"

I had no answer to that nor any idea why anyone should do so. "Besides," added he, "if the boots are as big as you say they would not have fitted me." And he twirled a trim ankle for us to admire the delicate size of his foot.

"As to that" I said, "both Miss Trueblood and I were

31

initially misled by the hugeness of the prints and assumed that the person who made them had to be a man of immense stature or at least in possession of large feet. Mrs. McAdam claimed them as hers but belonging to her husband, on whom, being deceased, no suspicion can fall. But while big feet cannot be forced into small shoes, I quickly came to realise that anyone with smaller feet might have donned them to put us off the scent."

"You are quite the detective, Mrs. St. Claire," said Devoy, that sneer in his voice again as he spake the name. Could it be that he guessed at my true identity?

"Just common sense based on experience, Mr. Devoy," I replied. "In any case, it was Miss Trueblood who first had the idea to examine the soil outside the window and found the traces I have described, following the earlier sighting of the smiling man. It is she who is the detective."

The young lady smiled with pleasure at my remark.

"But who could be doing this and why?" said the doctor. "Have you any notion, Bastable?"

The old man shook his head, but I detected a furtive expression in his eye. However, he looked all in and the present moment seemed unpropitious for further questioning.

"I think what you need is a good rest," Mortimer continued. "With Devoy's assistance, I propose to take you to your bedchamber."

I was tired myself after the excitement of the day and, since I am in the habit of rising at dawn, it was already well past the time that I usually retire. However, I like to take some light reading matter with me to bed to ease me into slumber and therefore enquired of Miss Trueblood if she had any such to lend me.

"In the study," she said, "my grandfather has a large library of books. I am sure there will be something to divert you. Come with me." Then adding in in hushed tone, "I wish to speak to you anyway on a most private matter."

Much intrigued I followed her across the hall and into the study.

"Can you imagine," said she on entering the dimly lit room, "that Charles, Mr. Devoy, who has always treated me in a special way, has this very day made me an offer of marriage? Oh, Mrs. Hudson, what am I to do?"

I was about to enquire if she had strong feelings for a young man who seemed to me sorely lacking in charm or allure, but any further confidence she intended to divulge was suddenly dispelled by her sharp cry. I followed her gaze and cried out too in surprise and shock.

"Good heavens! What is that?" exclaimed Miss Trueblood. "It was not here before."

As for me, I recognised it at once. For there, propped on the mantel, firelight flickering over it in uncanny fashion, was the same ghastly face that I had but recently seen at the dining-room window. On examination it was revealed to be a wooden mask of primitive origin, crudely painted, teeth grinning white between carmine lips, big eyes with peepholes bored into them, bulging under a thatch of real hair (horsehair, I sincerely hoped).

It should be said that it was not the only mask on show. The room was bedecked with all manner of exotic objects, including naked forms roughly hacked, no doubt part of the collection that had instilled such unease in the residents of N, so many years before. But of all that were there, the smiling man was the most grotesque.

"It is the very face," I informed her. "The face at the window. Someone in this house is perpetrating a cruel jest to who knows what end."

I remembered that it was from this very room that Charles Devoy had emerged sometime after the apparition had terrified Mr. Bastable, but on this subject for the time being I held my peace. However, it was telling to observe that behind imperfectly drawn drapes were French windows leading to the outside, facilitating unobserved egress and reentry.

"I do not understand," Miss Trueblood said, sinking into a chair. "What is happening?"

"From the extremity of his reaction," I said. "I imagine your grandfather holds the key to the mystery, but is unwilling to divulge what it is. We could take this mask upstairs and confront him with it, but I fear that in his weakened state, the effect might be disastrous."

"I agree," said Miss Trueblood, "maybe tomorrow he will be stronger."

"In the meantime, I suggest we remove the mask to a safe place. If you like, I will bring it to my room." I added this even though the thought of having the thing anywhere close to me filled me with revulsion.

"An excellent idea," said Miss Trueblood. "I knew you would help me through this, Mrs. Hudson. Thank you so very much."

She reached up and pulled the mask down and none too soon for we could hear the gentlemen approaching across the hallway. I just had time to seize the thing from her and press it to my stomach, wrapping the shawl around all, when the door opened. It was the doctor, alone.

"Your grandfather has settled. I gave him a dose of laudanum and he will surely sleep well this night. I will return in the morning to check on him again."

"That is indeed good news," said Miss Trueblood, "but Mrs. St. Claire," turning to me, "should we take the doctor into our confidence?"

He raised bushy eyebrows at that. For my part I could not see any reason to keep our discovery from him, since there seemed no way that he could be involved. I brought out the mask to show him.

"As you see," I said. "It was no hallucination."

34

"And," added Miss Trueblood, "I know for certain it was not here in the house before."

Dr. Mortimer held the thing for a moment before handing it back to me.

"Strange indeed," said he. "Some relic from your grandfather's explorations, perhaps. If it were not here before, how did it come to be here now? And why?"

"To terrify Mr. Bastable further, no doubt," I said. "But I propose keeping it secret from the rest of the household for the moment, in the hope that the person responsible will shew his hand in some way when it is found to be missing.

"And also to spare my grandfather further turmoil," added Miss Trueblood.

It was agreed again that I should hold on to the thing at least until the morning.

The doctor then addressed himself to my companion.

"Devoy has expressed an anxiety about you, Beatrice my dear," he said, "and has requested me to examine you."

I took this opportunity, bidding them both a good night, to slip out into the hall. It was most unpleasant for me then to find the secretary standing there waiting, for me or for what I did not know. Clutching my shawl the tighter to myself and conscious of his mocking gaze, I hurried past him up the stairs and did not feel safe until I had shut my bedroom door and positioned a chair in front of it.

I then examined more closely the mask, a distasteful thing which would have been more at home in some native village or remote jungle than in a respectable English country house, although I now noticed fine enough carving upon it. Turning it over, I examined the manner in which it would have been affixed to someone's face. This was by means of two thin lengths of hide knotted and then drawn through holes drilled beside each eye. Then I gasped with astonishment. For there, caught in one of the knots, was a small clump of hair and, upon studying this closer by the light of my lamp, I had not an instant of doubt as to whose hair it was, although it was perhaps almost the last person I might have suspected.

The next day dawned foggy and chill. When I looked out of my window I could see only ghosts of trees through swirls of mist. I had slept at last though fitfully, and disturbed thoughts had followed me into my dreams. Why, was the question which had haunted me on the preceding eve, but upon wakening it seemed to me that the answer had revealed itself, if only I could remember what it was.

I arose, washed and dressed and then ventured downstairs. At such an early hour hardly a soul was stirring in the big house except in the kitchen, where all was business and bustle, as well it should be, Mrs. McAdam preparing for breakfast in that slapdash way of hers. The devilled kidneys sat next to the bloaters and muffins all of a heap, while she assayed some sort of a kedgeree, ladling in the mustard and curry powders till my eyes watered at the very sight. She gave me a look which clearly expressed her mixed feelings for me, dislike and disdain warring with her wish for assistance. The second won out on this occasion and her regard clearly demanded are you going to stand there or are you going to help out, which I would gladly have done, had I not a more pressing mission.

"I am looking for Elsie," I stated.

McAdam merely shrugged and tossed a little more powder into the puddingy rice, to which she then added flakes of last night's fish, the which I feared she could only have collected from the leavings on our dinner plates. I shuddered and resolved to break my fast only with toast and anchovy paste.

Elsie, as I correctly surmised, was engaged in trying to light a fire in the dining room grate, though she did not possess my knack and could not get it to catch. Getting down on my knees, despite her protests and my rheumatics, I was soon able to

36

coax a decent flame out of the mess of paper and twigs which she had placed there. Once these had caught I added some coals and small logs.

The girl started to thank me but I hushed her and said, "You can thank me, Elsie, by telling me the truth at last."

She raised fearful eyes to mine.

"And start by explaining what is Ned Tilling to you? Your brother, is it."

"Oh no, ma'am." And her pale face became red.

"But," (this had come to me just that morning after suddenly recalling the cook's sharp words to the maid the night before) "you have the same last name, not to mention the same look."

"Ned's my... my cousin, ma'am." "You are fond of him, I see."

She gave me the how can you tell look I was starting to recognise.

"You blush when he is mentioned and a little smile plays on your lips when you say his name." Her silence informed me that I was right. "You would do anything for him, Elsie, would you not?"

"I'd die for him." Stated with all the fervour of a fourteen- year-old in love.

"That sacrifice will not be necessary at present. But come, tell me why he prevailed upon you to don the mask and topcoat and stand outside the dining room window to frighten poor Mr. Bastable near to death."

Now Elsie's eyes were almost popping out of her silly little head.

"He didn't... I didn't ..."

I looked at her sternly. "Come now, Elsie, none of that. The truth if you please."

"How did you know, ma'am?"

"I found long red hairs caught on the mask. Your hair for

certain. By the way, I suppose it was Ned's idea too, then to place the mask in the study, so that it would the first thing Mr. Bastable saw this morning when he entered the room. You did not, I suppose, expect Miss Trueblood and myself to pre-empt you."

"I meant no harm, ma'am, and that's the honest truth. When Ned found the mask, he said it would be a good joke on the old man and serve him right for not selling the copse. We never thought Mr. Bastable would take that bad, ma'am, honest we didn't.

"Ned found the mask, you say. Now where would that have been?"

Elsie bit her lip and stared at the flickering flames. "Elsie?"

"I don't want to get him into trouble, ma'am."

I must have raised my eyebrows for she added, "More trouble, ma'am."

"I hardly think either you or he could be in more trouble than you are already, Elsie."

She still seemed reluctant to speak but I fixed her with another stern stare.

"In the copse," she said finally.

"The copse belonging to this estate?" She nodded.

"And what, pray, was he doing in the copse?"

She shook her head, those treacherous tresses bobbing. I remembered something Mr. Bastable had said. "Poaching, was it?"

She fired up again, no doubt repeating pat what her cousin had told her. "There's rabbits and all sorts in them woods, Mrs. St. Claire. Mr. Bastable don't want them. He never goes near the place."

I did not care about the poaching. I am not an officer of the law nor yet the estate gamekeeper. But I was bewildered.

"This all sounds most unlikely, Elsie. However did the

38

mask get into the copse?"

"I don't know, ma'am. Ned said it was in some old box buried beside a tree. Only for the tree having fallen down in the storm he wouldn't have found it."

"Elsie, I need to talk to Ned and fast. Can you fetch him here?"

She shook her head. "Oh no, ma'am," she said. "I cannot leave my post with so much to do."

I wondered that she would have a post any more, once I had revealed her part in the business, but did not voice the thought.

"And what if I said I had sent you to the village on an errand for me?"

She thought for a moment.

"Maybe after breakfast then, ma'am."

"So be it."

I thought Miss Trueblood looked more wan than she should that morning and seemed listless. I asked what the doctor had diagnosed and she told me, with a maidenly blush, that he had enquired if it was a certain time of the month, and when she said no, he had simply patted her hand and told her it was nothing to be fearful of, no doubt just some woman's thing. I proposed fetching her a dose of the cordial her grandfather recommended and she screwed up her face in disgust at the thought, but acquiesced.

"He likes me to take it twice in the day," she said.

The bottle stood among the wines and spirits in the press and was easily recognisable by the fact that it had no label. I opened the bottle and, because Miss Trueblood seemed so averse to the taste, I sniffed at it. The odour was pungent and bitter and stirred a recent memory in me. An unpleasant memory, it has to be said. I poured a little into a glass and dipped my finger into it, assaying it.

39

"It is indeed extremely unpleasant," I said, pouring the drink back into the bottle, which, unseen by Miss Trueblood, I then placed in my reticule. "I think that after all I will spare you from this concoction today."

"That," she said, "makes me feel better already."

"But maybe," I added, "we should keep it the matter a secret just now from your grandfather."

To which she nodded agreement.

We served ourselves breakfast from the platters on the sideboard. I am exceedingly partial to devilled kidneys and risked taking one. It was rubbery and the spice too strong for my taste, but all in all not as bad as I had feared, so I helped myself to another. I stayed away from the kedgeree and advised Miss Trueblood to do likewise. Indeed, she seemed to have little appetite.

To tell the truth, I myself ate less than usual for I was troubled on many counts. The situation in this gloomy house seemed far more serious than that engendered by a mere prank on the part of the Tillings. There was something horribly sinister here and I feared it would be beyond my powers to get to the bottom of it all, though my worries were now less for the grandfather than for the young lady herself.

The same old man appeared at breakfast as I was finishing my last piece of toast. Apparently well recovered after his good night's sleep from the previous evening's ordeal, he must, I judged, have a constitution of iron. He ate greedily, particularly delighted with the kedgeree. No doubt his palate had become inured to strong spices, he having lived for so many years in foreign parts.

There was no sign at all of Mr. Devoy and I wondered was he still abed. However, when Mr. Bastable enquired of his granddaughter, she replied that the secretary had headed out for an early walk and was not yet returned.

"Devil take him," the old man said gruffly and went for a

40

second portion of kedgeree.

"And did you take your cordial this morning, my dear," he soon asked his granddaughter in oilier tones.

Miss Trueblood glanced at me and I understood she did not wish to tell a lie.

"I offered it her," I said, "since she seems a little under the weather."

"Capital, Mrs..." He had forgotten my name, but no matter. It was not my name anyway. "Make sure to take it regularly, my dear."

I patted the bottle, safely secreted in my bag, and withdrew. I wished more than ever that Mr. H was present with his skills, to confirm my suspicions. But in his absence I would have to proceed by myself.

It was later that morning when, having returned from a walk in the grounds, I managed to accost the doctor on his way into the house. Indeed, I had been looking out for him.

"Ah, Mrs... Yes." He pretended to be delighted to see me, and made some friendly remarks, but soon observing that something particular was on my mind, he turned more serious. No doubt, when I asked for a private word, he feared to hear a litany of old lady complaints, and emitted an inward sigh of resignation. I walked him into the grounds a small way and into the fog as well so that we might not be observed or overheard. I then produced from my reticule a vial into which I had poured a sample of the cordial Miss Trueblood was taking. I informed the doctor that a friend of mine had recommended it for my rheumatics, but that I was fearful of taking it after one ingestion had produced an adverse effect upon me.

As I had done, Dr. Mortimer sniffed the contents of the vial and screwed up his nose.

"A friend of yours?" he said. "By heavens, it is strange friends you have, Mrs..."

"St. Claire," I said.

41

"I would have to do some tests," he continued. "But I strongly suspect this is a tincture of oleander, and as such quite poisonous in sufficient doses."

"I knew it," I exclaimed, whereupon he raised his eyebrows. "That is to say," I added, "I thought there was something not right about it."

In fact, I had recognised the odour from a recent occasion when Mr. H had allowed both myself and Dr. Watson a sniff of it, Mr. H having recovered it from some dastardly villain or other. But how such a fatal concoction had ended up in the hands of Mr. Bastable, and whether – but surely not – he knew of its true properties, was for the moment a matter of speculation beyond my ken.

"You must imbibe no more of the stuff, Mrs. St. Claire," the doctor pronounced firmly. "If you wish, I will take it upon myself it have it examined to further confirm my suspicions."

"Thank you but no need," I replied. "It happens that I have close access to someone with considerable chemical knowledge. In the meantime, I beg of you please to say nothing of this to the company. I have particular reasons."

He gave me a shrewd look then, but nodded and together we made our way back toward the house.

In the hallway we were met by Miss Trueblood who answered the doctor's query by stating that she felt somewhat recovered. And indeed the roses had begun to return to her cheeks. Her grandfather, as she told Dr. Mortimer, was in the study and, since Mr. Devoy had not yet returned, in high bad humour.

"So he is recovered, too," quoth the doctor jovially. "I will call upon him instantly to be sure."

Everything thereafter happened at a rapid speed. No sooner had the doctor disappeared into the study, than Miss Trueblood and I heard the clatter of a vehicle outside and, on opening the front door, found there Ned Tilling and his wagonette, carrying Mr. Devoy together with a lady of ancient appearance. Devoy leapt down and then lifted his companion from the contraption. The secretary turned an unpleasant smile upon me, but the elderly lady looked bewildered until her eyes fastened on Miss Trueblood.

"Beatrice, is it?" she asked in quavering tones. "Dear little Beatrice."

"In a moment, great aunt," Devoy said. "Come away into the house first and warm up."

"Who is she?" I whispered to Miss Trueblood.

"I have not a notion," came the puzzled reply and she followed the old lady and grand- nephew into the house.

I meanwhile turned to Ned Tilling. I wanted a word with that young fellow before he had a chance to make off. He was reluctant at first, yet when he discovered that my interests lay not in exposing his and Elsie's foolish and ill-considered prank – I was willing to accept it as such – but in the circumstances of his discovery of the mask, he took me into his full confidence. And most interesting, instructive and shocking this proved to be.

It was thus a good half hour later that I entered the parlour where the rest of the party was assembled, having first made a foray to my bedchamber. Mr. Bastable was sunk in an armchair by the fire, the doctor standing beside him. The elderly lady was seated upon a couch, next to Miss Trueblood, who was holding her hand. Mr. Devoy stood by the window.

When I entered, all eyes turned to me. All but Miss Trueblood's decidedly unfriendly. For her part, she looked flushed and uncomfortable and lowered her gaze.

"Here is the woman at last," said Mr. Devoy. "I was starting to imagine," he now addressed himself to me, "that when you set eyes upon my great-aunt you decided to do a bunk."

"Do a bunk?" What expressions these young people use! "Why ever should I do that?"

"Can you tell me who you are?" he said.

43

I glanced at Miss Trueblood, who almost imperceptibly shook her head.

"I…" I started to speak. Then stopped, not quite sure how to proceed.

"You are reluctant, I perceive. And rightly so, madam. Then let me introduce my great-aunt." Mr. Devoy was grinning now like an alligator from the river Nile. "Mrs. St. Claire meet Mrs. St.Claire."

A gasp arose from the company, Miss Trueblood included. I suspected Mr. Devoy had merely hinted at my subterfuge until my appearance could make his revelation the more dramatic.

"What have you to say to that?" His eyes gleamed with triumph and I understood now the reason for his past hostility. "Explain yourself, madam."

I doubt that he was expecting the response I gave, for I could no longer contain myself and burst out laughing.

Everyone now looked at me in astonishment.

"Oh, dear," I said. "You must have suspected me of all sorts of underhand purposes, Mr. Devoy. But Miss Trueblood can clear this up in an instant. It was she who insisted I take on your aunt's identity."

Now everyone looked to the young woman of the house.

"It is true," she said. And explained all. "I was so frantic with worry," she concluded, "that I prevailed on Mrs. Hudson to accompany me here but did not wish her true identity, as an associate of Mr. Sherlock Holmes, to be common knowledge. It was a foolish deception and I apologise to Mrs. St. Claire for putting her to the trouble of a long journey in such inclement weather."

I was still debating if I should clear up any misconception of my role in Mr. H's household – an associate, indeed! – and reveal myself simply as his housekeeper and landlady. But all around me now was a buzz of conversation, in which I noticed Mr. Bastable took no part. He seemed to be debating something with himself and finally rose from his chair and fixed me with an angry stare.

"You are not welcome in my house, madam," he said. "You will be pleased to remove yourself forthwith."

A silence followed his words. A silence I had to fill, even though all was still not clear to me.

"I will go and gladly," said I, "but not until you have explained yourself, sir." And I pulled from under my shawl the same mask that had so terrified the man on previous occasions.

I have to say I expected the sight of the thing to produce a reaction, although perhaps not as strong a one as it did. The old man let out a bellow of pure rage and threw himself upon me. He wrenched the mask from my hands and flung it upon the fire. Quick action on the part of Mr. Devoy in recovering it with the poker, not to mention the lucky inadequacies of Elsie's fire-building skills, meant that only the hairs on its head became singed.

Meanwhile, Dr. Mortimer was having, with difficulty, to restrain his patient, who suddenly seemed possessed of some superhuman strength which, if he were released, looked to be directed towards inflicting harm upon my person.

But I was by no means finished with him.

"Perhaps," said I, producing the brown bottle from my reticule, and advancing towards him "you should partake of the same restorative with which you have been dosing your granddaughter."

"You devil," he shouted, again trying to break from the hands now not only of the doctor but also of Mr. Devoy.

"Don't you want some?" I opened the bottle and proffered it to him, he recoiled.

"What is this about?" Miss Trueblood asked, staring at the bottle.

"Why," I asked, still addressing my words to the old

45

man, "have you been trying to poison your granddaughter?" Bastable stared at me now with wild eyes.

"It's a damnable lie. I have not. I was given the medicine in good faith by a South American native tribe. It is herbal that is all."

Dr. Mortimer shook his head and, emboldened, I continued, "Do you deny this to be a concoction of oleander berries, which in low doses produces sickness and fainting, but which in higher ones can lead to death. Your own doctor will confirm this. While seeming to care for her well- being you were planning to kill her."

The old man's fire seemed to go out. He shrank down within himself.

"Grandfather?" said Miss Trueblood in horror. "This cannot be. It cannot. Why, would you? Why?"

"I think," Mr. Devoy stepped forward, "that I may be able to throw some light on the matter. While of course never being privy to any such murderous plot, I suspected that something here was not right. I have to confess further that I did not arrive here by chance. My great-aunt had kept in touch with her godson, Miss Beatrice's father, until his untimely death. Trueblood, it seems, had gone on to amass a huge fortune in the diamond mines of South Africa, a fortune Miss Trueblood was to inherit upon reaching the age of twenty-one, which she will do, I believe, in several weeks' time." He then pulled some papers out of his breast pocket.

The old man snarled and tried to rise up at the sight of them but was again held back by the doctor.

"These documents," Devoy continued, "which I found in the course of my research, hidden in a secret drawer in the desk in the study, the which however was no match for my ingenuity," (he smirked) "give the proof to all I have said. And if, God forbid, Miss Beatrice should die first, we can assume her fortune will pass to her grandfather, as sole next of kin."

"It is true," the young lady interposed in trembling tones, looking at Devoy. "My grandfather made his will only a few weeks ago, just before your arrival. He furthermore suggested, nay insisted, I should do the same, he naming me as beneficiary and me naming him likewise. I thought it strange, but he is a man of strange ways and..." here she started to break down, "someone never happy to be thwarted."

I could well imagine the mental pressure this man exercised over his powerless granddaughter, and shivered at the thought.

"It was apparent," Devoy continued, "from the correspondence conducted between my great-aunt and Miss Beatrice, which she shewed me, that the young lady was entirely unaware of the circumstances relating to her inheritance. So, partly to appease the concerns of Mrs. St. Claire, I offered my services free as secretary to Mr. Bastable, claiming as reason enough my heartfelt admiration for his work and my fervent urgings that it should be disseminated to a wider public. This, of course, without revealing my true identity. He accepted my offer to work unpaid with alacrity, this man whom you must all now recognise as the most miserable of misers. I knew that he expected to gain and enrich himself from the publication of his discoveries, and suspected moreover that he had designs on his granddaughter's inheritance. But never, never, never did I dream of his true and terrible plan. That money could mean so much more to Bastable than his own flesh and blood, well, it is past conceiving." And he shook his head sadly.

If this revelation were not astounding in itself, what happened next had us gaping with amazement. Suddenly, old Mrs. St. Claire rose up, signs of her dotage seeming to have passed for the moment. It was with a strong, clear voice that she announced, "There is no flesh and blood at issue here for there is no Mr. Bastable present."

"Now, now, aunt," Mr. Devoy said. "You are mistaken.

There sits Mr. Bastable, by the fire."

"I know Arthur Bastable well enough," quoth the old dame, "and that is not him. That is McAdam, gamekeeper to the estate in the old days. You are changed mightily, but not past recognition, sir."

Upon launching this bombshell, Mrs. St. Claire sat down again and resumed her vacant stare.

"I fear she is sorely bewildered," Mr. Devoy whispered. "The lady speaks only the truth."

At these words, we all turned now to view the speaker, newly arrived in the manly form of Ned Tilling, and bearing the very box I had requested him to bring, the box wherein he had found the mask of the smiling man. It was a large receptacle of black metal with a heavy clasp, somewhat dented and showing signs of the burial in woodland to which until recently it had been subjected.

"This box contains some most interesting items." The young farmer opened it to our view.

Indeed, it was piled full of a miscellany of objects: a strangely carved pipe, various foreign coins, a pocket bible, letters and other papers, photographic images. A swift perusal of these latter indeed confirmed Mrs. St. Claire's assertions. For the picture of the gentleman smoking the same distinctive pipe that was to be found in the box, a picture inscribed on the back as being of Arthur Bastable, shewed a person though somewhat like, but evidently not the one sitting in front of us. That gentleman, meantimes, had sunk deep into his chair, watching all with chilling malice, as if he intended that arrows from his eyes might pierce each one of us to the very heart.

I understood at once why he had been so enraged at the prospect of meeting Mrs. St. Claire, a person who could expose his imposture. I remembered the handkerchief over his face at our first meeting and the glee with which he had discarded it, upon realising that I was not the woman I pretended to be. And then something further struck me.

"McAdam?" said I thoughtfully. "Something to the cook, then?"

"His daughter, I imagine," quoth Devoy. "Such an ill-tempered, ill-favoured woman could surely never have found a husband."

Letting this ungallant remark pass, I went on to wonder aloud how a box containing such incriminating evidence should have come to be concealed in the copse and its contents not destroyed.

Mr. Bastable, or rather, McAdam, did not respond to my query, or did not have time to before Ned Tilling again broke into the conversation.

"You may ask that, ma'am, but the box was deeply buried and might never have been discovered but for the storms. Perhaps more to the point," he went on meaningfully, "is to wonder what else is buried in the copse along with the box."

A shrinking dread possessed me at these words. For the question must arise that if this man is not Mr. Arthur Bastable, then where in heaven's name IS Mr. Arthur Bastable?

The young farmer explained further. "The storm that uprooted the tree under which the box lay buried has, as I discovered on revisiting the site this very morning after fully perusing and reflecting on the contents of the box, also laid bare a quantity of bones which might have been casually assumed to be those of some large animal that strayed into the copse, only to be dismembered…"

Here Mr. Devoy broke in, "Good God, fellow whoever you are, please remember that there are ladies here present."

"Fellow?" said Ned, looking hard upon the other. "We'll soon see which of us is the 'fellow'…" He addressed himself to Miss Trueblood. "Will I continue, Miss Beatrice? I think you should hear this."

She, with a swift glance at myself, nodded her

49

acquiescence. "The bones being hung about with rags, we can assume them to be human. And this I discovered stuffed down beside them."

He delved into his pocket and pulled out a filthy handkerchief, allowing us to examine it. Clearly borne upon its corner were the embroidered initials, AB.

With a cry, Miss Trueblood fainted away, falling to the floor. "You see, you devil, what you have done," cried Mr. Devoy, leaping to the maiden's assistance. But the doctor was there ahead of him.

"She has suffered no great harm," said he, raising her up gently on to the couch. And indeed she very shortly opened her eyes.

"I consider," said I, "that the truth, however painful, needs to be revealed and we should be grateful to Ned here for his efforts."

"Grateful to a thief! Grateful to a poacher!" shouted the secretary. "What about me? Am I not due some gratitude for all that I have uncovered?" And he waved the documents in the air.

"Indeed, Mr. Devoy," I replied, "if the selfless motives you ascribe to yourself can be believed then you are surely due our gratitude. However, the fact that you arrived incognito and have been here many weeks without making any attempt to enlighten Miss Trueblood as to her inheritance, rather casts your motivation in an altogether more self-seeking light. Is it not the fact that you inveigled your way into the household expressly to woo and perhaps wed a woman you knew was about to become immensely rich?"

"Did I not tell him?" Mrs. St. Claire had perked up once more and spoke eagerly. "Did I not tell him Miss Beatrice would make a fine match for him? An heiress! And," she patted the girl on the hand, "she could do much worse than my Charlie." Glowering at Ned Tilling.

"Is it then proved," Miss Trueblood rose unsteadily to

her feet, "that I am to inherit a fortune?"

Dr. Mortimer, having taken the documents from Devoy, perused them for several minutes. "So it would seem," he said.

Whereupon Miss Trueblood started to laugh and then could not seem to stop, a terrible, hysterical laugh that went on and on and on. I stepped forward and slapped her face hard and then she fell into my arms and started to sob.

There is much more I could relate. How the police were called and indeed unearthed the bones of poor Arthur Bastable in the copse where they had lain ever since his return from foreign parts. At least he could now be afforded a Christian burial. McAdam, for his part, tried to claim that his master had died a natural death and that it was only then that he had decided to take on the other's identity, knowing nothing at that time of any inheritance and not knowing either that the elixir he gave to his "granddaughter" was a slow-acting but deadly poison. His daughter-in-law (she had indeed been married to his late son, despite Devoy's unflattering remarks as to her person), had attempted to flee but had been apprehended at the railway station about to board a train to London. She proved less than loyal and provided all the evidence required to convict her father-in-law as a murderer, no doubt in hopes of mitigating her part in the business. According to her story, McAdam had accompanied his master to South America, where they remained for many years. After hearing of the death of his daughter and son-in-law in the influenza epidemic, Mr. Bastable had indeed confided to McAdam that at least the young orphan would be very well provided for on reaching her maturity through her father's investments. He also expressed the intention of bringing her to Braxton Parvis, if she so wished, on his return from South America. It was then McAdam hatched his evil plan and, before any of the neighbours set eyes on the lord of the manor they had not seen for over twenty years, did away with him, burying his body in the copse, along with anything that might reveal the truth. He had thrown the mask of the smiling man in with all, having apparently a superstitious dread of the pagan object, the face of a god which the natives claimed foretold calamity.

McAdam's similarity to his master in build and general appearance and the fact that he presented himself as a recluse, only permitting those to visit who had never met him before, such as Dr. Mortimer, ensured that his secret remained such. He brought his daughter-in-law to the house as cook, a position, it was understood from her demeanour in mentioning this, that she deeply resented. However, she acquiesced on the promise of a goodly share of the loot once they had got their hands on Miss Trueblood's inheritance.

"I never knew 'e was a-poisoning of 'er, sir," she told the chief detective. "'E told me she was feeble and not long for the world."

Her father-in-law, on learning of her damning testimony, suffered a severe stroke and was not to be revived in possession of his wits, thereby dodging the executioner's rope. He was however, confined for the rest of his days in Bedlam, which some might consider a just enough punishment. His daughter-in-law was sent to Newgate but escaped with a light sentence due to turning Queen's evidence, though in my judgement the baggage knew all well enough and indeed connived with it.

The role of the Tillings, Ned and Elsie, was considered not worth prosecuting, since they had been instrumental in bringing villains to justice. Indeed, Miss Trueblood insisted on gifting the copse to Ned and his family in gratitude for his discoveries. My own modest role was also praised but mostly by Miss Trueblood alone. It is strange how gentlemen do not like to see women making advances over them, but I have often observed this to be the case.

It was some months after the events I have described – Miss

Trueblood in the meantime having reached maturity and inherited her fortune – that I met the young lady again.

I was in the kitchen remonstrating with Phoebe, who had once more burnt the porridge, when the knocker sounded on the door. Soon thereafter Clara called me to my parlour where she had seated my unexpected visitor. At first sight this was a very grand lady indeed. She stood with her back to me, looking out the window, in a coat of moss-green velvet edged with golden fur. A splendid hat with feathers and veil. Fine yellow gloves. Whoever could this be, I wondered, rather thinking it must be some caller for Mr. H who had mistaken the bell. As I entered, however, she turned, and I recognised the lovely features of Miss Trueblood. Despite her finery and my old floury apron, she fell upon me with expressions of joy.

I sat her down and she removed her gloves. I noticed a ruby ring set amid tiny diamonds sparkling on her finger and asked to which of the young men of her acquaintance was she engaged.

"None of them," she replied laughing. "Devoy has gone back to Brighton with his aunt, his tail between his legs, Ned I expect will someday marry Elsie, unless she finds better, and Dr. Mortimer…"

"Dr. Mortimer!" I interposed with amazement. "Was he also one of your admirers?"

"The most pressing," said she. "But he is an old man of thirty- five and I cannot be bothering with that. In any case, I am planning on travelling to see the world, to go on the Grand Tour."

"All by yourself?"

"Yes indeed, all alone apart from Elsie who will accompany me as my lady's maid." I wondered at the wisdom of this but said nothing. "You see, Mrs. Hudson," she continued, "a new century is about to begin, bringing with it new ideas about the position of women within society. No longer will we be the chattels of men, forever following behind them. Indeed, one day we may even lead the way."

I laughed heartily then at her jesting.

"Anyhow, I have brought you a gift," she went on, "since you refused any monetary reward for all that you did for me." (The which was exact. Discovery of the truth being the only reward I required). "Here," she said, proffering a box which by its shape and size I assumed to contain a hat, maybe almost as fashionable as the one she herself was wearing."

"Thank you kindly," I said, opening the gift, in expectation of feathers and net.

But what did I find inside, wrapped in tissue paper and only slightly singed from the fire? Nothing more nor less than the fateful mask of the smiling man.

Mrs. Hudson and the Demon Within

It was a balmy morning in spring and I was sitting in my front parlour enjoying the unaccustomed sun that poured through the window, busying myself with some small items of sewing. The doctor was away, but I could hear the restless pacing of Mr. H above me. He must, I thought to myself, be lacking an intriguing case to divert him and lift his spirits, which I feared had been quite down of late.

Suddenly there came a-knocking on the front door of an urgency which indicated to me that this was no casual caller. I hastened to answer, since Clara was busy in the kitchen and Phoebe had, by my instructions, been sent to the market to purchase some herring, chops and other comestibles. God only knew what the silly girl would bring back, but I still lived in hope that she might be trained up to the tasks allotted her.

I opened the door to find standing there a very fine lady indeed.

At the same moment, Mr. H leaned over the balustrade and called down, "Someone for me, I warrant, Mrs. Hudson."

And indeed, I was about to show the lady to the staircase when she hastily interposed, "Mrs. Hudson, it is you I wish to consult."

Mr. H continued to wait in expectation, evidently having failed to hear the lady's statement, which had been uttered in low tones.

"It's someone for me, Mr. H," I called up the stairs, whereupon he disappeared, muttering discontentedly, back into

55

his rooms.

I conducted the lady into the front parlour, hastily gathering up the remnants of my sewing.

"Please do not trouble yourself on my account," she said, with an elegant gesture. "I see that I interrupt your work."

"It is of no consequence," I replied, glad that the room otherwise was in good order, thanks to the sterling efforts of dear Clara. "Please to be seated."

The lady arranged herself in an upright chair with a great rustling of the watered silk grey gown she was wearing. She then lay down her parasol and, since the room was warm in the sun, removed the silver fox fur from around her shoulders, placing it beside her. Her hat which she retained, was no simple poke bonnet, but a pastel concoction of ribbons and plumes wrenched, I feared, from the bodies of many unfortunate and exotic birds of the Southern hemisphere. The face beneath was small (indeed I wondered that narrow neck could bear the weight of the hat), with fair and delicate features marred only by a troubled frown between fine pale brows. Her age, I assessed, as being in the middle twenties, and I detected the outline of a wedding band under the grey kid glove of her left hand.

"Can I offer you refreshments?" I asked as a preliminary. "You are kind," she replied in the same low tones. "Beatrice told me you were. Yes, a light China tea, if you have it, would be most agreeable."

"Ah," I said, understanding dawning as I rang the bell to summon Clara. "You are a friend of Miss Trueblood." This was a lady I had recently been privileged to assist out of a most hazardous situation.

"Beatrice is a dear, dear friend of mind from schooldays," the lady replied. "But permit me to introduce myself. I am Louisa Pym, Mrs. Ernest Pym, if you will, and I reside in the county of Kent, near Bromley."

At that moment a tap on the door was followed by the

appearance of Clara, tidy enough I was happy to note, despite her labours in the kitchen. I instructed her to bring us a pot of Souchong and some wafer biscuits.

Clara bobbed a curtsey and departed.

I regarded my visitor. Then, since she showed no sign of dispelling the silence, I asked, "In what way do you think I can help you, Mrs. Pym?"

At this, she leaned forward and clutched my hand, deep emotion etched on her pretty face.

"Mrs. Hudson," said she. "I go in very fear of my life."

To say I was taken aback, would do no justice to what I felt at that moment.

"My dear lady," I said, after a moment spent collecting myself. "I fear you misapprehend my abilities. I have no experience in such matters and the fact that I was able to assist Miss Trueblood out of her difficulty arose more from luck than judgment. I suggest you consult..." And I raised my eyes to indicate he who still restlessly paced the upper floor.

The lady stood abruptly and walked to the window. She looked out for a moment and then turned to face me.

"I know to whom you refer," she said. "But I cannot share my story with a man, Mrs. Hudson. It is too, too delicate. Modesty forbids. And in any case, I feel only a woman, nay a woman of your maturity and perspicacity, would be able to understand my predicament. If you will not help me, Mrs. Hudson, then all I can say is, God help me, wretch that I am." Whereupon she collapsed in a heap on the floor.

I hastily summoned Clara again and together we raised Mrs. Pym to the chaise longue, where I administered the sal volatile that I keep always in my purse even though I make no use of it myself, having, I am pleased to say, never been subject to fainting fits of any kind.

Clara left us to fetch the tea and it was only as Mrs. Pym sipped the hot brew that she seemed to recover.

"You had best recount your story to me," I suggested gently.

It seemed that Louisa, as she wished me to call her, had been married for some six years to a man many years her senior, a wealthy businessman with interests in the East Indies. These caused him to travel extensively, leaving her often alone in the house in Bromley with little Timothy, their son of five years.

The marriage at first was as happy as, said Louisa, one between two people of such different ages and interests could be. She enjoyed the arts, music, poetry, opera, the theatre. He regarded such as fitting diversions for ladies but certainly not for gentlemen and, when not occupied with his business interests, liked to go hunting and shooting through the Kent countryside, activities which she, as an animal lover, abhorred (at this point, no doubt in memory of so many needlessly slain creatures, she pressed a lacy cambric handkerchief to her eye). The couple had at least been united in love for their son, Timothy, that is (and her voice faltered) until very recently.

She took a sip of her tea and nibbled the corner of a wafer biscuit. It seemed such slight nourishment gave her the strength to continue.

"My husband," she said, "is a complex man, Mrs. Hudson. If you meet him, and I hope you will very soon, you will immediately judge him someone of gentle temperament, agreeable, even, in his way, charming. However, I have to tell you that he is a man of deep dark passions, as I have discovered to my cost. A man obsessively jealous who now throws in my face the fact that… that he doubts the paternity of his son."

After this shocking revelation, she tossed her head, the feathers and ribbons on her hat quivering as if infused with the lady's own strong emotion.

"Oh, Mrs. Hudson," quoth she, "I can bear insinuations against myself, knowing I am innocent of all. But, when he turns from my son, his son, with hate and revulsion on his face, that I cannot endure."

It seemed once more that she was about to succumb, and I stood to assist her, grasping again the bottle of sal volatile, but instead she rallied and waved me to be seated again.

"Whatever has put this notion in his head of a sudden?" I asked.

Louisa turned tear-filled eyes toward me.

"I will be entirely frank with you, Mrs. Hudson," said she. "There is a young man of my acquaintance..." She paused for a second. "A very dear friend of mine since childhood. While I have always regarded him as a brother, I suspect his feelings for me are... well... you understand." I nodded. The young man was in love with her. "But Gabriel was then and still is without wealth or indeed prospects, through, I must add, no fault of his own. Life, Mrs. Hudson, has conspired against him. Following my marriage to Ernest, he instantly left to try to make his fortune in South Africa and was gone for nigh on five years. Recently he returned and took up residence near us in Beckenham, where he scrapes a living as a clerk in an office."

She toyed with the tail of the fox.

"My life, Mrs. Hudson, has been a lonely one, without a soulmate to share my interests. Despise me if you will but when Gabriel came back into my life, it was with a mad joy that I received him. Not, I hasten to say, as a lover. No, I respect my vows of fidelity too much for that. But as one who can share with me my interests, one who can accompany me to the theatre, the opera, discuss books with me. One moreover without the blood of innocent creatures on his hands for Gabriel abhors the hunt as much as I do. Ernest was away at the time of Gabriel's return, but when he came back it seemed at first that he also was pleased. Even he could see that I had descended into a decline, and was happy that Gabriel could distract me from those dark places. Then suddenly, I know not how it came about for we gave him no cause, last evening he started ranting at me, that I had betrayed him and even claimed (oh, I feel ashamed to even utter it) that Gabriel was the true father of Timothy."

Her face radiated with the horror of the accusation.

"You see now, how I cannot confide in a man, even he…" and she raised her eyes to the ceiling. "It would be too shameful. And anyway, men see these things differently from us women, is that not the case."

I nodded, though by no means convinced. In my experience, my dear late husband Henry and I saw eye-to-eye on all things. But the young lady no doubt had her reasons if her husband was as merciless as she claimed. For sure, it was at the very least rash of her to encourage a young man who in the past had nurtured romantic feelings for her. However, young ladies, in my experience, tend to lack sagacity and no doubt she was flattered by the attention.

"I tried," she continued, "to convince my husband of the absurdity of his notions but he was having none of it. Mrs. Hudson, I was terrified. Ernest grabbed one of his pistols and waved it in my face, saying that if he found Gabriel and myself together in anything resembling a compromising situation, he would kill the two of us without an instant's care for the consequences. Oh, I could relinquish my miserable existence in a second, but what then of Timothy? What would become of my darling son?"

And she threw herself across the chaise longue in a paroxysm of emotion.

Louisa Pym's story had made me curious for several reasons and I felt it incumbent upon me to try to prevent any violent outcome resulting from the sorry situation she had outlined. However, there were complications attendant upon my immediately accompanying her to Bromley. Above all, I had to make arrangements for the welfare of Mr. H. Clara was as good a maid as I could hope for, but I would not trust her to prepare the hearty repasts that Mr. H required, and I knew that he would not care for himself. Assuming my absence would be but for one night, I sent Clara to call upon my neighbour, Mrs. Dixon, who is well aware of my tenant's strange proclivities, and thus unlikely to be shocked by them. She is also, and I do not say this boastfully but as a statement of fact, almost as good a cook as I, so Mr. H would not suffer too badly while I was gone.

Mrs. Dixon arriving within the half-hour, I collected together the few items I would need for a night's sojourn and duly set off with Mrs. Pym for Kent. What I could do there I had little idea, but the very fact that I would be with her, maybe to intercede with her husband on her behalf, seemed to reassure her, and she settled down most comfortably in the first-class carriage of the train from Victoria station.

On the way, I tried to impress upon her the need to cut all ties immediately with the young gentleman.

"But Mrs. Hudson," said she, "will that not give credence to my husband's accusations? Surely we should continue as before to show that there is no truth in them."

"If Mr. Pym is as volatile as you say, Louisa," I replied, "I fear that would be a most dangerous course to take. At least for the time being. Let me perhaps speak to your husband privately in an attempt to assuage his anger."

Louisa looked out of the window, a frown on her little face as she considered my words, tapping her parasol nervously on the floor of the carriage. She then turned back to me with a smile.

"How wise you are, Mrs. Hudson," she said. "Yes indeed, speak to Ernest by all means. But not immediately. Get to know him tonight, if you can see through the genial mask that he will surely don for your benefit. Then, talk to him later or perhaps in the morning."

I acquiesced to this and we continued the journey in relative silence, each with our own thoughts.

In due course, we arrived at Bromley station and took a cab the mile or so to the Pym residence, a medium-sized, block-shaped house, unattractive to my eyes, set in its own grounds, with a short drive to a front door flanked on either side by large stone urns embellished with the faces of smiling lions. A small boy was playing on the front steps with a middle-aged woman I took to be the nanny, dressed as she was in a plain blue gown and white apron. The boy looked up as we arrived but showed no further interest in us.

"Timothy," called Louisa.

"Go and say hello to mamma," said the nanny.

The boy came over to us, it seemed to me without enthusiasm. "Kiss your mamma, Timmy," called the nanny.

"Yes, but you are dirty, Timothy," Louisa said. "Mind Mamma's pretty dress." Almost as an afterthought, it seemed to me, she ruffled the boy's curly blond hair. "This is Mrs. Hudson, dearest," she continued, "who will be visiting us for the evening."

The boy looked at me with the suspicion the young often show to a stranger, but I am used to my own grandchildren and smiled easily, saying "Hello, Timothy. Is that a sword you have in your hand? I hope you are not intending to fight me with it."

"Oh no," he answered. "Nanny and I were playing knights and dragons. Nanny was the dragon and roared very loud. You should hear her."

"I should very much like to," I said. The woman smiled but Louisa frowned.

"It sounds like a rough game," she said. "I wish you would not play it, Timothy. Nanny, please take the sword away. He might hurt himself with it."

Timothy held fast to the wooden thing. "But Papa gave it to me. He made it."

"Nanny...Take the sword." Louisa said in a stern voice. "And the child is filthy. He must be washed this instant.

Whatever will Mrs. Hudson think of us?"

"Can I see your sword?" I asked the boy. He held it out to me to take and I examined it. It was well-crafted and sturdy, and unlikely to do more harm than any stick a boy might pick up off the ground.

At that moment, a man of unusual height appeared on the threshold. Though of advanced years, he looked fit and strong, with the tanned skin of one often in the open and – since I guessed him to be the jealous husband and knew of his occupation – one who spent time frequently in warmer climes than ours. He stepped toward me, an inquiring expression on his face.

"I hope you do not intend me any harm," he said. I did not follow his meaning until I saw him smiling at the sword still in my hand.

"Mrs. Hudson," said Louisa. "This is my husband Ernest." She turned to him. "Mrs. Hudson is a dear friend of Beatrice Trueblood and a great lover of music." Am I? It is news to me although I admit that I enjoy an occasional evening of parlour songs. I am often diverted as well by the more melodious pieces played by Mr. H on his violin. But a "great lover," that I would never claim to be. Louisa, however, continued. "She has kindly agreed to accompany me tomorrow to the concert in Sevenoaks."

I had no recollection of any such thing, although there is nothing wrong with my memory. Moreover I had not come prepared for illustrious company, nor for more than one night away. The young lady really did seem to presume too much.

"I am delighted to meet you, Mrs. Hudson," said Mr. Pym, striding forward and shaking my hand in his firm one. "But what of poor Gabriel, Louisa? Are you throwing him over at last?"

"You know more about that," muttered Louisa, shooting me a meaning glance.

Her husband, I have to say, seemed puzzled, as was I. There was no rancour at all in his voice when mentioning the name of the presumed lover.

"But we linger too long on the doorstep," he said. "Please to come in, Mrs. Hudson," and, taking my arm, Mr. Pym led me into the hall.

"My sword," said Timothy, scampering alongside us. I gave it to him but heard behind me the tut-tutting of his mother.

"Really, Ernest," she said, "Timothy should not be encouraged to play such war-like games."

"Timmy needs no encouragement," came the reply. "Boys, Louisa, will be boys."

"Then," she replied tartly, "perhaps you should have given me a daughter."

"Timothy tells us you made the sword," I said quickly in order to soften harshness of her words. "It is a fine piece of work."

"A hobby of mine," Mr. Pym said. "Woodworking, don't you know."

I thought I heard another dismissive "tch" from the lady close upon my heels.

A maid showed me up to a neatly furnished guest room on the first floor of the house, with a view over a kitchen garden and beyond it, an orchard of apple trees, prettily coming in to flower.

I sat for a moment on a comfortably upholstered chair, trying to gather my thoughts. Before I could marshal them in any satisfactory way, the door burst open after the briefest of taps, and Louisa entered, placing a finger on her lips.

"Mrs. Hudson," said she, in low tones. "I understand you must be wondering at what you have so far seen. No doubt my husband has managed to charm you as he does all who do not know him intimately. I hope you will believe me when I say that Ernest is skilled at presenting a pleasant demeanour to the world

64

while concealing absolutely the demon that lurks within."

"I admit to finding nothing here as expected. Your husband shows no enmity at all to your friend Gabriel and treats his son Timothy with love and affection."

"That is indeed his base trickery, Mrs. Hudson. Oh please, I beg of you, do not turn your face from me. You are my only hope." And she gripped my arm.

"Forgive me, but you speak to him quite sharply," I said.

"And do you think I should grovel?" A flame flared in her eyes.

"No, but I assure you, he will make me pay for it later, when we are alone."

Unless the lady were a superb actress, I could not doubt the anguish on her face.

"Well, well," I soothed. "Let us hope my words will bring him round and call a halt to any unfounded suspicions."

"Yes, but you have promised not to speak until tomorrow morning," she said.

"I understood later tonight."

"No, better leave it till the morrow. Tonight he will take wine and spirits, which often affect his temper severely. I should not like you also to be victim of his wrath."

It was now the afternoon, and Louisa asked if I wished to have a rest after our journey.

"The maid can bring you refreshments here if you will."

"That would be most kind," I replied. "I admit I am somewhat fatigued."

This was, I am afraid, a white lie. I am not at all in the habit of resting during the day. But the truth of the matter was that I required a break from the fervour of the lady, time indeed to think.

"I will send Perkins up with some tea and pastries forthwith," she said. "Rest well." And she swished from the room.

Refreshed shortly after by the brew brought me by a sullen enough girl I would have chastised for her manner had I been mistress here, I lay down for a moment on the bed. But I am loath to be without occupation and the sun, dappling through my window, together with the soft and aromatic breeze that accompanied it, tempted me to try for a walk in the garden. Passing through the house I heard no one except, faintly, the childish voice of little Timothy, protesting as nanny scrubbed the mud from his body.

I made my way first to the kitchen garden and examined the flourishing herbs that grew there, pinching some sage leaves between my fingers to release the scent. Although it was early in the year, already some vegetables were showing themselves: the overwintering broad beans were coming on nicely with their black and white flowers. Pea plants were flourishing too, their blooms a delicate white, and pink and purple sweet peas gave fragrance to the air. I noted with approval that the spring spinach was up and spotted beds of lettuce and radish. Even the first early potatoes looked ready. All in all, it was a neat and well-tended place and I mentally congratulated whoever was responsible for it – not, I suspected, the lady of the house.

I then walked into the orchard through a gate in a high stone wall, prettily aged with mosses, lichens and sprouting ferns, stepping into a veritable fairy-land of flowers, from the palest pink blossoms on the trees to vivid pools of bluebells beneath and the occasional tuft of primroses that grew between them. Bees buzzed busily and birds chirped among the branches. How, I wondered, could violent emotions thrive in such a peaceful place?

A seat had been positioned against the wall and I sat upon it to take in the beauties around me.

Maybe I dozed a little after all, one of those waking sleeps that Mr. Shakespeare talks about. After some moments, I was roused by hushed voices from the other side of the wall. One

I recognised as belonging to Louisa Pym, the other that of a man, though not her husband. The voices were so soft that much of what was spoken was lost to me and in any case it is not my habit to eavesdrop upon private conversations. However, one or two words gave me pause and, I confess, I strained my ears to hear more.

"Tonight" and "she will be our witness," from Louisa, though the man's response was carried away on the breeze.

"I will leave it..." Then something that sounded like "Ern..." Possibly a sobriquet for her husband.

A murmured demur from the man. Then "Do not hesitate now, I entreat you, after all that I have done," came quite clearly from the raised voice of the lady. A pause and she added, more softly, "it will all be over soon. And then, my dearest ... to Southern Africa and the diamond mines ..." The silence that followed spoke more to me than any words.

I prayed to God that neither party would enter the orchard and discover me. I could only feign sleep if such occurred and positioned my body accordingly. However, there was no more to be heard save sounds of departure in opposite directions and I sat up, pondering what further action to take. The deceitful character of the lady did not, I confess, come as a great surprise to me. The truth was that from the first I had not warmed to her. There was a slyness in her manner that revolted me and I had already observed a lack of accord between her vaunted adoration for her little boy and her cool and unmotherly behaviour toward him. However, I was not yet inclined utterly to dismiss her dread of her husband, no matter how apparently absent the evidence of his jealous and vindictive nature. Let me admit it: I was intrigued. Something was happening in this household below the surface of things and I wanted to find out what it was. Lucky chance, then, led me out of the orchard a different way and past a small wooden hut whose door stood open. Inside I spotted the master of the house intent on constructing what, as I stood on the threshold, I observed to be a small sailing boat. Here was a perfect opportunity to examine further into his character.

I stood watching him for a moment. The intensity with which he concentrated on the matter in hand reminded me of my own dear departed Henry, when engaged on one of his own hobbies. I coughed quietly and Mr. Pym turned towards me.

"Mrs. Hudson," he said. "How delightful! Please to come in.

As you see, I am keeping out of mischief here."

"Is it for Timothy?" I asked, indicating the boat.

"Indeed, for his birthday. He will be six next month. A big boy already."

"You love him very much," I ventured.

"He is the very apple of my eye." Said with such vehemence, I could not doubt the gentleman. His voice, his eyes, his smile attested to the truth of that which he spake. The weight of evidence seemed to swing away from his wife. Nevertheless, I had promised to speak. But how could I approach the subject which now weighed heavily on my heart without appearing a meddlesome old woman. In any case, for whatever reason, Louisa had made me promise not to say a word just yet. I could not help but wonder why.

I watched him for a moment as he adjusted the boat's mast. "It will have sails?" I asked.

"That is the plan but alas I am all thumbs and suspect my attempts will prove a disaster. I would ask dear Nanny Grimes, but she is so busy already, caring for Timothy every hour of the day."

"Mrs. Pym, can she not sew the sails for you?"

"Louisa?" he laughed. "I think you cannot know my wife well if you imagine she would sit quietly with a needle and thread."

"Indeed," I replied, "my acquaintance with your wife is

very short."

"Is that so?" He turned to look me in the eye, his own keen and bright. "Strange then, you should agree to accompany her down here. Where is it that you live?"

"In the middle of the city of London, though I am country born. One reason why it is always a pleasure for me to leave the smoke and bustle behind me even for a few hours."

"Then you are quite the opposite of Louisa, who, I think, would like nothing better than an establishment in London, near all the theatres and shops."

I smiled. "Indeed, London has a lot to offer in that respect." "And did I hear aright," he continued, "that you are friends with Beatrice Trueblood?"

"I am, a lovely lady."

"Yet one who has experienced great trouble in her life." That keen glance again. He must know of Beatrice's tangled history but presumably not of my role in unravelling it.

"So I understand," I said and hastened to change the subject, expressing admiration for the grounds and appurtenances of the house.

"Yes, you see I am completely happy to be here in the countryside, cultivating my garden, as M. Voltaire put it, and would hate the noise of the city."

"Mrs. Pym told me that, as a consequence of your interests abroad, you travel widely."

"I have done so in the past, yes. But now I think I will stay here for good. Timothy needs his father and I am getting too old to be travelling so much."

I smiled at the "too old" and disputed it, assuring him that I had seldom met a man of any years so obviously full of energy. Why did I say such a thing? Perhaps Louisa spoke truly and I was taken with his charm. However, what I said seemed to me simply the plain truth. I found myself adding, "I would be pleased to sew the sails for you, if you wish."

"Mrs. Hudson," he said, "I could not presume on your generosity."

"Not at all," I replied. "For me it would be the work of a half- hour at the most and I would enjoy it."

That agreed, he gave me the pattern for the sails along with some linen scraps he had gathered for the purpose. I assured him that I always travelled with a small sewing kit in case of emergencies, so no need to provide anything further.

"Mrs. Hudson," he said merrily, causing me to blush. "If I wasn't spoken for already, I would marry you on the instant."

I made my way back to the house and up to my room, luckily unseen by any denizens therein. Sewing I find conducive to thought and, after all that I had seen and heard, I needed seriously to think. Though I had certain fears for what might be about to transpire, I yet considered nothing would occur before the evening. It would have given me comfort to confide in Mr. H or even the doctor, but alas, that could not be.

By the time the bell announcing dinner had rung, I had completed the little sails and had also time to compose myself for dinner and whatever might ensue thereafter.

It turned out to be an uneventful enough meal, and one the cook might be proud of except that I found the veal escalopes a trifle overcooked and hard and the sauce for the potatoes lacking in seasoning and containing a few lumps. But the mulligatawny soup that preceded it was excellent, as was the trout, and the fruit pie had a fine crust upon it. Louisa Pym ate little and was mostly silent unless addressed. Her husband made up for it with his bonhomie and showed no sign upon his mood of the adverse effects of the Rhenish wine, even though he consumed several glasses of the same.

Dinner having finished, Louisa rose to conduct me back to the withdrawing room, while Ernest Pym sat with his thoughts, his cigar and a bottle of port.

"You see how he is," she said to me. "Charm itself."

"It is true he is not at all as I pictured him from your description."

She rose abruptly from her chair. "I fear he has woven his spell around you too, Mrs. Hudson," she said.

"I hope," I replied with dignity, "that I am able to keep an open mind. Yesterday I knew nothing of the existence of either you or him. And to be perfectly frank, I am puzzled at the chasm – there is no other word for it – between what you have told me and what I see. I hope you appreciate my difficulty. However, I am not inclined to judge at the moment and am still happy to fulfil my pledge and talk to your husband on your behalf."

"Thank you, Mrs. Hudson. But not tonight, I implore you. Not tonight."

I promised her that I would not.

We were joined shortly after by Mr. Pym and spent a short but tranquil enough evening while Louisa played some pieces on the pianoforte. An awkward moment occurred when I, as a supposed music lover, failed to identify an apparently famous piece by Frederic Chopin, though it was Mr. Pym who diffused the moment by suggesting that it was so ill-played as to be unrecognisable to such a connoisseur as myself. Whereupon we laughed it off, though that little frown again corrupted the perfection of Louisa's visage, after which she played only old favourites that even I would know.

I sensed, however, a tension below the surface of our genteel conversation and strongly felt that both the Pyms, for whatever reasons, were anxious for me to depart. Since anyway I am in the habit of retiring early in order to rise at dawn or shortly thereafter, I started yawning after nine of the clock.

"Poor Mrs. Hudson. Your music is sending her to sleep, Louisa. We must not keep her any longer from her bed," Mr. Pym said, and he stood politely as I rose from my chair.

I thanked him and bade goodnight to the two of them. However, I had little true thoughts of retiring. That "tonight" I had heard in the orchard was playing on my mind and I resolved to keep my wits about me in case anything untoward should transpire.

With that in mind, I performed my ablutions and changed into my nightwear but sat up in bed perusing the latest novel from the pen of my favourite, Marie Corelli.

It was perhaps an hour later that I was awakened (for I had dozed off sitting up over my book), that I heard a piercing scream. For a second I thought it was a dream inspired by Mrs. Corelli's melodrama. However, the scream was repeated and came, I soon realised, not from the pages of my book but from downstairs. I seized my shawl and hastened to my door, hurrying along the corridor and towards the staircase. As I reached it, I heard voices shouting angrily.

I descended in haste and, entering the withdrawing room illuminated only by the last flickerings of the fire, was indeed confronted by a sorry sight. Louisa stood transfixed in horror, hand to her neck, while a young man unknown to me brandished a pistol towards the shadows of the window drapes.

"You villain," cried the younger man. "You will pay for your cruelty... You must..."

But before he could finish his sentence a shot rang out and he crumpled and fell to the floor. Heedless of danger, I sprang to his assistance.

"Mrs. Hudson," came the familiar voice of Mr. Ernest Pym, though now there was a bitter edge to it that I had not heard before. "Just in time for the fun."

I looked up, and, my eyes adjusting to the lack of light, now made out his tall frame against the curtains.

"What have you done!" I said, and bent down to attend to the prone man. It seemed the bullet had entered his upper chest above the heart. He was bleeding profusely and I used my shawl to staunch the flow.

Behind me, I heard steps and a gasp of horror. It was Nanny Grimes just entered, bearing a candle.

"Oh, Mr. Gabriel!" she exclaimed.

"Gabriel?" I repeated and regarded the wounded man with curiosity. He was very young and, despite all, of a most prepossessing aspect. No wonder perhaps that Louisa's head was turned.

"It was him or me, Mrs. Hudson," Mr. Pym said. "You heard how he threatened me. You heard him say that I must pay…"

"Liar," screamed Louisa. "He was defending me."

"Defending you, my dear. From what exactly? From the cruelty you have attributed to me?"

"You were trying to strangle me."

Mr. Pym actually laughed, although what was amusing here when a man was bleeding maybe to death was beyond my ken.

"Light the lamps, Nanny if you would," he said. "And let us get to the bottom of this charade."

"Never mind the lamps, Nanny," I said, careless of the rules of etiquette in another's home. "Pray fetch warm water and bandages and send for a doctor."

"He will live," said Mr. Pym lightly. "If I had intended to kill him, I assure you I would not have failed."

While he sat himself in an armchair, Louisa and I managed to raise the young man and set him on the chaise longue. He was of a deathly pallor and I feared, despite the assurance of his attacker, that without professional assistance, he might yet succumb.

But Nanny returned in haste with a basin of water and clean linen bandages and I think I did a reasonable job patching up the young man's wound while Nanny left us again to send for the doctor.

"So let us establish what exactly has happened here," Mr. Pym remarked. "Mrs. Hudson, I fear my wife invited you to our humble abode under false pretences, not for the reasons she gave you, which was some frippery or other, I am sure. And of course nothing at all to do with concert parties in Sevenoaks. No... She brought you here simply to be witness to a killing. You were to be roused by her agonising screams, rush down and find what you thought was her ladyship under attack by me."

"He did attack me, Mrs. Hudson," Louisa said. "He tried to throttle me. See here the marks upon my neck."

Her throat was indeed mottled with the imprint of a rough hand.

"They faked it," Mr. Pym said. "Her lover put those marks there himself to incriminate me. And then in the throes of this supposed attack, the young man you see lying here was to spring to her defence, accidentally shooting me dead in the ensuing struggle. Is that not so, my lady?"

"No," Louisa said. "At least, I wanted a witness to your cruelty, that I admit, one not subject to the blind or bought loyalty of the servants. But for the rest, no, we did not intend to kill you."

"And yet the young man has a pistol. One of mine, I perceive." He gestured to the weapon lying on the floor by my foot. I picked it up and examined it.

"It was just for show," Louisa cried out. "He did not intend to shoot it."

"Just for show. Do you hear that, Mrs. Hudson? Can you credit it?"

"In fact I can," I said. "The pistol is not loaded."

"You can tell that, I suppose, by looking at it," Mr. Pym jeered.

"I grew up in the country, as I told you. I had brothers and a father who shot and who taught me to shoot. I am well

74

acquainted with such weaponry."

The young man groaned and I noted with alarm the blood seeping through my bandage.

"If he dies," I said, "you will have killed an unarmed man."

"But I honestly believed the thing to be loaded," Mr. Pym said. "Why would I not?"

"Can you tell me," I went on, "how you yourself come to be armed with a loaded pistol? It seems a strange thing to have about you."

"I heard noises and thought it was an intruder. As indeed it was," he said glaring at Gabriel. "I entered this room and found my wife in the embrace of this young man whom I trusted. What a betrayal!" And he shook his head sorrowfully.

"There was no embrace," Louisa said.

Suddenly a feeble voice broke the silence. Gabriel.

"It was to have been loaded. She told me it would be loaded." "Do not be ridiculous," said Louisa, but she had paled.

"You see, Mrs. Hudson," Mr. Pym said gleefully, "he admits it. He admits I was to be killed. You as witness would then be called upon to state the case for the defence, my wicked cruelty, the young man acting to save his old friend's life. After which, when the furor had died down, the two of them would dance off together with my considerable money to start their new life, somewhere or other. Let us say to Southern Africa. The diamond mines perhaps." He laughed dismissively.

"Ah," I said.

"The pistol was presumably, and I am only surmising this, to be concealed somewhere that Gabriel could retrieve it easily" the name at last expressed with venom. "He would then lurk outside the French windows previously left open. My wife would enter here and scream, bringing me running, and I would be shot dead... Witnessed by Mrs. Hudson here, an elderly lady of impeccable respectability, whose objective testimony would leave no doubt as to the truth of the matter." He turned to his wife. "You should really have remembered to load the pistol, my dear."

"I had no need to load it," she said. "It was loaded already. At least... I am sure..." She then staggered at the momentousness of her admission.

"I think you will agree, Mrs. Hudson," he said, "that I have had a very lucky escape."

"Oh no," I said. "I do not consider that luck came into it at all." That "elderly," I admit, had rankled somewhat, and my tone was perhaps sharper as a result.

I looked from one to the other, at the now unmasked hatred that flew between them. If the young man were not lying desperately wounded upon the couch, I should almost imagine I was part of some parlour game the two of them were playing. Both parties, it seemed to me now, had tried to use me for their own nefarious ends.

"Not luck," Mr. Pym asked, seemingly amused. "What then." "I think like me you overheard a certain conversation in the garden this afternoon." (Louisa starting perceptibly at this revelation.) "Yes, I was there, having taken a turn in the orchard, although unlike you, Mr. Pym, I did not deliberately set out to listen in to a private exchange... No doubt, seeing your wife making her way to the garden, you followed, to see what she was up to. Then, after the two lovers had gone their separate ways, you hastened back to your workshop where I found you soon after, apparently working hard on Timothy's boat... No, Louisa," I said as the young lady started to interrupt, "there is no need to dissemble further. The true nature of your relationship with Gabriel is quite clear to me now."

I turned back to Mr. Pym. "The substance of what you overheard gave you pause. I think you must have heard more than I, for, as I have stated, I was not inclined to listen. Hearing the plot afoot, you realised how you could turn it to your own

76

advantage and take revenge upon those who had betrayed you. I was to witness, not your assault on your wife and her defence by her friend, but instead you defending yourself against a villainous and unprovoked attack."

The man laughed. "A pretty fantasy, Mrs. Hudson. I think you must read too many sensational novels."

"There are two pieces of evidence that back up my theory," I persisted. "In the first place, you have just mentioned the diamond mines of Southern Africa. How could you know that the lovers intended to make their new life there unless, like me, you had heard Louisa state it in the garden?"

"A lucky guess," he responded.

"Luck again," I said. "You seem to be a very lucky man, Mr. Pym. But, as I have said, I do not think luck came into it, at least with regard to the pistol. This is my second point of evidence. Like me, you heard that Louisa intended hiding the pistol for Gabriel to retrieve. I thought at first that she said "Ern", being a nickname for you, but now I realise the word was "U-R-N". The pistol was to be concealed in one of the stone urns by the front door. It was there you found it and removed the bullets, thus ensuring an unfair fight. I have no doubt, by the way, despite your vaunted marksmanship, that you fully intended killing your rival, but missed."

"Villain, murderer," Louisa intoned.

"Self-defence, my dear. Pure and simple." He smiled again this time, with all the charm of an Egyptian alligator on the Nile. "I fear, Mrs. Hudson, you will have great difficulty in proving the case you have so cogently put before us…"

"The police…" I started to say.

"I do not think," Mr. Pym interrupted me, "that either dear Louisa here or I want any truck with the police. My evidence could send the two of them to Newgate. After all, as we know, the law favours the husband especially when the servants can back him up as, be assured," added in icy tones, "they will."

Louisa hissed, "You villain," again.

I regarded the lady then but she turned away, unable to look me in the eye.

It was some two months or so later when I found myself in tea rooms in Piccadilly, sitting opposite dear Beatrice Trueblood, who was breaking her grand tour of the European Continent with a brief sojourn in London.

"Louisa Pym," she said thoughtfully. "Louisa Baggot that was. Yes, I remember her, although we were hardly friends, she being several years my senior. At school she was a schemer, gathering around herself a group of admiring peers who enjoyed nothing more than to make game of the less fortunate, less pretty, less rich. I was the butt of her mockery a few times, though I managed at least to stand up to her, for which I garnered some grudging respect. She ignored me thereafter."

I explained my brief involvement with the lady.

"She used my name to gain your confidence! How typical of her," Beatrice remarked. "So what has become of her? I think I heard some scandal. Did she not elope with her paramour?"

"Indeed. That is the given story. In the end, it was all about money, Gabriel, her lover, being penniless and Louisa unable to bear the prospect of renouncing her lavish ways, her gowns, her jewels, her fine house. Their only hope, as they saw it, of a good life together was with her husband dead and Louisa the inheritor of his fortune. Their crude plan failed, they being no match for Ernest Pym, the true master of manipulation. I have no doubt, by the way, having seen the man unmasked, that he was indeed the cruel tyrant his wife described."

"It sounds to me," Beatrice remarked, buttering her scone, "that the two of them deserved each other."

"Yes, I rather fear the young man was a mere puppet in the lady's hand, someone she could inveigle into her plans."

"But not you, Mrs. Hudson. You saw through her at once."

"Not at once, my dear." I demurred. "But quickly, I admit it. And him too, despite his smiles and compliments."

"So how did the matter resolve itself?"

"I suspect Louisa came to a financial arrangement with her husband in order to avoid an ugly court case."

"And the child?"

"He has stayed with his father. Despite her professed love for Timothy, Louisa has proved content to abandon him, while Ernest Pym loves his son sincerely and so must have no doubts as to his true paternity."

"But for a mother to give up her child! How horrid. I cannot imagine such a thing."

"Indeed. It seems inhuman."

"And tell me further, did this Gabriel then recover from his wound?"

"He did, although I understand it has left him with a permanent weakness."

Having consumed her scone, Beatrice cut into a fruit bun. "How was it explained to the doctor?"

"As a sad accident. Mr. Pym claimed he heard noises below and, suspecting an intruder, came down in the dark with his pistol which he discharged before recognising his "dear friend" Gabriel. You should have seen him weep, Beatrice. The man is a consummate actor and almost deceived even me."

"And the doctor accepted that story?" She popped a small morsel into her mouth.

"We were all to back him up," I replied. "I, however, could not bring myself to do so, untruths being anathema to me, and merely stated that I could not speak of that which I did not know."

"Very circumspect, Martha," said Beatrice, and sighed. "Well, I suppose justice has been served in an oblique way at least. I am glad that I am not married and remain solely responsible to myself for my destiny…" She looked at me with her clear grey eyes. "But do try these buns, Martha, they are most delicious." And she tempted me with the cake stand.

Mrs. Hudson and the Vanished Man

Mr. H and the doctor being away on the continent of Europe for a spell, I decided to take advantage of their absence to pay a much delayed visit to my sister. I had not seen Nelly for over a year and her reluctance, given her age (she is quite several years older than I), to make the long journey to London, it was incumbent upon me, if I wished to see her, to travel to the northern city where she resides.

Thus it was that I boarded the train from King's Cross station on the dreary November morning in question, little suspecting what an eventful journey it was to become.

Having found, with the help of the porter who carried my bag for me, the first class compartment that contained my reserved seat, I settled myself down, noting with satisfaction that a corridor ran the length of the carriage, nay, one might conveniently walk into the next carriage and on and on the length of the train if one so wished, something that proved, as it happened, most significant in this case. However, at that moment, I was merely happy to observe the fact. A means of egress is always useful, I find, in case one needs to stretch one's legs or request some refreshment from the attendant, although I had the foresight to bring with me a small package of comestibles prepared by my invaluable Clara.

I was soon joined in the carriage by a most respectable-looking couple, the gentleman however with the unhealthily pale complexion and blue-hollowed eyes that reminded me of Mr. H when he was having one of his spells, while his companion, most probably his wife, was a rosy- cheeked young person, dressed modestly in a dark blue dress and coat, a neat bonnet over wayward curls of brown hair. The gentleman failed to acknowledge me, being occupied with stowing their bag in the luggage rack, but the young lady nodded politely. I had come armed with the latest Marie Corelli novel – the author being a firm favourite of mine despite what the doctor jests about her – so was not inclined to converse. Apart from the odd whispered exchange, my travelling companions sat quietly, he holding her gloved hand in his.

The train left promptly with blasts of whistles and much waving of flags from the guard, and for me, who have not travelled extensively, it was thrilling enough.

It is in any case always pleasant to leave behind the smoke and dirt of the city and emerge into the clean air of the countryside where I had been raised. I soon put aside my book and studied the landscape flying past, the meadows with their cows and sheep and horses, the little towns we sped through, or occasionally stopped at, the canal that ran beside the railway for many miles, with its colourful horse-drawn barges. I thought of my childhood and the rural place where we lived, my musings then turning to dear Nelly and how changed we had both become from the girls we once were.

I was roused from this reverie by the sudden noisy opening of the carriage door. A man of extraordinary appearance, of a girth almost as wide as his low height, had burst in upon us. He had the swarthy features of the Mediterranean or beyond, a broad-brimmed hat rakishly askew on straggling and greasy black hair, his clothes of a stained and dusty condition, a thin line of a moustache underlining his bulbous nose, small eyes set in folds of flesh, like currants in a Chelsea bun.

He looked at each of us in turn, his glance lingering longest on the gentleman, then threw himself down opposite the young couple on my side of the carriage, though happily an empty seat's distance away. I must have been staring, for he turned to look at me and said, in oily tones with a distinctly foreign emphasis, "I trust this place is not taken, madam." His lip curled in a sneer that belied the politeness of his words.

"It is not," I answered.

I turned away and opened my book at the place previously marked and looked down to continue reading, but not before I had noted the evident discomfiture of the gentleman at the sight of this new arrival. He had barely suppressed a gasp when the man entered and now, I saw, clutched harder the hand of his companion, who looked at him with concern.

"It is nothing. A touch of dizziness," he reassured her in low tones.

"Oh, William," she replied, and I understood from her tone that she worried for his health.

A few moments passed in which I became conscious of a change in the atmosphere in the carriage. I looked up to see the newcomer still staring at the couple, an unpleasant smile upon his face. He next took a paper bag out of his pocket and removed from it a fistful of seeds, biting into them to extract the sweet kernel within and spitting the discarded husks on the floor. I was quite disgusted and coughed meaningfully. He turned to me with a grin that exposed stained yellow teeth and offered me the bag.

"Sunflower seeds," he said. "Please to try."

"No, thank you," I replied coldly. "And here in England, you know, we don't like to foul our own nest," indicating with a gesture the mess on the floor.

"Oh, pardon me, Madam," and he kicked the seed husks under his seat, as if not seeing them would make them disappear altogether.

"Tch," I said and shook my head. The scoundrel simply grinned.

Suddenly the gentleman opposite muttered something to

his companion, stood up abruptly and left the carriage, turning right, towards the rear of the train. The foreigner looked after him for a moment and then addressed himself to us.

"I hope he is not going to complain to the guard," he said, though his tone was unworried. "I should not like to be put off the train."

"Not at all," the young lady replied. "He is going to smoke his pipe." She turned to me. "He knows I do not like the smell of tobacco."

I smiled. In truth, I do not mind it myself, having been inured to it first by Henry, who liked to indulge in an after dinner cigar, and later by Mr. H and his briar. However, I agree that, in a confined space, tobacco smoke can be quite overpowering. In addition, her words tended to confirm my suspicion, having noted by certain tell- tale signs that the young lady found herself to be in an interesting state.

"It is a good idea," the foreigner said. "I think I will take a turn myself and enjoy a cheroot. Excuse me, ladies." And with what seemed to me, although I might have been wronging him, a mocking bow, he left us and walked off in the same direction as the gentleman.

I glanced at the young lady and she looked back at me with a relief I imagine was mirrored on my own countenance. She then turned her head to look out the window and I resumed my book.

After about twenty minutes, the door again opened. I looked up but it was only the foreigner returning, the sour smell emanating from him indicated the low quality of the substance that he had inhaled. I continued my reading.

The story I found so absorbing, indeed, that I lost all track of time and it was only as the train started to slow down approaching our destination that I looked up again. Her companion not having returned, the young lady appeared quite agitated.

"Can this be M…. already?" she asked me.

I replied that I thought it must be.

"But where… oh God!" And she pressed a gloved hand to her cheek in distress.

"What is the matter?" I asked, noting in passing the keen interest of the foreigner in our conversation.

"William," she said, confirming my suspicions. "Where is William? Wherever can he be?"

"Is that your husband, my dear?" I asked.

"Yes. William…"

I had no better idea that she of the whereabouts of her spouse, but in order to provide a crumb of comfort I suggested that he might have met a friend on the train and become so absorbed in conversation as to forget himself, the way gentlemen sometimes do.

"I suppose so," she said doubtfully. She then addressed herself to the foreigner. "Did you see him when you went out to smoke your cheroot?"

"Alas, no," he replied. "I stayed here in this corridor. He must have gone further. I cannot say where he is."

At that moment, we had no reason to doubt the veracity of his words.

By now the train was already pulling into the outskirts of the city. It was clear we would arrive within minutes.

"He went towards the rear of the train, is that not right?" I asked.

The young lady nodded agreement.

"And did not pass by again in the opposite direction?"

"I am sure he did not. At least, I was looking out most of the time and think I must have seen him had he passed."

"Then I suggest we make our way to the very front of the train and be among the first to alight. We can watch everyone getting off."

"But if William returns and finds me gone? What then?"

I refrained from requesting the foreigner to pass on a message as to the young wife's whereabouts, since he looked to be an untrustworthy type. Instead I replied "I am sure he will assume that you are waiting for him at the barrier. Which indeed you will be. Come let us take down our luggage and make haste."

The foreigner making no move to assist us, we lifted down our cases, both luckily being quite light, and hurried down the corridor towards the front of the train. As we passed each compartment, we glanced in without however catching sight of the lost husband, Florence Maybury, for that was my new friend's name, becoming ever more agitated by the moment. As the train pulled into the station, we were among the very first to get off. We stood at the ticket barrier and watched the crowds surging towards us.

Among those passing us was the same foreigner, tipping his hat towards us, an insolent glint in his small eyes. He even hesitated for a moment, as if about to address us, but I looked pointedly away and he continued toward the gate. Then, the last passenger having finally left the train, with no sign of the missing husband, I took it upon me – Florence being in no fit state to do so, having by now become convinced that her William had met with some terrible accident – to speak to one of the porters. This man, a short and wiry individual, looked doubtful at my insistence that William Maybury had vanished.

"You be sure then 'e didn't get off someplace else?" he asked. I assured him that the train had not stopped since our last sighting of the gentleman.

The porter turned out to be obliging enough, however, though somewhat garrulous, and agreed to accompany us on a search, even insisting on carrying our cases, which left us conveniently unencumbered as we once more swept down the corridors and through the different carriages. Finally, both first and third class, having been searched and found empty – our porter constantly reiterating a tiresome refrain of "Well, taint be 'ere" – all that remained was the guard's van. It seemed unlikely that we would find William within but, leaving no stone unturned, we prepared to enter it.

Florence preceding me into the space, it was that lady's sharp cry that alerted me that all was not as it should be. The porter, following her, was equally astonished and bawled "Blummin' 'eck!" or some such exclamation. I clambered in behind them, to be met with an alarming sight.

A man in his shirtsleeves was lying bound and gagged on the floor, wriggling in a hopeless attempt to free himself of his shackles. It was immediately evident that this was not the missing husband. Nearby, however, neatly folded, was a jacket, overcoat and top hat. Florence leaped on these garments.

"They are William's," she cried. "Oh heavens, what has become of him?"

The porter meanwhile was freeing the unfortunate captive. "Harold," he said. "Oo be doin' this to ye?"

"I dunno," the man I now took to be the guard replied. "'E 'it me on the 'ead, din' 'e."

"Where's yers cap 'n jacket?"

The guard, now sitting up, looked round and shook his head. "Them's gorn."

A horrible suspicion overcame me. Could it be that for some as yet unknown reason, William Maybury had entered the guard's van unseen, overcome the guard, knocking him unconscious and, having relieved him of his official jacket and cap, had exchanged his own clothes for those, afterwards tying up the guard to prevent him alerting anyone? Thus disguised and hiding his face, it would have been a simple matter for him to slip past us at the barrier. We would not have been looking for anyone in railway uniform. Unfortunately, this seemed the most likely explanation to me, for certain it was that there was nowhere in this carriage – nay, nowhere on the whole train – for him to hide. But what could have driven a gentleman to take such extreme measures? I could not begin to guess.

I looked at Florence. Her open face expressed nothing more than puzzlement mixed with ever-growing panic and I felt certain that whatever was behind the behaviour of her husband, she was not party to it.

Meanwhile, the porter was apparently quick to make the same connection as I.

"So this here's yer man's clothes, say ye," he remarked, looking at her appraisingly. "And Harold's is gone. Seems to me, yer man needs to answer some hard questions, milady."

"But where is he?" she asked and started to sob.

I spoke quietly to the porter, indicating that the wife seemed to be no more informed of the facts of the case than I was myself. He was sympathetic enough, seeing the evident distress of the lady, but insisted that she accompany himself and the guard to the station master.

"This here's a very serious incident indeed," he said. "Harold might ha' bin killed. His Gertie might ha bin left a widderwoman. His childer fertherless…"

I doubted all that. The man seemed relatively unaffected by his experience and I rather mistrusted his claim to have been knocked unconscious. There was a definite smell of drink off him, so it seemed likely that he had been too intoxicated to put up much of a fight or might even have been sleeping on the job and thus easily overcome. I also deduced that he had divested himself of his jacket prior to the attack in order to consume some meat pie or other, whose juices had spattered his shirt and the remains of which I observed, in the form of crumbs, upon the floor of the van. The said stains were surely fresh, for no wife worth her salt would allow a husband to go to work wearing a shirt in such a filthy condition, even if concealed under his official jacket. However, I held my peace on that subject, not wishing to antagonise the men. I also agreed to Florence's plea that I accompany her to the station master. I felt that I could not leave her, even though my sister would worry that I did not arrive, should I be delayed for any great length of time. However, I must admit that my motives were not wholly altruistic, being frankly intrigued by the whole business.

The station master, a florid self-important class of a man by the name of Samuel Briggs, as indicated by the brass plaque on his office door, having heard the testimony of both the guard and the porter, was at first most stern with both Florence and myself, clearly suspecting us of being part of some gang that operated on trains with a view to robbing the passengers. I soon convinced him of my own irreproachable respectability, especially after I mentioned my famous lodger. Nay, the very name gave this Briggs pause, as if he suspected that I was even now assisting Mr. H in some investigation, and he became quite obsequious in his manner towards me. Under the awkward circumstances I found myself in, I was not about to correct this impression.

Having exhausted his questioning of us, and in truth we were unable to enlighten him very far, Briggs stated with some smugness to Florence that she was free to go "for now," but that if her husband were to "show up," she was immediately to inform the authorities. He meanwhile would be conducting his own enquiries through the medium of the railway police.

"But where am I to go?" she said. "I do not know the name of the lodging William reserved for us. He always saw to such matters."

William, it seemed, also kept the purse, so that Florence had insufficient moneys to take a room for herself. Now, while I am no advocate of this new movement towards female emancipation and while one could hardly anticipate that one's husband would vanish in the course of a train journey, it would still seem to me only provident for both parties at all times to have recourse to sufficient funds to cater for an emergency. Certainly, my dear Henry and I used to practise this sensible precaution. However, given the sorry situation in which poor Florence found herself, I could see no other course than to bring the lady with me to my sister's residence, at least for the moment. Luckily, my sister is of a kindly disposition and, I hoped, would not object to another guest.

"Oh, Mrs. Hudson," Florence said, throwing herself into my arms and sobbing afresh when I told her of this plan, "whatever would I have done without your kindness!"

I provided Briggs with my sister's address, rather reluctantly, it must be said. To have uniformed railway officials calling to the house in full view of the neighbours might be a step too far even for Nelly. However, needs must and I led Florence to the cabs waiting outside the station.

It was only after I had provided the driver with the necessary information and seated Florence and myself inside, that, glancing out of the window, I spotted, to my dismay, a familiar figure. It was none other than the swarthy foreigner lurking in a doorway nearby, spitting his abominable sunflower seeds on to the ground and watching us with sardonic eyes.

Dear God, had he overheard the address I gave to the driver?

Did he now know where my sister lived?

Nelly's delight at seeing me was tempered somewhat by my tardiness she fearing all manner of catastrophes had befallen me – and at first by the unexpected presence of my companion to a house where nothing was prepared for an extra visitor. There really was no need for anxiety, as I hastened to point out. Nelly had ample space now that the children all had establishments of their own, and her maid-servant, Gladys, was well able to make the necessary arrangements. Moreover, once I had taken Nelly aside to apprise her of the mysterious events on the train, leaving out the more sensational aspects of the case such as the attack on the guard and the presence of the sinister foreigner, she became all tender solicitude towards poor Florence, as I knew she would. All she needed to know, I reckoned, was that Florence's husband had unaccountably disappeared, leaving the young lady in a kind of limbo. And she expecting a child.

Naturally, Nelly, who likes to peruse those newssheets that deal in society scandals, horrific murders and white slavery, immediately concluded that Florence had been abandoned, not by her husband – she dismissed the notion that the pair could truly be married but by some heartless ravisher, and that it was only lucky chance that I had been there to help the poor girl so that she, penniless and friendless, would not end up on the streets. She spoke in a whisper so loud I feared that Florence must have overheard, but a glance through the half-open door of the parlour showed that young lady to be lost in thought, gazing out of the window on a prospect which, though pleasant enough, she had by no means been expecting or wished for.

I turned back to Nelly and asked her, even if that were the case, which I very much doubted, having observed a true and unfeigned tenderness between the couple, how it was that Mr. Maybury had thereafter disappeared so completely. I proposed taking a walk to place a notice in the local newssheet informing "William" how he might contact his "Florence" through the same office (not intending to reveal Nelly's address to all and sundry). I asked both ladies if they wished to accompany me, but I could see that Florence was very much in need of a rest, so my sister said that she would stay with her. Indeed, she suggested that Gladys might be sent on the errand in my place, to save me the trouble of venturing out after my long journey, but I demurred, not wholly trusting the maid to fulfil the mission properly, and anyway wishing for time to myself to ponder a few matters. Armed with instructions on how to reach the said office – not above a mile's walk – I set off forthwith, certain in my mind, though unsure quite why, that there was no time to be lost.

Florence had informed me, in the course of our ride in

the hansom cab, that her husband had sprung this trip on her only the previous evening, vouchsafing her hardly time to pack the necessaries. When she had asked him why so soon, he had replied that a break in the country (though M is hardly that) would do them both good, and she was glad to agree, having observed in his demeanour recently evidence of stress and strain. When I enquired as to his occupation, she replied rather vaguely that he worked for the government, although she was not quite sure in what capacity. I concluded that William was one of those traditional men who keep their work life and their family separate, considering it unsuitable for a wife to know too much of her husband's business. Florence was apparently happy enough for this to be the case, showing no curiosity about William's work. Henry, on the other hand, liked to share everything with me, and I appreciated him for it. However, there are no God-given rules about such things and everyone, I suppose, is different.

It seemed to me, as I walked the cobbled streets of M towards my goal, that, given his ravaged appearance, William had already been in a state of anxiety when he and Florence first entered the compartment but that this had increased considerably after the arrival of the foreigner. Whether it was the man himself who had caused this or whether his presence had simply aroused a memory, I could not say, but almost certain it was that a fear of something terrible had suddenly overcome the gentleman, causing him to flee.

So wrapped up was I in my thoughts that I walked past the very office I wished to visit. Turning back abruptly, having realised my error, I thought that I caught a glimpse of the self-same swarthy personage dodging into a doorway. On reaching this however, I found no one concealed therein so concluded that, the man being uppermost in my mind at that moment, I must have imagined his actual presence.

My errand completed with assurances from the clerk that

the notice would appear in the newssheet on the following morning, I returned to my sister's house without, thank goodness, seeing any more sinister apparitions, although there was so much of dross and filth to step over and round that I was concentrating more on that, not wishing to get my good bombazine soiled.

Returning to the house, I found that Florence had retired to her room to lie down, so I sat with Nelly in the parlour and, after further discussing the situation of the poor young woman, we took to bringing each other up to date with news of our respective families, which would not advance this story and which would be without interest for the reader.

Later, at dinner, at which Florence partook only a small dish of broth and a single slice of capon, despite Nelly and myself urging her to eat to keep up her strength, I apprised her of the success of my enterprise in placing the notice, and expressed more confidence than I truly felt as to its happy outcome. The young lady seemed to revive somewhat at this news and stated her intention of retiring early after the upsets of the day, while Nelly and I settled down for a companionable game of whist.

It was not long, however, before we were again joined by Florence, who entreated me to accompany her to her room where she had something to show me.

She had evidently been unpacking her case, for it lay open upon the bed. Various items of feminine wardrobe were scattered in a haphazard fashion that I could scarcely approve of. There were also intimate garments belonging to a gentleman, as well as a clean shirt which she had evidently been in the process of hanging up to eliminate the creases. But none of these was the object of her interest.

"What, Mrs. Hudson," said she, "do you make of this?" throwing aside yet more of the contents of the bag. I stared at the now empty space and then back at her in some puzzlement. Suddenly, with a grand gesture, she pulled at a riband I had previously not noticed and the base swung up.

93

"A secret compartment!" breathed Nelly, who had crept up behind us.

We gazed somewhat aghast, for the space contained a quantity of papers that to me, anyway, looked to be official.

"Did you not know of this before?" I asked Florence, who shook her head.

"It is William's case. I simply placed my clothes and necessities on top of his. Just now I pulled the riband in error, thinking it part of my wardrobe and these tumbled out." She gestured at the papers.

"I wonder," I said, "if there is anything here that might explain his sudden disappearance or give us a clue as to where he might have gone."

"But would it not be very wrong," Florence replied, "to look among his private papers? I think that William would not want me to. His work is quite secret, you know."

"Is it?" asked Nelly all agog. I could just imagine which way her mind was now working.

"Oh yes," Florence replied. "All I can say is that it is connected in some way to a war in...in... India or somewhere."

"Africa, perhaps," I said, having read in the papers of battles and a war in that same far-flung continent.

"I don't know," she replied. "Only that I overheard him talking to Mr. James about it."

"Mr. James?"

"A man he works with who called round one morning. They withdrew to the study but not before I had heard a few words on the matter they were to discuss. Then William shut the door, smiling at me and saying that they would not be long. Indeed, they were not. Mr. James left but I have to add, however, that after that..."

She paused.

"Yes," I said encouragingly.

"After that I noticed that William seemed not himself.

Lost in worrying thoughts, you know. Troubled in some way."

"Well, war is a serious enough matter. I suppose that was it."

"Perhaps." She looked doubtful.

"I still think that the answer to some of our questions might lie in these papers," I went on. "It is your bounden duty to examine them, Florence."

"You think so?" She was still reluctant, although, I felt, wishing to be urged.

"I do. For William's sake." I turned to Nelly. "Perhaps, dear sister, you could ask Cook to prepare us each a glass of smoking bishop, made with port wine if you please. We may need it to give us courage for the work ahead."

Nelly gave me a look. I think she realised the chief reason for my request was to remove her from the room, when she would as lief stay. It was with reluctance then that she left us, but I felt that, if secrets were to be revealed here, the fewer people who knew about them the better.

The papers upon examination proved indeed to deal with recent events in Africa, specifically in a place named Sudan, with much about Egypt, a certain Mahdi and also a Major Jean Baptiste Marchand, a Frenchman. I gathered from a brief perusal that some sort of confrontation was expected between British forces under their commander, Horace Kitchener, and the latter. I wished the doctor were present to throw more light on the matter since he had great experience working for the British army in foreign parts and was well-versed in the politics in such places, having occasionally mentioned to me something called the "scramble for Africa" which I admit usually sent me into a doze.

While I read on, Florence was rummaging further to see what she could find.

"What can this be?" she exclaimed.

I looked up to see that she had pulled an envelope from

amongst the papers. It had been opened and then clumsily resealed and was addressed to William Maybury Esq. in a crabbed hand.

"We should open it," I said at once. "Oh, do you think so? I fear not."

I took it from her briskly, glad to leave the commander as well as the generals, the majors and major-generals to their unfathomable devices for a spell, and easily broke the seal. I withdrew what turned out to be a thin sheet and cast my eye over it. What was written there must have caused my expression to darken, for Florence cried out, "What is it, Martha? Oh, pray, what is it?"

I could not but show it to her, though I was loath to do so. The letter made her start, she clutched at her heart, her eyes rolled in her head and, fearing that she might faint quite away, I hastened to her side and supported her in my arms.

"William! Oh, William," she whispered. "Whatever have you done?"

It was at that moment that Nelly re-entered the room with the smoking bishop. In one way it was timely because both Florence and I were both in need of a reviving drink. However, I was certainly not inclined to apprise my sister of the contents of the letter and so hastily thrust it into my reticule.

Luckily she failed to observe my movement for would have surely questioned me on it. Instead, she busied herself around the now weeping form of Florence.

"What has happened?" she asked me. "What have you discovered?"

"Nothing of purpose," I replied. "Florence, given the delicacy of her condition, is simply overcome by today's events. I think perhaps we should help her to bed and let her sleep. Tomorrow we will all have gained the strength to face the problem. And who knows, tomorrow Mr. Maybury might walk through the door and explain all."

This agreed on and Florence assuring me that she would prefer to be alone, although I offered to stay with her, I retired to my own room, taking with me the steaming and fragrant glass, to think deeply on events and to try and decide what next course of action to take. Clearly the danger was far greater than I had anticipated, the danger not only to the gentleman himself but also to Florence and their unborn child, as the letter made clear. It was to be hoped that the enemy knew not of the young lady's whereabouts, but I feared, alas, that unknowingly I had placed her within the reach of the very villains who threatened her well-being. It would be imperative to move her on the morrow to somewhere further sequestered.

But reader, you will be anxious to learn the full contents of the accursed letter, writ in the same crabbed hand as on the envelope. I copy it here.

Maybury, it started, *you think you can escape your obligations so easily, with a few pieces of information that any fool could learn from the daily newssheets in an instant. No, no, my friend, your indiscretions, your weakness for the opium pipe and for the gambling den, have placed you in a position of indebtedness that can only be alleviated by provision of the papers we earlier requested from you. You say you would prefer to die than betray your country. That may be so, but what of your wife and unborn child? Could you continue to live (for we would certainly spare you) knowing that you have cut short both their beings as effectively as if you yourself held the knife to that pretty throat and let the life-blood run out of it. But, friend, how simple after all the remedy! A few trifling sheets of paper in exchange for all your debts and for the safety of those you love! Do not think too long about it. Our patience is running out.*

The letter was unsigned.

Reading it again sent a chill down my spine. Clearly William had fled rather than give in to the blackmailers' demands. Yet something had happened on the train to make him flee again. But why abandon Florence and her unborn child to their fate? Or did he flee hoping to draw the pursuers after him and leave them be? I puzzled over all this long into the night and once, glancing out the window at the blackness beyond, seemed to my horror to see pressed up against it, the sneering visage of the swarthy foreigner. A vision that frightened me beyond words, even though a vision was certainly all it could be.

I fell at last into a broken sleep, the disarray of the sheets when I awoke evidence of my restlessness. I hastened to find if Florence had slept better than myself, but judged not when I saw the pallor of her countenance. I had immediately to tell her of my fear that her whereabouts was known to her husband's enemies and urged that she be up and dressed as soon as possible, so that we could move her to another place.

"But Martha," said she. "I am so very tired. And this is where William will come when he sees the notice in the papers."

If he sees it, I thought to myself. If he is any position to see it. "Nelly or I will be able to direct him once we have you installed elsewhere. I am sure Nelly will know of a respectable establishment where we can place you until this business is sorted out." Though how it was to be sorted, that I could not tell.

I descended to breakfast, followed shortly by Florence. Neither of us had much appetite. I could barely manage two kippers, a small scone and some buttered bread, and Florence ate hardly at all. Nelly was in better order, unaware of the dire threat that hung over one of her guests.

It was while we were finishing our tea that the doorbell rang. Gladys announced that a gentleman wished to speak with Mrs. Maybury.

"William," exclaimed Florence jumping up in excitement.

"I have taken the liberty of showing the gentleman into the parlour," Gladys went on.

No sooner said than Florence ran from the room with

Nelly and me following fast behind.

We both heard the disappointed "Oh," that emitted from the young lady on entering the room. The visitor then was not William but turned out to be a tall lean man, dark-haired with a moustache and small beard in the French style.

"Mrs. Maybury," said he in warm tones. "How pleased I am to see you so well, under the most trying circumstances."

"It is Mr. James," Florence explained to us, performing the introductions. Mr. James, the work colleague of her husband's whom she had mentioned to me already. Whatever was he doing here?

Nelly begged him be seated and soon we were all around him. "My dear friend, William, has taken me entirely into his confidence," he explained. "He cabled me yesterday and so I took the morning train in order to be here as soon as I could. Circumstances that I cannot at this moment reveal have prevented him attending you, but he has instructed me to take you to a certain place where he will shortly be joining us. I have a carriage waiting outside."

Florence was overjoyed. "You see, Martha," she said to me. "An answer to my prayers. But Mr. James," and a shadow fell over that lovely face again, "is William unharmed? Is he truly safe?"

"I can assure you that all is well and all will be well," he replied.

"Oh then, Mr. James, I will collect my things and be with you instantly."

She left the room, attended by Nelly.

"The morning train," I said, consulting my timepiece which showed it to be not yet eight of the clock. "I did not think there was one so early. When I looked to come here, Bradshaw's showed the first to arrive a good hour or more after this."

He smiled. "Ah, but you see, dear madam, I did not come from London. I happened to be visiting my family not so very far

99

from here. The train from there is most convenient."

"How lucky then," I replied, "that Mr. Maybury happened to know that you were away from the city and where to find you."

"Indeed," he smiled again. "So very very lucky."

We sat in silence. There was something I did not like about this gentleman but I could not say exactly what it was. That ingratiating smile perhaps which he put on every time I looked at his face.

"Where is this place of safety?" I asked at last.

"Ah, dear madam, I am sure if you were to be acquainted with the full details of the case, you would agree that it is better for you not to know."

"Hmm," I said. "I still should prefer to be informed."

"I am sure you would, Mrs. Hudson, but I am afraid it is not to be."

More silence until Florence veritably bounced down the stairs and into the room.

"I should like to come with you," I said to her.

She glanced at Mr. James, who shook his head. "You must come alone, dear Mrs. Maybury. For now. Your friends can join you later."

We went out into the hall, an anticipatory dread overcoming me, as Gladys opened the door. There a carriage was indeed standing but in front of it – oh, heavens – the swarthy foreigner. All my fears were realised. They were in it together.

But no! To our horror and shock, on seeing this individual, Mr. James instantly pulled a revolver from his belt and fired it towards the man, shooting him in the leg so that he stumbled. However, he too managed to draw a pistol and shot back with a truer aim, hitting Mr. James where he stood between myself and Florence in the middle of his chest, causing him to fall to the ground.

Florence and Nelly screamed and I called to them to get

back into the house at once and lock the doors, which they did without hesitation. At the first shot, the cab driver had leapt from his vehicle and run away. Some hero, he! However, he would undoubtedly raise the alarm so that we might expect the forces of law and order to appear forthwith. Meanwhile I knelt beside Mr. James to try and staunch the bleeding, tying my shawl tight across the wound. I cared little for my own safety. Surely even a foreigner, however villainous, would not shoot a defenceless woman while she was involved in trying to save a life. The man in question himself appeared to be intent on using his soiled cravat to bind his leg. Mr. James's revolver lay by my side, where he had dropped it, so I seized the thing. I know from my youth in the countryside a deal about firearms, and pointed it at the murdering scoundrel.

"No, no," he said. "You are wrong. I was sent to save the lady."

"Oh really," I mocked. "So that is to be your story, is it?"

"By Allah, it is the truth," he said and started to reach into his pocket.

I cocked the gun but was by no means sure if I could bring myself to fire it even in self- defence. However, what he pulled out was not another firearm or knife, as I had feared, but an envelope.

"Read this," he said. "And you will begin to understand." He tossed the letter in my direction. It was addressed to Florence but was unsealed and so I wasted no time in perusing it.

My dearest girl, it said. *You will be surprised and shocked at my sudden disappearance but believe me when I tell you that it had to be. All will become clear soon. But I exhort you to trust with your life the bearer of this letter, namely my good friend Omar Elhusseiny. So that you know that this is truly from me under no duress I ask you to remember Box Hill and the Adonis blue butterflies that entranced you there. I pray to God that we will soon be restored to each other and that in due course of time we may together take our child to see the butterflies dancing there too. Your own loving William.*

I confess that I was astounded to read this, but before I could begin to gather my thoughts, I caught sight of two constables running up the street, followed by a man who turned out to be a doctor.

Dear reader, you are no doubt as puzzled as I was at these latest developments, but before all can explained I must hurry over the more humdrum events of the next hour; the attention paid by the doctor to both wounded men, brought into Nelly's house (to her great consternation), and laid one on the couch in the parlour (Mr. James), the other (Omar) in the pantry; the questions of the constables who looked, as you may imagine, with the deepest suspicion on the foreigner, Florence however attesting that the handwriting on the letter that proved the man's innocence to be indeed that of her husband and recalling (with a tear in her eye) how truly the Adonis butterflies had delighted her so at Box Hill.

Once more, sometime later, a knocking came at the door; once more Gladys announced a gentleman asking for Mrs. Maybury. This time she showed less alacrity in going to see who the new visitor might be, but quite burst into a fit of weeping when she saw that it was, incontrovertibly, her own William restored to her at last and looking in turn relieved to find her unharmed. Mr. Maybury was accompanied by two other gentlemen, one of whom identified himself as a chief inspector of police, the other an assistant to the minister in whose department Mr. Maybury worked.

Mr. James now having been dispatched to hospital accompanied by a burly constable, we all assembled in the parlour to find out the truth of the matter at last. There were many interruptions, exclamations and digressions in the course of this, so I will summarise as best as I can.

William Maybury, it seemed, as the inspector explained,

held a position of trust high in the ministry but his weakness for opium and gambling had almost led to his downfall, and he fell prey to a villainous plot to extract secret plans regarding the war in Sudan and the struggle with the French, papers that, had they fallen into the wrong hands, could have brought about much bloodshed and loss of life, to the severe detriment to the honour of the British Empire. It was true that the first demands of the plotters were for innocuous information that, as the letter had stated, "any fool could learn from the daily newssheets." However, once they had Maybury, as they thought, in their clutches, they increased their demands as well as their threats. Maybury, however, showing a degree of sense previously absent from his undertakings, felt that if he acceded to more demands, then even more would be made in a never-ending spiral. Instead, he confessed all to his superior, throwing himself on his mercy, and asking for advice. This man, now present in the room, had agreed to overlook Maybury's previous indiscretions, particularly in the light of his wife's condition, if he in turn agreed to help expose the plotters. It was suspected that one at least worked in the ministry itself, though without access to the high level of information that Maybury enjoyed. Following the latest demands, a plan was hatched to draw the villains from their cover. Maybury would pretend to flee and, particularly in view of the threat to Mrs. Maybury, a bodyguard was provided to accompany the couple secretly, an Egyptian whose life Maybury had saved while working in that country before his marriage, and whose loyalty could not be doubted. This personage was, of course, none other than the same swarthy foreigner who had dogged our footsteps and whom I had taken for an arrogant scoundrel.

On the train, his joining us was a signal to Maybury that Omar needed, with some urgency, to talk to him. Thus Maybury, agitated, left the compartment in order supposedly to smoke his pipe, shortly followed by Omar, who informed him that at least one of the suspected plotters, the miserable wretch, James, had indeed followed him on to the train. The two men then proceeded to the van where Omar incapacitated the drunken guard, while Maybury took his clothes.

"Oh, William," cried out Florence at this point. "I knew you could not have done violence, even," she added, glancing at Omar now present, and clean bandaged, "in a good cause."

The inspector smiled indulgently at the interruption, and continued his narrative. Thus disguised, Maybury had left the train, just as I had supposed, at the terminus, slipping past his wife and myself, and, according to a prior arrangement, informed the police authorities there to watch out for James. Omar meanwhile had earlier returned to our compartment to safeguard Florence, but when he saw how I had taken her under my wing, he let me unknowingly assume the role of protector, as being more to the comfort of the lady, but with himself keeping an eagle eye on us betimes.

The plotters having been outwitted for the moment, were not aware that the identity of at least one of them was become known. James was followed to an hotel in the centre of the city where he made contact with his fellow conspirators, three Frenchmen and an Arabian who, while being the ringleader, had pretended to be the servant of one of the others. The next morning, perusing the early edition of the local newssheet, James must have observed our notice for he shortly after visited the office pretending to be the William mentioned therein. As the clerk had explained to the police, somewhat red-faced, he had had no cause to doubt such a respectable-looking gentleman and so revealed to him the address where Florence could be found. The result of that we already knew.

The rest of the gang, having been seized at the hotel, were now awaiting interrogation. James, in hospital but out of danger and able to speak, had tried to present himself, as he had to William, as another unfortunate who had fallen into the clutches of the spies. This, as the chief inspector now informed us, was very far from being the case. It seemed that money was behind all, as his co-conspirators were now pleased to reveal, having assumed that he had betrayed them. James had been promised a large bribe to get to Maybury and persuade him to give up the papers. His first attempt at persuasion having failed, the gang then planned to resort to more violent measures. Had they succeeded in whisking Florence away, in order to blackmail Maybury further, the inspector went on, the outcome would certainly have been a tragic one, since, James's identity now known to her, she would not have been allowed to live. (At this moment, William put his arm around his beloved Florence with great feeling.) Luckily, the inspector continued, nodding to that personage, the faithful Omar had been on hand to prevent the worst happening. Although James's condition was still grave, no proceedings would be initiated against the Egyptian for the wound inflicted upon the scoundrel since we three witnesses could testify that James had drawn and fired first.

I felt remorse at suspecting Omar of villainy, although I must state in my defence that his behaviour had at no time inspired confidence. However, the ways of foreigners are not our ways, and I was most grateful that he had turned up in time to save the day. I pride myself, all the same, that I would not have let James, whom I did not trust, carry the young lady off to some destination unknown, having it in mind, had Omar not just then appeared upon the scene, to call a cab myself and follow them wherever they might go.

I was now able to spend the rest of my holiday most enjoyably with sister, Nelly, while the Mayburys returned to London. We kept in touch and in due course of time I was informed how a fine baby girl was born to them. To my great delight, I even had the pleasure, come the following summer, of attending the christening of young Elizabeth Martha. Meanwhile, the villains received their just punishment, each condemned to a long spell in Pentonville prison, and, their dastardly plot having been foiled, great loss of life was prevented in far off Sudan, Lord Kitchener, as he came to be called following the Battle of Omdurman, overcoming peacefully the Frenchman Marchand.

The events which form the substance of this narrative were reported but briefly in the national press and my own small contribution went completely unrecorded. The doctor, over his breakfast kedgeree (the gentlemen having meanwhile returned from abroad), happened to observe that a shooting incident had taken place in M while I was there, adding in his jocular fashion and twirling his moustaches, that it was lucky I had not been in the line of fire. Since any exploits of mine in the past have met with mirth or belittlement by both the doctor and Mr. H, in this instance I merely smiled, though a chill went through me as I recalled the swish of Omar's bullet passing between myself and Florence, and concluded how lucky we were that the swarthy foreigner had turned out to be such an accurate shootist.

Mrs Hudson and the Darlin' Boy

My endeavours thus far have been to recount those cases in which I was able to perform some little good and resolve a sorry situation. I should not, however, consider it honest to omit that one instance where vanity blinded me so far that I was unable to prevent a catastrophe. You might ask, in mitigation, after perusing the details, how I could in truth usefully have intervened, being so little cognisant of all the facts and not in the confidence of the main players? Even so, the following, I am afraid does not place your narrator in a good light and yet I include it as a warning lesson to others of my impressionable sex.

It all started one fine morning in late spring. My housemaid Clara and I having an urgent errand to perform, I had requested Phoebe, the kitchen maid, to see to the gentleman's breakfast for once. A simple enough task, as you might have thought, even given Phoebe's well-known propensity for disaster. On re-entering the house, I heard the doctor's loud laughter, alongside disgruntled murmurings from Mr. H, and immediately suspected something amiss. So, sending Clara below with our purchases, I climbed the stairs to my lodgers' chambers.

I tapped on the door, which anyway stood ajar, and entered. Phoebe stood as gawky and awkward as usual, her face redder than ever and tears in her eyes. Mr. H for his part looked anything but pleased while the doctor seemed in high good

107

humour and forthwith explained to me the cause of his mirth (and the dissatisfaction of Mr. H).

It seemed the eggs were raw, the tea was cold, the toast was burnt and there was salt in the sugar bowl.

"Although," he added, "Phoebe at least had the wit to place the burnt side down so that the black part only became apparent when one lifted the bread up."

Now Phoebe, ever clumsy and slow, had proved a trial to me since she entered my service some eighteen months previously, but I had tolerated her for the sake of her poor mother, a widow with five children to rear, of whom Phoebe, at fourteen, was the eldest, and in the hope that, with dear Clara as a model, the child might eventually develop some sense. However, it seemed at that moment that my hopes were in vain. I had asked so little of the silly goose and yet still she was unable to do things properly.

"Do not look so discomforted, Mrs. Hudson," the doctor continued, observing my expression. "I strongly suspect the reason for young Phoebe's distraction is that she is in love."

To say I was dumbfounded at the suggestion would be putting it mildly. Mr. H, too, for once looked astonished. I suspect that, clever as he is, affairs of the heart largely fall outside his area of experience. We all then regarded Phoebe, a maiden undeniably homely and entirely lacking the qualities of a romantic heroine, being plain of face and lumpy of body. She looked back for a second, pulled her apron to her face and fled the room weeping copiously.

"Explain yourself, Watson," quoth Mr. H. "Whatever could have drawn you to such a conclusion?"

"Why, the maid's demeanour, of course, Holmes," the doctor replied, with some satisfaction. "The distracted, dreamy air. The little smile from time to time playing on her lips. The attempts to improve her appearance. Did you not notice the blue riband in her hair, the blush on her cheeks where she had recently pinched them? I am astounded you did not observe such telling signs for yourself."

"Hmm," was all that Mr. H vouchsafed in reply.

"In addition," the doctor went on, smiling. "I have seen a certain prepossessing young fellow in conversation with her on more than one occasion."

"Not in this house, doctor," I exclaimed. If so, that would certainly prove to be the nail in Phoebe's coffin as far as her continuing in this establishment were concerned.

"Not at all, Mrs. Hudson. There has, to my knowledge, been no impropriety. The young man in question is the bread boy, delivering the morning loaf which Phoebe managed to burn so efficiently today. I have simply observed them communing briefly outside our windows, the young man then smiling and sauntering off, leaving Phoebe staring after him with what can only be described as adoration."

"Hmm," Mr. H commented again, and I could tell he was displeased that for once he was the one asking the questions, rather than explaining something that puzzled the rest of us but which always seemed to him so obvious. He now took refuge in a change of subject. "Well, Mrs Hudson," he said in sarcastic tones. "I hope it would not be too much trouble to bring us a decent breakfast after all. We have been waiting long enough."

"Of course," said I, gathering up the debris. "I have some nice fresh buns newly bought in the market. And be sure, sirs, that I will have strong words with Phoebe. She cannot presume on my tolerant nature forever."

"Ah, Mrs. Hudson," the doctor intervened. "Be merciful. She is a good girl and with your example before her cannot fail but to learn in the end. And I must add that the young man in question was so exceedingly well-formed as to turn any young girl's eye."

My curiosity aroused, I descended to the kitchen with the laden tray. There I found Phoebe, her face swollen with tears, in

109

the comforting arms of dear Clara.

"She is very sorry, ma'am," said Clara. "It won't happen again, will it, Phoebe."

"Ah no, mum," the girl managed to stammer. "I swear to God, mum. I'm so sorry, mum."

"Now Phoebe," I said as soothingly as I could, for it is a weakness in my character that the girl's helplessness never fails to move me. "Our first duty is to prepare a proper breakfast for the gentlemen and then you must explain all to me. Clara and I will see to it, while you dispose of this." I indicated the miserable contents of the tray.

So it was that some ten minutes later, I sat the girl down with a cup of sweet tea and urged her to confide in me.

"For you know," I said. "In lieu of your mamma, I am responsible for your moral well-being as much as for your physical."

She looked blankly at me and I translated my words into simpler ones.

"I hope and trust you are a good girl, Phoebe, but have to ask.

Is there, as the doctor suggested, a young man in the case?"

She looked down, looked up, looked down again, fumbling with her crumpled apron.

"Phoebe?"

"Oh, mum. There's no wrong in it. He's just a merry fellow who delivers the bread of a morning."

And her eyes brightened at the recollection.

"He always has a smile on his face and he whistles, too."

"Whistles?"

"Such a jolly tune. It makes me laugh, it does."

"And has this young buck a name?"

"Jimmy, mum. And such a queer way of talking."

"Indeed?"

"He's Irish, mum. From Ireland." She made it sound like Timbuctoo.

"And you are sure he has made no improper suggestions."

"Not at all, mum. Except…" She looked down again.

"Yes? Come on Phoebe."

She was clearly reluctant to speak.

"Well, I don't knows as it's improper or not, mum," she said at last in a rush. "He says I looks pretty when I smiles."

She raised her eyes then and looked at me inquiringly.

"Oh," I replied. "I don't think there's any great harm in that, if that is as far as it goes." Although, my thoughts were that, while a smile in most circumstances cannot but enhance a person's appearance, I could not help but feel that "pretty" in Phoebe's case must be something of an exaggeration. However, as my dear late husband Henry used to say "beauty is in the eye of the beholder," and was that not a good thing, too. "As long," I continued, "as it goes no further than that, and the young man attempts no liberties."

"Oh no, mum… though he did ask me," Phoebe went on, and I have to confess I had never found the girl so eloquent before. Rather she was mostly stuck for words and given to mumbling, "He asked me, mum, if there be any situation in this house that he could suit, since he is not at all happy where he is, having to work through the night and all."

"I hope you told him there is nothing for him here."

"I did, mum, but then he says if there be any odd job round the house he might help you with, to be sure to call upon him."

Now it just so happened that there were some tasks that, though trifling, were beyond the strength and capabilities of Clara and myself, but which would present no difficulties at all to a strong young man possessed of the correct tools. A back door that swelled in the rain and would not close easily, or once

111

closed, would not open. A gutter clogged with leaves. A broken kitchen press. A loose floorboard above my bedroom that creaked whenever Mr. H took to pacing about in the middle of the night, which was often, disturbing my rest. And such like small but vexing domestic issues.

I thought for a moment. "Very well," I finally said to Phoebe. "You can ask the young man to call upon me when next you see him, and I will decide if he can be trusted to help out." There could after all be no harm in speaking to him. Indeed, I could then perhaps judge at the same time if he were a trustworthy acquaintance for Phoebe.

"Oh thank you, thank you, mum," she cried. "You're so good." I feared the girl was about to fling her arms around me but instead she just burst into tears again in an excess of emotion.

To be honest, I did not feel so very good. What moved me most, I confess it, was a curiosity to meet this merry fellow who had so turned the head of my kitchen maid that she mistook salt for sugar.

For someone so generally a laggard, it was quite astonishing how rapidly young Phoebe managed to pass on the message. On the afternoon of that very same day, a sharp rat-a-tat-tat sounded on the kitchen door. Clara was engaged in gutting the rabbit for the gentlemen's stew, while I was descaling the haddock. Phoebe, well, Phoebe was lurking near the range popping peas from their pods into a bowl on her lap. At the sound of knocking she jumped up, and the bowl fell to the floor, its contents flying far and wide. Luckily there seemed to be not too many peas in the bowl, possibly because a large number had instead found their way into the girl's mouth. Before I had time to remonstrate, the rat-a-tat-tat sounded again and this time in response to my "Come in" the door (sticking as usual) was pushed open, revealing a young man of an exceedingly charming aspect. The somewhat arrogant strut of his walk was counterbalanced by the frankness of his gaze, and when he smiled it was as if sunshine had burst into our dark kitchen. I heard a little gasp from Clara and could see that even she, who in general has eyes only for her beau, Walter, the butcher's son, was struck by this apparition. Of medium height and spare build, the young man possessed a skin that shone with the creaminess of the typical Celt. Beardless, the spattering of freckles across his nose and cheeks resembled crumbs of gold. His heavy- lashed eyes were green flecked with brown. Most striking of all was a head of glittering black curls that shook in all directions whenever he moved his head but a fraction, which he did almost continuously.

"Mrs. Hudson," said he with a lilt to his voice that I recognised as Hibernian. "How delightful to meet you at last. I have heard so much from Phoebe." Who even now lurked in the corner of the kitchen, endeavouring to push the spilt peas out of sight with the toe of her shoe. "She never stops singing your praises."

"Indeed?" I replied. I was somewhat surprised at this report from Phoebe, and glanced at the girl, who for now, at least, was struck dumb.

The young man extended a hand for me to shake, but I was most conscious of the fishy scales upon mine and excused myself to wash them off first under the tap, before returning this unusual salutation (finding his hand firm and hard, no doubt from labouring in the bakery).

"I hear constantly of your virtues, so I do," he spoke on. "Your kindness and goodness. Your generosity." He was looking into my eyes and still holding my hand. Recollecting myself, I pulled it away.

"Well, young man…"

"James Murphy…" he said, "but most people call me Jimmy.

Like in the song, don't you know."

"The song? I don't know it."

113

"Ah, sure you do." And to our astonishment the lad there and then picked up the refrain: *"Now Jimmy Murphy was hanged not for sheep stealing, But for courting a pretty girl and her name was Kate Whelan."* Then added, "But I hope I will not get hanged either for stealing or for courting." And he smiled a wide smile that revealed even white teeth.

"Well, James," I interjected before he could come out with more verses or more compliments. "I understand from Phoebe that you are willing to do a few odd jobs around the house for us."

He nodded and every curl on his head seemed to quiver with pleasure.

"Starting, I think, with that door," he smiled and pointed at the way he had entered.

"You had better," I said, "come through to the parlour so that we can discuss the matter in peace and let these young ladies get on with their work." Without the distraction that you present, as I might have added.

I of course only had Phoebe's most unreliable assurances as to the boy's good character (he was no more, I am sure, than nineteen or twenty), so I quizzed him mightily as to his present and past occupations. He explained that he was from the County of Cork, his father there employed as a stableman on the estate of a mighty lord, whom he named. James, having wanted to better himself had come to London but a few months previously, to make his way in a place where great opportunities must be open to an energetic and willing young man. He spoke modestly and with no further flattery and I was pleased with what he told me. As to his present employer, all he had managed in that regard was, as I already knew, a back-breaking turn in the bakery.

"But will you have time to take on extra work?" I asked. "I presume that your hours of labour are already long and hard."

"It is true," he said, "that I work by night. But I need very little sleep, so I can take time occasionally to earn some

114

extra shillings. You see, Mrs. Hudson, my father is now advanced in years and unable to work as before, so it is my fervent wish to be able to send money home to support the family in some small way."

I was most pleased to hear this. A young man undoubtedly of a good and honest nature.

"A big family?" I asked, knowing that the Irish tend that way.

"Not so very big," he replied. "There are just seven of us children, most mere chisellers."

When I raised my eyebrows, he went on to explain "chiseller" as an Irish expression for a young child.

"I cannot, I am afraid," he continued, "furnish you with a character reference. I should not like Mr. Judd, my present employer, to know that I am looking elsewhere for work. However, if you are willing to trust me," and here he looked deep into my eyes again, "your trust I assure you, Mrs. Hudson, will not be misplaced."

For myself I could not see any harm getting him at least to fix the troublesome kitchen door. I or Clara could keep a sharp eye on him the whole time. He was so willing, it seemed churlish not to give him a chance and we agreed on what seemed to me a fair payment.

"As well," I said, "as your dinner and a glass or two of ale."

He extended his hand to shake on our agreement. This, I thought, must be an Irish custom, I being unused to such a procedure. However, I happily took his hand again and again had some difficulty in extracting mine, since he clutched at it so hard while speaking with emotion at last of the difference his earnings would make to his poor mother.

"One more thing, though," I said, "with regard to Phoebe."

"A sweet girl," he said. "She reminds me of my little

115

sister, Maria."

"That I am glad to hear," I replied. "But I fear you have inadvertently turned her head. She is in my care and – please understand me, James – I cannot but worry…"

"Say no more," he broke in, somewhat shocked, I fancy. "She is a child. You need have no concerns on that score, I assure you."

It was as I had thought. The young man's kind words and merry demeanour had kindled in Phoebe's young breast a wholly misplaced affection. I would have to make sure that her heart was not broken utterly and suggested that he explain his brotherly feelings to her in as discreet a way as possible, which he agreed to do as soon as an opportunity presented itself.

To say I was pleased with the young man's work would be to fall far short of the matter. His diligence in applying himself to any task I offered was exemplary. He was also in the habit of whistling while he worked, tunefully, various Irish airs including my favourite "The Last Rose of Summer," as well as a selection of jaunty shanties, so that it livened up the house no end to hear him. I found myself praising him to my friends, in particular to my neighbour Mrs. Dixon, who was thereafter most curious to meet this paragon. The upshot was – and foolishly I found myself a touch jealous – that he started doing little jobs for her as well. Soon enough, indeed, for my other neighbour, Mrs. Melrose. It was astonishing that he could find the time and I wondered if he ever slept at all, to which query he laughed merrily and shook his curls.

It was Mrs. Melrose indeed – a Miss O'Kelly before her marriage, hailing originally from the County of Wexford – who took a particular interest in Jimmy and dubbed him "the darlin' boy", an epithet that seemed to suit him perfectly.

I presumed meanwhile that, as instructed, he had spoken to Phoebe, although it was clear to me that she continued to moon after him. Possibly he had expressed himself with such a subtle delicacy that the silly goose had not picked up on his hints. I decided to sound her out on the matter and found that this indeed was the case.

"Oh, mum," she sighed, "he talks of bringing me to Ireland to meet his sisters."

Now this was not at all the line I had expected the young man to take, although I supposed that Phoebe had mistaken his meaning. I felt, however, the need to discuss the matter once more with him and discovered him in the parlour where he was fixing a few loose tiles in the parquet floor.

"I can assure you, Mrs Hudson," said he, rising from the floor, like a phoenix from the ashes, his shirt unbuttoned at the neck to reveal a comely sliver of hairless chest, like milk new drawn, "that Phoebe has taken me up wrong. I may have suggested that if she ever visited Ireland, she would get on famously with my sisters, but for her to imagine I would bring her there, well…" and he laughed.

"I thought it must be so," I said, "but still, you need to tell the girl quite firmly that if there is any love on your side for her it is only of the brotherly sort."

"I have said it, Mrs. Hudson," he insisted, "but I think Phoebe only hears what she wants to hear."

That was true enough and not just in matters of the heart. As I had often observed, any time she was given an uncongenial task to do, Phoebe had the tendency to become irredeemably deaf of a sudden.

"I should perhaps inform her more forcefully," he went on, this time looking at me intently, "that I am drawn not to young girls, however superficially pretty, but to more mature women. Women of experience, women who have lived."

Goodness me, I thought.

"Mrs. Hudson, forgive me but I understand you have been a widow for many years."

117

"True enough," I said. "My dear Henry passed away more than twelve years since."

"And how is it that you never remarried?"

It was presumptuous of him but I had to laugh. He looked so earnest.

"Me," I said. "Remarry! I have never thought of such a thing and now I am far too old."

"Not at all," he said, approaching close. "No, Mrs. Hudson... Martha... You are still a fine woman. It would be a terrible waste..." And he actually brushed my face with a light finger. I felt his warm breath on my cheek as he drew even closer.

Who knows what might have transpired but at that moment, with me all of a fluster, the front doorbell rang. I almost ran out of the room to answer it. Someone for Mr. H, a portly gentleman, whose name I was in too much of a tremble to understand.

I went upstairs to announce him all the same, and must have looked sufficiently flushed for the doctor to ask if I was all right.

"You seem," said he, "somewhat feverish."

Under the circumstances, so would you, I thought. However, I explained that indeed I felt a trifle dizzy but it was nothing serious.

The doctor looked at me, considering, but let it pass. As for Mr. H, he was solely interested in his latest visitor.

I showed the portly gentleman up to the chambers and then went back to the kitchen, quickly and quietly passing the parlour door. The darlin' boy was still there, whistling a tune I now knew to be "The Wild Rover."

Indeed, I was so discomforted that I poured myself a small glass of port wine and, mumbling an excuse to Clara, retired to my room with it.

There I sat at my dressing table and regarded myself in

the mirror with what I imagined to be another's eyes. I saw a plump – but could one not also say fine? – figure of a woman, certainly no longer young but hardly, at not yet fifty, old either. Not so very many greys in my hair. The few lines on my face more related to smiling than frowning because I consider myself a happy enough body. But am I really happy? I asked myself. Suddenly I found I was missing the gentle touch that love inspires. Oh Henry, I thought, while at the same time thrilling to the much more recent memory of the darlin' boy, his hair, his skin, his touch, his breath. Those strong, firm hands... I took a goodly swallow of the port wine and at least had not lost my wits sufficiently that I could not laugh at myself. However, for the rest of the day I found myself humming "The Wild Rover."

I have said that Mrs. Melrose took a particular interest, a motherly interest I presume, in her young fellow countryman. Now, it just so happened that Mrs. Melrose's sister was milliner to a certain Lady X, who during a fitting and in the presence of Mrs. Melrose started complaining bitterly about one of her stable boys, a lad of intemperate habits and surly demeanour. Mrs. Melrose immediately remarked that she knew a young man who would suit the post perfectly. Indeed, quite possibly, in the telling, she so exaggerated her degree of familiarity with, as well as the virtues and lineage of, the same young man, our darlin' boy of course, that Lady X could not wait but must have him call upon her immediately upon her return from the country, in a week's time.

When next the dear boy called around, I congratulated him on his opportunity but his countenance for once was gloomy.

"How can I call upon such an illustrious personage as Lady X," he asked, "when I have only these rags to my name?" He indicated his clothes which, for the first time I noted were indeed shabby and even torn in some places.

"Good Heavens," I exclaimed. "Why did I never think of

it before? Come with me and we will find if we can dress you somewhat better."

The fact was that I had preserved my Henry's clothes over the years, not willing to throw out good quality tweeds, cottons and gabardines, and it now seemed to me that I could do no better than to present these to this worthy young man..

I confess I had not considered the propriety of bringing a man into my bedroom, even one young enough to be my son. It was only when the door closed behind us, however, that I realised that our presence there together might be seen as compromising, especially when I noticed the smile playing on my companion's lips as he looked upon my bed, the way his eyes shone and his curls quivered more than ever. I therefore did nothing more than fling open the wardrobe door and bade him take whatever he wanted, before hastening from the room. Luckily neither of the servants was witness to the scene.

He took so long, however, that at last I had to go and find what was the matter. I tapped lightly on the door but there was no reply. Had he then left without a word? Surely not. I opened the door, and gasped in amazement at the sight before me. The darlin' boy lay on my bed, in only long undergarments, my Henry's clothes scattered under and around him. He was fast asleep.

"Oh mum," I heard a sigh. It was Phoebe, who had crept up behind me and now was as transfixed as I. "Don't he look just like an angel."

An angel indeed, though perhaps, as I thought even then, a fallen one.

Although Phoebe in her innocence did not question why her beloved should be lying on my bed in a state of undress, I felt that since she was sure to relate the matter to the much more canny Clara, I must explain about the clothes.

"Very good of you, mum," Phoebe said, still staring at the youth.

The sound of our voices roused him. He stirred charmingly, opened his eyes and smiled and yawned. Then, realising his situation, he leapt out of the bed and clutched the sheet to himself, while laughing at the belated attempts at modesty.

"I must be more tired than I realised," said he. "A million apologies, Mrs. Hudson."

"We will leave you to collect yourself," I remarked rather primly, and pulled Phoebe from the door, which I then closed fast.

I cannot say that Henry's clothes fitted to perfection when Jimmy eventually emerged, my late husband having been taller and considerably stouter. However, some small adjustments could easily be made, and I took the necessary measurements, assuring the young man who had been grinning like a maniac during this operation, insisting quite falsely that I was tickling him, that his clothes would be ready the next time he called around. I was as good as my word, setting aside the coat I was knitting for Phoebe's youngest brother to work hard at the task.

The transformation when the darlin' boy tried on his new garments was astonishing. Clara clapped her hands and said he looked quite the country gentleman, to which I agreed with somewhat mixed feelings. The fact of the matter was that Henry had worn the very same Norfolk jacket in blue and grey dogtooth tweed with the matching breeches on our last outing to Hampstead Heath, before the heart attack that fatally struck him down. The suit that held such special memories for me now graced (the very word) the youthful frame of Mr. James Murphy. I was sad and glad at the same time. Glad at least that use would be got at last out of such good cloth, even though Jimmy complained, laughing, of the smell of moth balls. It was a pity, though, I considered, looking at the battered and muddy boots on the boy's feet, that Henry had been possessed of such a very large shoe size that his would not do in the present circumstances.

"If only," Jimmy went on, opening the jacket, "I had a gold fob watch and chain to hang across this splendid waistcoat.

Of a sudden, an evil and unworthy thought crossed my mind and I wondered had Jimmy, while alone in my bedroom, chanced to glance in my jewellery box. If so, he would have spotted the very items he described, Henry's great pride, since they had belonged to his father and grandfather before him. We had no son to pass them to but yet I was not so besotted that I was about to gift them to some young stranger, however charming. I smiled back at him impassively.

Even without a fob watch, it was thanks to me that, despite the sorry condition of his boots (as I then thought), he was able to call upon Lady X in a presentable state of dress. The great result for him was that he was immediately taken into service by her, the sorrier one for the rest of us was that he no longer had the time to wait upon us as he was used to. However, in any event, I was finding that I was running out of jobs for him to do around the house and only persisted for the sake of his poor family.

Some two months passed and the darlin' boy had not been seen once in our neighbourhood, much to the grief of young Phoebe, who for some time was become even clumsier and distracted than before. For my part, I experienced a mixture of regret and relief. Life turned humdrum again, which was surely for the best, even if the chance sound of someone whistling could cause my heart to leap in my breast. Then, one day, I happened to find myself in the vicinity of Hyde Park. It was a fine August afternoon and I decided, time being light on my hands, not to hasten back immediately to my duties but rather to take a stroll. I ambled along to Rotten Row, where riders were exercising their horses, and sat on a bench to watch the fun, and admire the elegance of the gentlemen, the style of the ladies. One of the latter in particular caught my eye, in her Lincoln green velvet, a peacock feather in her jaunty hat. A lady no longer in her first youth, but with a stern beauty all the same. She rode well on her gleaming chestnut mare, sitting straight in the saddle.

How astonished was I then, a moment later, to see none other than the bold Jimmy Murphy, rigged in the smart costume of a groom, standing across from me, his eyes fixed on the same lady. I was about to jump up and call to him, when he ran towards her and caught her in his arms as she, seemingly, was about to fall from her horse. Strange, I thought, since a moment before she had been wholly in control of her mount. Did I then imagine it, or did he hold on to her a little longer than necessary? Did he smile at her in that all too familiar way? And was the answering smile on her face not one of a secret pleasure shared? Such questions were troubling and I tried to slip away unseen, but in my haste I must have called attention to myself, for, having relinquished the lady, he looked up straight across at me and raised his hand in a natural and friendly way, gladness on his face. I waved back and he indicated I should stay where I was. He then bowed to the lady and helped her into her carriage which was then driven off. He tied the horse to a post and came over to join me, holding out his hand for me to shake, which I did.

"How are you, Jimmy?" I said. "You look well." I indicated his dress.

"A servant's livery all the same," he said. "I prefer the suit you made for me."

"But you like your new situation, I trust."

"I love working with the horses."

"And the lady?"

"Oh yes," he said offhandedly. "That is my employer, Lady X. She likes to ride here when she is in town."

"A fine looking woman," I commented, studying him carefully.

123

"So they say." He smiled in that disarming way of his. "But she is a proud cold woman, you know, and beauty is no substitute for heart." Spoken with such sincerity I knew I must have mistakenly interpreted what I had seen. He gazed at me with those fine eyes, a soft smile playing on his full lips

"You must come and visit us again," I said. "We all miss you."

"I will be sure to call," he said, adding in hushed tones. "I have missed you too, Martha."

Well, there we are. I never saw the darlin' boy again.

You will no doubt have read of the ensuing scandal. How Lady X absconded with a servant boy, half her age and more, abandoning without a thought her distinguished husband and three young children. How the couple have been reported from time to time travelling to fashionable watering places across Europe, Lady X being a woman of independent wealth, although, as Mrs. Dixon remarked sourly to me over tea one afternoon, how long would that last with the darlin' boy's hands in the purse? She was particularly bitter because from her own small savings she had purchased for him a pair of elegant boots of fine Spanish leather, the money for which he had promised to pay back but never had.

"And to think someone from my own County of Wexford behaving in such a manner," added Mrs. Melrose. "I should never have believed it."

"No," I said. "You are mistaken. He was from Cork."

"He told me Limerick," said Mrs. Dixon.

"Son of a big family," I said.

"An only child," said Mrs. Melrose.

"An orphan," said Mrs. Dixon.

We looked at each other speechless for a moment. "Was he even Irish?" asked Mrs. Dixon at last.

"Who knows?" I said. "But sure it is that he played us for

fools."

And then we laughed.

"I miss him sorely all the same, the darlin' boy," said Mrs. Melrose, and took another buttered bun.

Mrs. Hudson and the Gentleman in the Next Room

Along with the whole world, but from a much more personal perspective, I had been shocked beyond words to learn of the death in Switzerland of Mr. H. The good doctor apprised the tragic news to me by telegraph so that I would not first hear of it through the newspapers or by word of mouth from idle gossipers. I was indeed touched at his consideration for me, at a time when he himself must have been in no fit state to think clearly, the friendship between the two gentlemen being of such a deep and abiding nature; and that despite Mr. H's occasional sharp tongue and, I am sorry to say, often sneering tone. It was the great man's way, nonetheless, and we all put up with it.

By now, of course, everyone is aware that Mr. H somehow miraculously survived the plunge into the watery abyss of the Falls, but that he decided to keep this a secret for three long years, for his own, I am sure, very good reasons. How and ever, I still cannot think but that it was a cruel trick to play on his good friend even though the doctor has assured me since that it was for all our sakes and safety.

I say it was a secret, but there was one whose discretion he trusted implicitly, his brother Mr. Mycroft Holmes. In the days after the supposed fatality, when we were all still in a state of high confusion, a missive arrived addressed to me from that gentleman. It informed me how his brother had left instructions, that, in the event of his passing, all his worldly goods as found in

126

the Baker Street apartment were to be maintained there and not sold or distributed, and that arrangements had been made through a solicitor for the rental on the rooms to be paid as usual. At the time I thought it a strange and even shocking requirement, but, well-acquainted as I was with Mr. H's unaccountable ways, I felt there must be some purpose behind it without for a moment guessing what this might be.

I still do not know, and have never asked, if the solicitor too was aware that the news of Mr. H's death had been greatly exaggerated, as the supposed late detective himself recently quipped to me in a rare moment of levity, but I suspect that it must be so. In any case, the matter has only a sideways pertinence to this my next narrative, in that the distressful mourning for my lodger caused me to long for an immediate change of air and it just so happened that an old school friend, with whom I had kept in touch over the years, had sent me a timely invitation to visit. This Dolly, Miss Eames that was, Mrs. Butler as she was now, kept a boarding house on the southern coast of England, and indeed, over the years had frequently urged me to come and see her, most particularly following the death of my poor Henry. On that occasion and on others, I had found myself too preoccupied with domestic duties to consider taking a holiday. In any case, I have always found that keeping busy is the best medicine for grief. Now suddenly, with the cessation of my duties as a landlady (the doctor having an establishment elsewhere), I had nothing to keep me so very occupied, and decided to take up the invitation. I left the house in Baker Street in the capable hands of Clara, and for the nonce sent Phoebe back to stay with her parents in the country, the girl being sentimentally distraught at the supposed death of a master who alive, however, only seemed to notice her existence when she did something wrong. It would be a good opportunity, I considered, for Phoebe to help out her poor mother, recently brought to bed of yet another addition to the already numerous family.

127

Thus it was that in the early autumn of that year I took a railway train to the fashionable resort of Eastbourne on the southern coast of England. I was met at the station by Dolly's son Arthur in a pony and chaise. I had never met the lad before but he identified me from the photographic likeness I had sent Dolly at her request the previous year. ("We never meet," she had written, "so I do not know what you look like these days, Martha, or even if I should know you if we passed in the street.") She had likewise furnished me with a picture of herself, so that I was somewhat prepared for the stout red- faced personage that my slender school friend had grown into.

We met with much emotion, embracing and weeping, and it was only after a while that I was able to take in my surroundings. The boarding house, though narrow in its frontage, had a most respectable aspect and was but a side street away from the sea itself.

"You may wish tomorrow to take a walk along the promenade toward the pier," Dolly told me. "It is at that end of town that the fancy hotels are situated, where wealthy and titled folk like to stay. But we are happy here in our modest little establishment, and hope you will not take it amiss that you are not on the better side of town."

"Heavens, Dolly," I declared. "I am sure I am much more comfortable here with you. What would I be doing among the upper classes?"

It seemed that my friend, from her reading of the doings of Mr. H as reported by the doctor in his lively accounts, was under the impression that I was accustomed to the company of lords, ladies, earls and other prime movers of the country, as well as foreign dignitaries.

"I may on occasion have opened the door to such and shown them the way to Mr. H's chambers," I told her. "But I am certainly not in the habit of frequenting their company."

At the mention of my lodger's name, I am afraid I broke

down again, and more tears flowed. Dolly clasped me to her large and motherly bosom and then took me upstairs to my room. It had a pleasant enough though shadowed view over the little street, and if you stood sideways close up to the window, you could almost look down to the sea itself. The bed was covered in a crocheted blanket of red, cream and gold and I suddenly remembered that Dolly, as a girl, had liked to occupy herself with such work.

She confirmed that she had made it herself, and also the cushions scattered around, as well as the curtains of the same chintz material. This was somewhat coarse in texture, as I privately ascertained, and perhaps overly bright in design, but for a boarding house, with sometimes careless guests, I suppose the best, most expensive quality would hardly be warranted. A small table and upright chair, an armchair next to the fireplace, a dressing table and rustic wardrobe completed the accoutrements. All in all I was quite satisfied with the cosy room and felt that this, combined with chats with my old friend and exhilarating walks along the sea front, would work wonders on my mood and soften the grief I was feeling.

I asked Dolly if she had many visitors in the house at that moment.

"The season is coming to an end," she explained. "In the winter months business becomes slow although I have some regular travelling sales gentlemen who stay from time to time when in the district. There is a permanent resident too, a retired governess who still teaches drawing and German conversation to young ladies. Fraulein Franks is a pleasant enough woman, as you will no doubt find her, even though a foreigner. In addition, a young lady has also taken up residence for the past week, a Mrs. Braddon. She is very shy and not at all forthcoming, so I know nothing of her doings here or what she occupies herself with all day long." Dolly frowned somewhat at this and I suspected her of being one of those landladies who like to know their lodgers' business. "I also had a family staying here for two months over the summer," she continued, "a mother with her two small children, the father visiting on Sundays from London where he was working. One of the poor little mites was afflicted with a frightful breathing wheeze, and his parents wished to give him the benefit of clean sea air away from the city. But they could not stay forever and I fear that, although Bobby improved mightily while here, he will soon get bad again when the winter fogs start up. I do not know, Martha," she concluded at last, "how, having been reared in the countryside, you can bear London at all."

I smiled at that and replied that I was used to it.

"Well," she went on. "Now that you no longer have either husband or the burden of a lodger, perhaps you might think of moving down here. It would be delicious to have an old friend nearby."

It was perhaps crude of her to suggest as much, although I am sure she meant well. I was not, however, about to explain the strange instruction I had received, post-mortem as it were, from Mr. H since I could already tell that my friend had become a gossip and that this information would provide all the more grist to her mill. I am afraid, as well, that mention of Mr. H rather set me off again. Dolly patted my arm and asked if I would like to settle myself, Arthur having brought up my bag meanwhile, or if I would prefer to come downstairs and partake of some refreshments.

I opted for the latter course, agreeing that a cup of tea would be most acceptable, and we descended the stairs again.

"I hope," said Dolly, "you will not mind taking it in the kitchen. "It is such a fag to set up the parlour and we will be more comfortable there I am sure."

I certainly had no objection, often preferring the kitchen at home myself, and was pleased to meet there the cook, Mrs. Gunning, and the maid, Betsy, both solid, reliable looking bodies.

Dolly sat me down and, while the tea was drawing, produced a plate of warm scones, fresh from the pan, with some good country butter. I asked about her husband, whom I had not met since their wedding.

"Jeremiah is well, thank God. He still has the carpenter's shop down by the harbour. Arthur and Harold work there too and business is good enough. They mostly provide boxes and such for the fishermen but can also make furniture. They built the wardrobe in your room."

"I was admiring it. That is fine work." She was pleased, I could see, at my praise.

We drank our tea and I ate two scones, one more than I should have done and slathered in butter too but, as I complimented Mrs. Gunning, they were most delicious, packed as they were with currants. As I was sure Dolly had duties to attend to, I then expressed the intention of retiring to my room to unpack, politely declining the offered services of Betsy, since I like to put my things where I want them and not where a maid, however efficient, thinks they should go.

It was just as I went out into the hallway that the doorbell rang out with a shrill screech that quite caused me to jump. Dolly hurried out behind me, saying, "Whoever can that be?"

I of course had no answer to give, until Dolly opened the door on an undersized gentleman of decidedly eccentric appearance. He had a bushy red beard, and thick tortoiseshell-rimmed spectacles that covered the rest of his face. He was wearing yellow trousers under a yellow and brown checked jacket, a green scarf, lemon yellow gloves and brown boots on small feet, the whole surmounted by a brown and green deerstalker hat, ear flaps down. The latter item caused me to start, recalling as it did Mr. H's preferred headgear.

"Can I help you?" Dolly asked.

"A room," the fellow said in gruff tones.

131

"Well, sir, you are lucky, It happens I do have a vacancy at present," she replied and started to explain terms.

I took the opportunity then to ascend to my bedroom. I felt somewhat fatigued, no doubt from the journey, but also, to tell the truth, from the garrulousness of my old friend. Without even starting to unpack, I laid myself down on the bed for a rest.

"Well, Martha," I said to myself, at the uncustomary indulgence, "you are not as young as you once were." A truth brought home to me perhaps more particularly by the elderly and matronly appearance of one who, when I knew her in her youth, had been a pretty elfin thing. No doubt my appearance had also changed for the worse, but it was depressing to think on it.

I dozed a little, aware of noises from the adjacent room where it seemed the new arrival was to be installed. Then it seemed I must have drifted off to sleep altogether, for when I opened my eyes, the room was almost dark. I rose and quickly put my few things in order, hanging my dress in the wardrobe that smelt sweetly of well-seasoned wood.

I descended then to the parlour where I found a woman well advanced in years sitting over a book. I introduced myself and she spoke back with a certain intonation that I recognised as German.

This had to be the Fraulein Franks mentioned by Dolly, not a typical sausage-eater at all but a small shrivelled figure of a woman, white-haired, with sharp blue eyes. We exchanged a few pleasantries and then she returned to her reading, allowing me the freedom to sit at the desk and there pen a short missive to Clara, describing my safe arrival. Soon enough a gong sounded which was, apparently, the summons to supper.

Fraulein Franks showed me the way to the dining room, which was furnished with several small tables. I was somewhat at a loss. Would it be more polite to sit with the German lady or to leave her to the companionship of her book, which I had observed to be in her own native language? I decided on the latter course since I felt that we had already exhausted the usual commonplace topics. Furthermore, while she had proved civil enough, I had the strong impression that she was happier to be left alone. As indeed at that moment was I. I took a table near enough to her, all the same, and one that faced her, so that if she wished to resume our conversation it would be no great trouble.

We were shortly joined in the dining room by a young woman, presumably the Mrs. Braddon, spoken of by Dolly. A very young woman indeed, surely no more than twenty, of slight build, pale complexion and an abundance of fine auburn hair. She gave us a nervous nod and sat herself some distance away by the wall. Betsy entered with a tureen of soup, and started to ladle a few spoonfuls into the dishes in front of each of us, announcing the thick mixture as "mock turtle." It was while she was so occupied that the newly arrived gentleman made his entrance, both of the other ladies looking up as he came in. I could not tell which one of them it was that gasped, or indeed whether it was Betsy, but sure I was that someone did. The gentleman paid no attention to any of us and took the remaining table in the remotest corner of the room. He crouched over his bowl and slurped up the contents in a way that was unpleasant to behold, some of each spoonful dripping down his beard. I looked away and concentrated on my own soup, which would have been greatly improved, I thought, with less calves' brain, more oysters and a liberal glass of Madeira. Nevertheless, it was sustaining enough, as was the mutton course that followed and I was honestly able to tell Dolly, when she joined us at last, that it was all most acceptable.

"I expected you to dine with us," she said, seemingly put out, although she had conveyed to me no such thing earlier. "Jeremiah is agog to meet with you again, Martha. But it is no great matter. I suppose you are pleased to make the acquaintance of my guests. Fraulein Franks, Mrs. Braddon and Mr. um... Smith." She waved a proprietary hand over them but only Mrs.

Braddon responded with a small smile. "Perhaps you can at least join us for pudding, Martha. Mrs. Gunning has made a splendid jam roly-poly."

I thus spent the rest of the evening squashed into the kitchen with Dolly, Jeremiah, Arthur and Harold. The latter two boys were civil enough, but rose from the table immediately after finishing their meal to go, as they told their mother, "out." The husband, Jeremiah, meanwhile far from being "agog" showed very little interest in me at all, but was rather more absorbed in his pudding, his ale and his vile pipe. Dolly shared her time between praising to the heavens her offspring, announcing what a joy sons were (to me who have only daughters), and quizzing me about my late lodger.

"I have followed Watson's accounts over the years with such great interest," said she, her small bright eyes on me like a bird avid for tidbits. I was disinclined to satisfy her curiosity so she then started gossiping about her lodgers, being particularly interested in the latest arrival.

"Smith," she said dismissively. "Not his real name, I am sure. A strange, surly man who hardly addressed two words to me. There is a mystery here and no mistake. Oh, Martha," she exclaimed, "would it not be fun if he turned out to be a spy."

"A spy?" I replied. "What would he be spying on here and for whom?"

"For our enemies, of course," she retorted. "They are everywhere, you know, and ships come in and out of the harbour here all the time."

At this Jeremiah, silent up to now but for the occasional grunt or belch, emitted a loud bark of a laugh. "Ships! Ha! Fishing boats." And then after a pause, drawing deeply on the evil mess that was in his pipe (so different from Mr. H's aromatic weed. and indeed from my own dear Henry's cigars). "Spies, ha!"

It seemed that my friend had become addicted to the

more sensational yellow press and read little else. How different after all our lives had turned out to be. Well, here I was and determined that I would stay at least until the end of the week, but already found myself missing my own comfortable nest. Luckily my hosts, having to rise early, went early to bed, and I was soon able to betake myself to my room. There I indulged myself until quite late by reading the latest work from the pen of Marie Corelli.

There was no sound from next door and I supposed my neighbour had already retired. However, at past eleven of the carriage clock on the mantle, I heard a commotion from below, the loud and shrill ringing of the doorbell, Dolly's raised voice and the subsequent clumping of feet up the stairs, followed by the banging of the adjacent door and various noises that suggested a person preparing for bed. The next morning at breakfast (kippers in the kitchen), my friend informed me, still quite incensed, that Mr. Smith had indeed returned late and raised the household.

"If I had but known in advance of his intentions I could have furnished him with a key, as I tried to tell him. He just pushed by me. Can you imagine that! Not a single word of an apology. If he is not a spy, Martha, then I am sure at least he is up to no good. I would have a mind to tell him the room is took for the next night, only that he paid me in advance."

The weather being mild and bright, she then, having recovered her composure, suggested a tour along the promenade, assuring me that her duties were not so onerous that she could not spare an hour or two to entertain a friend. I gladly agreed: the house I had found cosy the day before was already become confining and even somewhat oppressive. Moreover, I was eager to see more of this most fashionable of watering places.

We walked down to the sea side and along the promenade which stretched far off into the distance. There being quite a breeze and the tide being high, the waves were choppy and splashed against the sea wall, sometimes throwing sparkling droplets of spray across our path. I thought it quite delightful but Dolly worried for her dress.

"Salt water, you know, my dear Martha. It stains badly."

I was admiring the prospect before me, the beach and crashing waves, the children playing merrily under the watchful eyes of their mammas or their nursemaids, the pier that almost miraculously it seemed to me, stretched out over the water on thin metal legs. Dolly's interest, in contrast, was all in the gentry promenading on the upper levels and particularly the ladies of fashion, although it seemed she was readier to criticise than approve. She was also keen to point out to me the fine houses, the expensive hotels where sometimes, sometimes (repeated in hushed tones) even royals were known to stay.

"Martha," she added solemnly, "I have seen with my very own eyes the Princess B. here in Eastbourne," pointing, "almost on that very spot." She looked there searchingly as if hoping this august personage would manifest herself once more.

I responded with an appropriate expression of surprise and awe.

"She perceived me regarding her and gave me a most gracious nod."

I said I was delighted to hear it.

"Although," Dolly continued, "the mustard velvet of her gown was, I felt, mistaken. She has a sallow complexion already, do you know, and the dress made her look even more jaundiced."

We walked beyond the pier and past ever grander hotels. Dolly explained that a walk much further on would bring us to the well-known beauty spot that was Beachy Head.

"But that," she said, "might be for another day when we have more time. Unless you wish to continue alone. I have to return home to supervise luncheon."

I said that I would be happy to stay in town for a while, and we turned to walk slowly back, Dolly's head turning to right and left not to miss anything and nodding at a few persons of her acquaintance. Just as we came up to the pier again, she gripped my arm and nodded to indicate a figure heading directly towards us.

"Why, Martha, is that not our own Mr. Smith?" she cried.

I had noticed already that the seaside crowd sported clothes of a brighter hue than those generally seen in the city, but even so, the yellows, greens and browns of the lodger's outfit were unmistakeable.

"I shall give him a cold acknowledgement," she said. "I am still suffering from a broken night's sleep."

Her plan, however, could not take effect since the gentleman swerved before our encounter (not, I am almost sure, having noticed us at all) and turned on to the pier.

"Oh Martha," Dolly exclaimed. "How I would love to follow him and see what he is up to, but I cannot. It is too late already." Then as if the idea had just struck her. "But you can. You have all the time in the world. Oh, follow him, Martha, and see what he is about."

"He is probably just a holidaymaker wishing to see the sights, like myself," I replied.

However, since I was greatly inclined to take a stroll along the pier, it was to the great satisfaction of my friend, that I agreed to visit that construction, assuring her that, after, I should be able to find my own way back to the boarding house.

"Be certain," said she, "to note any suspicious behaviour."

I nodded, without having any firm intention of fulfilling this latter instruction.

"You must hurry," she said, looking after our friend. "He is getting away."

Where she thought he could hide on a pier, I am not sure, unless she suspected he had a confederate at the other end with a boat moored ready for a hasty escape.

I waved goodbye to Dolly and paid my entrance fee at the toll booth. It was most pleasant, if somewhat windswept, to walk along the wooden planks of the pier, between which you could glimpse the wildly churning sea beneath, thus providing an enjoyable thrill of danger. Even though I am sure it was quite safe, it seemed to me that the structure was swaying about slightly, so that on occasion I had to put my hand on the metal railing to support myself.

With no intention of pursuing Mr. Smith, I could not help but observe his distinctively clad person still hurrying ahead of me. He certainly seemed a man with a purpose, not merely an idle sightseer, and I admit my curiosity started to get the better of me, even though I was momentarily distracted by a kiosk selling souvenir items. I bought two small clay ornaments of cottages each on a base that read "Eastbourne", one for Clara and one for Phoebe. I then strolled on. At the very end of the pier was a domed pavilion where it was possible to sit and look out and even partake of some refreshment. There I spotted the gentleman lodger sitting, a glass of some beverage in front of him. I seated myself at a distance and ordered a glass of lemonade, keeping him in view all the time. It seemed certain to me that he must be waiting for someone, looking around himself from time to time in an agitated manner. Eventually, after about twenty minutes, he suddenly arose and rushed out past me. I followed, more slowly, but, as I have previously stated, it was a simple enough matter, given the conspicuous nature of his dress, to keep him in view. He left the pier and came to a halt on the promenade, looking about himself in some perplexity. Then it was as if he found what he was looking for, because he took off again at high speed towards one of the hotels and indeed entered it.

I was unsure how to proceed – the place being far grander than any that I might usually frequent – but then bethought myself. If such a person as Mr. Smith could enter such sumptuous premises, then surely I equally had as much right. In any case, I was curious to view the interior. I walked with dignity to the entrance, the door being opened for me, before I could push on it, by a bowing lackey. I was pleased that I was wearing my most respectable black bombazine and not my workaday grey. Inside, the hotel was all white and yellow marble, thick red carpeting, a chandelier sparkling down on all, rather more alabaster nymphs and satyrs than I am used to seeing out of a museum, and a quantity of gold leaf on all sides. But nowhere could I spot the elusive Mr. Smith.

I fancied he must have gone into one of the dining rooms or salons, but felt that I could nose around no further without calling unwanted attention to myself. I sat me down in an armchair of great elegance but some hardness, intending to state, if approached, that I was waiting for a friend. No one, however, queried my right to be there and I must say that it was an entertainment in itself to watch the comings and goings of the fashionable ladies and gentlemen who frequented the establishment.

After a goodly time and it approaching the hour when I was expected back for the mid-day meal, I left the hotel without again getting sight of the mysterious lodger.

Dolly of course quizzed me mightily and oohed and ahhed a great deal regarding Mr. Smith's sortie into that particular hotel, known for its high prices and the accompanying high standing of its guests. I was unable to satisfy her more but she announced herself delighted with the unfolding mystery.

"I will be keeping a very sharp eye indeed on our gentleman lodger," said she. "And if he asks for a key after all, I think I shall not give it him."

The rest of the day passed with no further incident relevant to my tale. I had brought with me a small tapestry to work on and needed to go in search of a shop that could furnish me with a certain rust shade of wool. Dolly pointed me in the right direction and I spent a happy two hours wandering the little back streets of this most attractive town.

Mr. Smith turned up at last in time for the evening meal, but, since I was expected once more to dine with Dolly and her family, there was no occasion to observe the gentleman. In any case, given his lack of gracious table manners, I was by no means sorry to avoid the spectacle.

Supper concluded, we repaired to the parlour where we found Fraulein Franks and Mrs. Braddon, but no Mr. Smith. Dolly prevailed on the two ladies to join us in a game of Old Maid, which they did, though, as I could see, somewhat reluctantly. It was not a jolly evening, even though Dolly chattered away throughout, while Fraulein Franks won every hand and earned herself all of sixpence.

As early as I could, I again pleaded weariness in order to retire to my room and my book which I was finding most absorbing. Because it was a balmy night, I opened the window a little and was pleased to find that I could hear in the distance the pounding of the sea on the stony beach. Thus an hour or more passed most pleasantly.

I had been unaware of my neighbour and assumed that he was again out on the town. I was therefore surprised suddenly to hear from close by a voice raised and impassioned. Moreover, it was that of a woman. I rose and went to the window and ascertained that it was indeed from the next room that the voice was coming, the sash there also being slightly raised.

I tried to make out the words but apart from fragments: "the promises you made...," "you cannot but be aware of my situation...," "I shall be forced to take extreme measures..." all these repeated it seemed several times, I could make no sense of the dialogue. Although in truth, dialogue it was not. The woman did all the talking. I could hear nothing of the gruff tones of Mr. Smith and imagined him sitting slumped in a chair while she whirled about him with her accusations and reproofs.

But whoever could this person be? The doorbell had not rung and so I must assume that Mr. Smith had brought the woman back with him, having been provided with the key after all that Dolly said she would not give him. Yet I had not heard the opening of the front door which was strange for it was directly under my window. Could it be, then, that the speaker was actually one of the women already in the house? If so, I felt that I could safely discount Fraulein Franks, the servants and even Dolly herself, though it amused me to wonder if she might be in a secret liaison after all with this Smith. I reluctantly let go of the frivolous thought. No, the most probable speaker was the shy and troubled Mrs. Braddon. I was sorry to think it, however, since I had taken a liking to her.

The voice was now silent and stayed so and I imagined that its owner must have left the room, though most quietly. Long into the night, I wondered what to do about the matter. To tell Dolly that Mr. Smith had entertained a woman in his bedroom would certainly provoke a scandal and I firstly resolved to have a discreet word on the morrow with Mrs. Braddon.

However, I fell into a deep slumber towards morning and was let rest on by Dolly, who decided I must be in need of it. By the time I arose, Mrs. Braddon had already gone out, as Dolly informed me.

There was nothing for it but to wait. That or to set out in what had to be a needle in a haystack kind of exercise, trying to track her down.

I asked Dolly where Mrs. Braddon might have gone, making the excuse, to avoid arousing my friend's suspicions, that the young woman had promised me an embroidery pattern. Dolly not knowing her plans, I was about to go for another wander along the promenade when Fraulein Franks, who had overheard our exchange, stated that Mrs. Braddon was in the habit of taking a morning stroll up to Beachy Head. Since I was curious to visit the place anyway, I gladly set out in that direction, rather more pleased than disappointed that Dolly declined to accompany me.

"It is a long way and a steep climb, you know," she said, "and I am not well able for it. I thought we might go another day in a charabanc with a picnic."

"Well," I said, determined not to be put off, "if it as striking a place as you say, it is worthy of more than one visit, and anyway I am well used to long walks."

She could not but let me go, no doubt feeling I was a most unsatisfactory visitor. That I could not help. From the urgency in the voice I had heard the previous night, I had the feeling that it was of prime importance to reach Mrs. Braddon at the earliest occasion. I forthwith set out armed with directions, though, to be honest, it would be hard to miss the cliffs that loomed over the town.

"As you go, you might," Dolly added in a whisper, "look out for you know who. He also left the house early."

Perhaps, I surmised, the two were bound for a rendezvous away from prying eyes and ears.

The air on this September morning was again pleasant, the sun shining but emitting not so strong a heat as to prove uncomfortable while walking. I was surprised, then, to find so few people out enjoying the climate, and saw virtually no one once the town gave way to the countryside.

Walking a worn path over coarse grass, I clambered up the steep slope that eventually led to the top of the cliff. The prospect was quite daunting and I feared to go too near an edge that plunged down straight onto spume-covered rocks. It was with some astonishment, therefore, that I spied the figure of a woman sitting on the very brink of the precipice. I was every more amazed, drawing closer, to observe it to be none other than Mrs. Braddon, hatless, her beautiful hair blown loose by the wind and flying round her head in a mad dance. Of Mr. Smith, there was no sign.

I feared to frighten her by a sudden approach, so made

various noises as I walked nearer, coughing and seeming to stumble on stones and the like, and eventually she turned her face towards me. It was a face that presented a picture of such despair and misery that I hope I shall never see the like again.

"Mrs. Hudson," quoth she in surprise, trying to recover herself, "what do you here?"

"The same as you, my dear." Meaning enjoying the view.

"I doubt that very much," said she in reply, with a bitter laugh.

"But you make me nervous," I said. "Please come away from the edge."

"You think I might fall?"

I thought worse than that. I thought she might be preparing to jump, and was thus relieved when she rose and came towards me.

"I am here every day," she said. "But still cannot find the strength to go over."

Of a sudden, she subsided onto the grass beside me in a full faint. I knelt at her side and applied some of the sal volatile I always carry with me. She soon came around again.

"Tell me," I said, "what would drive a lovely young woman like yourself to commit such a terrible act?"

She started sobbing then, for which I was pleased. It is always, in my understanding, salutary when release occurs in such a way, making the desperate act less likely.

"Is it," I went on gently, "Mr. Smith?"

She then raised eyes to me expressing such bewilderment that I knew I had been mistaken. Hers must not have been the voice I had heard in the night. Yet the young woman was deeply troubled by someone or something.

It poured out. A story I must have heard with variations many times before. How she, of good family, had fallen in love with a pretty young man of a class considerably below hers. How

143

he had persuaded her to elope to France. How they had gone through a form of marriage which turned out to be nothing of the sort. How, when her family made clear they wanted nothing more to do with her, and her money all gone, he had abandoned her, laughing at her tears and pleadings. And when she informed him that she was with child, he had only laughed the more and told her that she and her brat could go to the devil as far as he was concerned. She had made her way home to England, thinking to throw herself on the mercy of her family, but once more they had thrown her pleas back at her.

"They sent such a terrible letter in response to mine," she said pulling the missive from her bosom, and thrusting it at me to read. It stated in hard and unforgiving words that she had brought such shame and disgrace on the family that it could only be expunged by her disappearing forever from their lives. "It must be as if," the letter went on, "you had never been born to us."

"How cruel," said I, holding her trembling body tight. "I understand you. And yet, you know a baby, a new life, is something precious and not to be destroyed."

"But I am ruined. It is death or the streets of shame for me. I fear for my immortal soul and yet I must choose death."

I think, if I had not been holding her fast, she would have broken from me there and then and flung herself from the Head.

I tried to reassure her and told, in soothing tones, of charitable houses that would take in a young woman like herself.

"I know of those places," she replied. "They are worse than anything. My mother, as patron of such an establishment, took me once to a house for fallen women, as they are pleased to call them. I will never forget the expression in the eyes of those poor girls. I will never go to such." She paused and then added, "How I wish I had been born a man, Mrs. Hudson. My brother, Charles, leads a life of no little dissipation and to my certain knowledge, and I am sure that of my parents, for they paid the girl off, got one of our maids with child. And yet he remains the apple of their eye."

What she said was true and I have often thought it myself: a whole different scale of rules apply to the two sexes and behaviour that is condoned and even lauded in menfolk, brings women only disgrace and blame. Perhaps one day the balance will be redressed and women will be judged equally with men but, sad to say, today, at the end of the nineteenth century, that is certainly not yet the case.

We both looked out across the wind-whipped sea that, from this beautiful but deadly place, had already gobbled down the lives of so many.

"My dear," I said at last. "What is your real name, for I suspect it is not Braddon?"

"I am Mary Wright," she replied.

"Well, Mary," I went on, having made a decision. "At the end of this week I will be returning to London. Following a bereavement, I am in need of a companion and would gladly offer you the position until you decide what you want to do."

She raised a face to me that expressed for the first time a faint gleam of hope.

"You do not know me," she said.

"I think I know enough. I cannot offer you much remuneration," I went on. "But a safe place is, I think, what you and baby need at the moment."

There were then tears on both sides, embraces and assurances, after which we made our way clinging together down the cliff top back to the town. To compose both ourselves, I treated us to ices from a booth on the promenade and we sat on a bench for a while each absorbed in our own thoughts and in enjoyment of the sweet.

Dolly was exceedingly surprised at the friendship which had sprung up so suddenly between the young lady and myself and was dying to know more of its cause. I however made light of it and certainly did not inform her of the plan I had hatched to

145

save poor Mary.

Through my own mistaken assumption, I had ventured far along a path away from the highway of my main concern and now felt the need to address this immediately. The question indeed had become all the more pressing. If the woman in the room with the gentleman lodger was not Mary Wright, then who in heaven's name could she be? The tragic conclusion was, as it turned out, not far off and must, I think, amaze my readers as much as it did us who had a small involvement in the unfolding events.

That night I was again reading in my room unable to tear myself, even at such a late hour, from the grip of the story. Marie Corelli has the true writer's gift to keep one enthralled. At a certain point, as the narrative reached its climax, I became aware of a sobbing in the next room which became ever more violent as I listened. And again I heard the female voice crying out for pity. Another wronged maiden, it seemed.

I became incensed on behalf of my sex and, although it was none of my business, I resolved to act. No doubt I was already fired up by the sad injustice and near tragedy of the situation of Mary Wright, not to mention that of the heroine of the novel I was reading. I rose from my chair, crossed the room and went out into the passage. Certain it was that the sobs came from my neighbour's room and I knocked sharply upon the door. Silence fell. It stretched out and I knocked again, even more sharply.

"What?" I heard the gruff voice of Mr. Smith.

"It is Mrs. Hudson. Open the door, please. I wish to speak to the lady within."

A pause, then, "There is no lady here."

"Come, come, Mr. Smith. I heard her voice quite plainly."

At this point I was joined by Dolly, apparently roused by our voices, clasping around herself a hastily tied robe.

"What is it?" she asked, keeping her voice low not to disturb the other residents.

"Mr. Smith has a woman in his room," I said. "I have heard her weeping and calling out."

Dolly then applied her fist to the door.

"Open up, Smith," she said. "It is Mrs. Butler speaking."

Now quite a crowd was gathering on the landing, Arthur and Harold, Miss Franks, Mary.

"Arthur," Dolly said. "Fetch my spare key."

At that the door opened a crack. Dolly pushed it open on Mr. Smith dressed as usual, even including his deerstalker hat.

"Come in if you must," said he. "There is no woman here." He went to the window and turned his back on us.

Dolly swept in with me behind, the others lingering on the threshold and indeed, clear it was instantly that no other person was concealed it there, even under the bed, which Dolly ascertained, or in the wardrobe, the sister to the one in my room. I was astounded, confused and embarrassed but still sure of what I had heard, as I insisted.

"Well Martha, there is quite evidently no one else here," Dolly said severely. "Unless, of course, they leapt from the window."

I went to look, despite her sarcastic tone, Mr. Smith moving to one side out of the way, and soon perceived that it was an impossibility, given the narrowness of the ledge, the sharp fall on to the street below.

"What you heard must have been outside. Or else," she added seeing the volume of Marie Corelli I still held in my hand, "your reading of fantastic fiction has quite turned your head and you dreamed the whole thing."

What could I say except to apologise to all, and especially to Mr. Smith, who barely nodded in my direction. Everyone then returned to their respective rooms, Mary giving me a sympathetic glance for which I was grateful, since the others seemed to regard me with either amusement (Arthur and Harold) or disapproval (Dolly and Fraulein Franks). I was glad Jeremiah had kept to his bed for I could only imagine the barks of scorn he would have directed toward me.

Once safe behind my own door I put my mind to the puzzle. I still had no doubt as to what I had heard. The evidence however contradicted this and I found myself sorely confounded. Suddenly a remark of Mr. H's, relayed to me by the good doctor, popped into my head, that when you have eliminated the impossible, whatever remains, however improbable, must be the truth. I tried then to imagine how Mr. H would have solved the contradiction and it came to me then that there was one explanation which, bizarre and shocking as it was, could cover the facts. Brooding further on this, I could find no desire in myself to go to bed, but sat in the dark.

It must have been a good hour later when I heard the stealthy sound of a door opening, my neighbour's door. Soon after, again softly, the opening of the street door. I peered from my window and, sure enough, saw Mr. Smith making his hasty way out. He paused to stare up at my window but I drew back in haste and so doubt he saw me among the shadows. I waited not a second to follow him, as quietly as possible, seizing my coat and hat from the stand in the hall.

By the time I emerged into the road I had to guess at the direction my quarry had taken, and took a chance, setting off down to the sea front. Once there, by the light of a crescent moon I ascertained that a figure was indeed striding west along the otherwise deserted promenade toward the fashionable end of town. It had to be Mr. Smith, for who else would be out at this hour and in such a hurry? Indeed, I could not keep up with his speed and for the first time started to wonder at the wisdom of my pursuit. Dear Henry had often laughed at my stubbornness in proving a point, calling me his little mule. In this present case I had been mocked for telling a truth and my pride was at stake.

Despite the possible incaution of my behaviour, I knew that I could not rest until I had got to the bottom of the mystery and vindicated myself.

It seemed nonetheless that my ambition in this regard was doomed to failure, for I reached the pier with no further glimpse of the subject of my pursuit. He had simply disappeared. Would I then have to abandon the search? It was at that moment, as I was about to turn back, that I caught sight of someone coming from the direction of one of the hotels, the very same that Mr. Smith had entered on the previous day. The figure, a man's, came furtively towards the beach, I managing to slip behind a booth to conceal myself. The newcomer passed quite near me and I saw that it was not Mr. Smith. However, as I continued to watch, he made his way over the beach and, the tide being on its way out, under the very pier itself.

Then, above the susurration of the waves, I heard a soft mumbling, as of voices. These soon got louder but I still could not make out the words and feared to come closer, since the stones of the beach would surely have given advance notice of my approach. Ah, but now that all has become clear, would that I had intervened: the consequences could not have been worse. For suddenly I saw two figures emerge from the darkness, engaged in a most terrible struggle. A cry of agony sounded out and one of the figures fell to the ground in a convulsion of movement. I waited no more and, without considering my own safety, rushed forward.

The crescent moon shone down on a sorry sight indeed. A young man lay in the final spasms of life, a sharp blade having pierced his breast. Beside him knelt the familiar figure of Mr. Smith, overcome it seemed with despair.

He raised a newly clean-shaven face to me and asked, "Can nothing be done?" in tones very different to the ones that usually came from his mouth. Indeed, I had guessed the secret already and this only provided confirmation.

I shook my head in answer to the query, for already the other lay still, eyes staring out but already beginning to cloud over. I instinctively reached out to shut them.

"He came to kill me," my companion said in wondering tones. "Oh Gerald," and flung himself across the body.

Or perhaps now is the time to reveal what I had already suspected, that the eccentric dress and ginger whiskers of Mr. Smith concealed nothing less than the tender body of a young lady. For how could I have heard the voice and sobs of a woman in a room which seemed to be empty except of Mr. Smith, unless the voice and sobs actually belonged to Mr. Smith? I had guessed her secret and had tried to prevent a catastrophe, but – alas – arrived too late.

The noise of the affray had inevitably roused people, who started to congregate near to us, among them a stout constable on his night-time rounds who had great difficulty in getting to grips with a case which was, understandably, almost beyond understanding, and sent a wide-eyed urchin for assistance, since it was clear he could not manage alone.

I will not detail the confusion that surrounded the subsequent enquiry, but simply summarise the main points of the terrible business that echoed in so many ways the fate of my poor Mary. The person we had known as Mr. Smith was in fact a young actress of the name of Susannah Golden. She had been admired on stage and subsequently pursued by a young man of wealth and fashion, of a family name that ranks among the greatest in the land and which, for that reason, I will not reveal here. Spoilt and thoughtless, he saw, wanted, and, what he wanted, had to have. Bewitched by his promises, she fell in love with this scion of the nobility. Unlike some others of her profession, however, she was virtuous and insisted on marriage before giving herself to him. He laughed and agreed, seeing it, his friends later revealed, as a great lark, considering that it would be no great matter to cast the girl aside once he had done with her. He had meantime extracted a promise from her to keep the union a secret until he had occasion to talk to his father.

A match having lately been announced between himself and a lady of his own class and great wealth, this came to the attention of Susannah. Shocked and disbelieving, she followed him and his intended to Eastbourne where they were preparing for the nuptials. She disguised herself as a man in order to more easily approach her husband in private and decided on outlandish dress and appearance to ward off others who might be inclined otherwise to try to make the acquaintance of a presentable youth on his own. The wardrobe of the theatre where she worked furnished an appropriate if rather too conspicuous costume, complete with whiskers.

Her encounters with Gerald having shown his true nature, she decided that her only course, despite her promise, was immediately to make their marriage public. He thereupon requested her to meet him on the beach at night before she took such an irrevocable step. Having already failed to move her with promises of money, he decided to kill her as a way of getting rid of his problem for good, and for that purpose brought a knife to the rendezvous. This, though his friends later tried to lay the blame on Susannah, stating that it was she who brought the weapon with murder in mind, was later identified by his valet as Gerald's very own letter opener, a stiletto he had purchased in Italy. In the ensuing struggle, the knife intended for Susannah was somehow turned and fatally pierced the breast of the villain himself.

That was what was argued by her defence, and the jury, I am pleased to say, believed it, despite the wealth and influence of Gerald's family that had been brought to bear against her. I was called to give evidence of what I had seen and heard, the which I think in no small way influenced the decision of the jury in Susannah's favour. The judge, however, who happened to be a member of the same club as Gerald's august father, ruled that manslaughter had taken place, dismissing the plea of self-defence, and sending the poor girl to prison for fifteen years.

I was deeply troubled, nay angered, by this outcome which just proved once more to me how the law is written and practiced by men for the greater good of men. Even though this Gerald had armed himself, clearly intending to threaten, wound or kill, it was he who was considered the innocent victim. Susannah's arrest also caused a falling out between myself and Dolly, enraptured by the attention she now received in the neighbourhood for harbouring the killer under her roof and under such sensational circumstances too: disguised as a man. The kitchen and parlour were ever full of gossips like herself. They delighted in the whole business and plagued me for more details, which, to their disgust, I refused to furnish. My thoughts were only for the poor girl, reviled and ridiculed. Come the time of my departure, relations between my old school friend and myself had cooled to such an extent that I had to hire a cab to take me to the station, because, as Dolly told me in a most offhand manner, neither of the boys could be spared from their employment. I still smile at the expression on her face when she discovered at the last moment that Mary was to accompany me. My last view of my old school friend was of her standing open-mouthed at the door of her house. Although, beforehand, we had exchanged an embrace of sorts and promises on either side to meet up again soon, I trust never to see her again.

As for Mary, she proved to be the worthy young woman I had first judged her to be. She stayed with me for some months until delivered of a fine baby she named Martin, as being as near my name as she could find for a boy. She also did me the honour of asking me to be godmother to the dear child. In the meantime I had been in touch with the Wright family on her behalf, endeavouring to explain to them how their impressionable daughter had fallen into the clutches of a plausible villain, believing herself to be honestly married until he revealed the truth. The family however was not to be moved, their hearts hardened against her. It was difficult for Mary to accept this rejection but in time, with the support of myself and particularly of dear Clara, as well as one other significant person, she did so.

You see, Mary being of a pious and God-fearing nature, she liked to attend the local church with me (we putting it about that she was widowed, to explain her impending motherhood). There she became acquainted with the young curate, Felix Goodhart. When her time came, and she was confined to the house, he took to visiting us at home, on many more occasions in fact than his parish duties warranted. I was not at all surprised then to discover that he and Mary had reached an understanding (she having frankly explained her circumstances to him) and that he wished to marry her, which in due course he did. Soon after, Felix came into a living of his own, in a part of the country much more suited to the rearing of a child than is London, and the new little family moved to Hampshire. I am in constant touch with Mary and have recently learned with pleasure that young Martin now has a baby brother to play with. Indeed, I plan a visit there to see them all in the very near future, Mr. H's return from the dead permitting.

Mrs. Hudson and the Sydenham Psychic

As my readers will have by now become aware, over recent years and rather despite myself I have become involved in various cases in which a modest search for truth has succeeded in uncovering a number of crimes and villainies. The happy result has been the just punishment of the culprits. However, there was one instance in which right and wrong seemed to me less than clear cut and which posed a not easy dilemma of moral choice. I set it here before you (having changed names to protect both innocent and guilty), that you might decide for yourselves if the course of action I finally took was the right one.

I would never have dreamed of going to a spiritualist meeting, excepting that my friend Mrs. Dixon was so urgent. Indeed, when she suggested it, I expressed to her quite forcefully my grave reservations about the business: all trickery and hocus-pocus in my view, not to mention that it is decidedly unchristian. Mrs. Dixon replied that, while, of course, some practitioners may be fraudsters, she had it on the good authority of several of her acquaintances that this Madame Kapoushka had genuine powers, which she used only for good. Her own reason for wishing to consult the woman was that her youngest son had recently died in a tragic accident at his place of work, and she missed him so very dreadfully that she would seek any means of trying to make contact with his spirit and ensure that it was at rest. I still argued reluctance and suggested that her husband or Mrs. Melrose might be willing to accompany her instead of me.

"Oh, no, Martha," Mrs. Dixon replied. "Mrs. Melrose is a Roman and don't you know they are quite forbidden from such practices."

As for her husband, she knew that he would have nothing to do with the business and indeed wished even to conceal from him her own intention of consulting the psychic, Mr. Dixon being a man of uncertain temper.

She would not dare to go alone and so in the end I agreed to accompany her.

"Perhaps you will be able to communicate with Henry," said Mrs. Dixon.

I hoped not for I imagined that my poor dear deceased husband, long reduced to dust, was by now incapable of speech and resting in the peace he so richly deserved after a life of good service. However, I admit that I was curious to see one of these supposedly psychic persons in action, even perhaps to unmask her trickery.

The woman lived in Sydenham, south of the city of London and near the location of the Crystal Palace Museum, a place I had always wished to visit. However, it seemed impossible that there would be time for that on this occasion and such proved to be the case. (I might add that I have since made time to go there and quite splendid it has turned out to be. I can highly recommend it for a pleasant day's outing. But let me return to the present account.)

It was on a fine afternoon in June that Mrs. Dixon and I took a train from Victoria to Sydenham railway station and from there a cab to a most respectable street of semi-detached houses, the which I for one was most relieved to find, having feared the premises might be tucked down some dark back alley where unsavoury characters lurked in the shadows.

Number 7 stood out all the same from its neighbours, not least because of a thick shrub of white wisteria that grew around and over the door and windows, its flowers hanging down like, as Mrs. Dixon poetically remarked, the tears of ghosts.

In response to our tap on the door – the brass knocker being of a most singular design, a demonic head with a grinning mouth – this was opened after a period by a young woman with the longest, plainest face that I have ever seen. Poker thin in a rusty black dress, and with arms like furled umbrellas, she looked sourly upon us.

Mrs. Dixon, already in a shook state and apparently incapable of speech, I introduced us, explaining that we had an appointment with Madame Kapoushka, wondering if this could be she. The female, however, named herself as Miss Quill and indicated that we should enter, leading the way down a dark passage, to a room at the back of the house. Several persons were already present, seated at a round table, and we took our places beside them.

The room was gloomy, being low ceilinged and decorated in the Gothic style, illuminated only by sconces holding wax candles. There were no windows visible to cast the bright light of day upon the proceedings. Three walls were covered in tapestries, whose dim mythological subjects seemed to shift and move in the flickering light. On the fourth side of the room, an iron fireplace stood cold but still full of charred logs, and surmounted by a mantelpiece of black marble on which stood a single lit candle in a holder grotesquely fashioned in the form of a skeletal hand. Above this hung the portrait of a most villainous-looking gentleman in ancient dress. Ill-painted, yet the artist had sufficient skill to devise it so that the man's piercing blue eyes stared straight back at you, wherever you stood or sat, seeming to wink occasionally above the wavering flame. The table and chairs were of dark, heavy wood, crudely fashioned and hard to sit upon. All in all, a room designed to send you into a mood receptive to the supernatural, if you were that way inclined.

I broke the oppressive silence that hung over us all by introducing myself and Mrs. Dixon to our companions. In turn, they revealed themselves to be a Dr. and Mrs. Agnew, a Miss Swift, a Mr. and Mrs. Beckett, and a foreign gentleman, a Signor Orsini. The Agnews were both of late middle age, he with a fine head of white hair and noble features, she tending to a soft pink plumpness but with vestiges of a pretty face. Miss Swift had to be in her thirties, with a sallow complexion and dark hair drawn so tight back that her eyebrows seemed pulled up, giving her a constantly startled look. The Becketts were an attractive young couple, almost I imagine newlyweds, he with dark curly hair, she fair and pale. A sadness seemed to hang over them, and I wondered had they, like Mrs Dixon, recently lost a child. As for Signor Orsini, he was a small, wiry man who smiled far too much, yellowing teeth gleaming in the candlelight out of his swarthy face, oily black hair hanging long over his collar in strands like tiny snakes. I did not, I confess, care for the look of him at all.

After the introductions, we relapsed into silence. This did not last long, however, since after a few moments Miss Quill re-entered the room and announced that Madame Kapoushka would be with us instantly. Indeed, she was followed by the medium herself, as round as her companion was narrow, and dressed in the loose flowing robes that, as I understand it, these persons often affect. A bandana of green silk spotted with livid yellow, like the shed skin of some venomous serpent, was tied around her head, and beads dangled from her ears, neck and fat wrists. Heavy gold rings were embedded in her swollen fingers.

This was my first impression, although I admit it was perhaps clouded by the dislike and distrust I felt even before meeting her. Mrs. Dixon had informed me that the woman was Polish or Russian "or something similar," and when she spoke her accent was certainly thick and slippery, with many English words mispronounced. However, I was almost certain I had seen her before, though in very different garb and setting and I caught Madame Kapoushka giving me a sidelong glance from time to time as if she too recognised me from somewhere. The psychic sat herself down with her back to the fireplace.

Her assistant then placed a dish of some confection next to the woman's right hand. It looked to be the sweetmeat known as Turkish Delight, pink jellified cubes under a heavy dusting of powdered sugar. I do not know if such it was, however, since she did not offer the plate round to us but fed herself continuously, her fat fingertips and puffy lips whitened by powder.

After staring at each of us in turn for a considerable time, making us all, I am sure, quite uneasy, she finally seemed satisfied and, pushing the dish of sweetmeats from her (Miss Quill leaping up to remove it), she pronounced herself ready to start the séance.

What can I say of what followed? We were instructed to hold hands around the circle while Miss Quill extinguished the candles one by one, excepting only for the thin flame over the mantelpiece, leaving us in almost utter darkness. She then seated herself next to the medium and joined the circle. My eyes eventually became more used to the gloom but all I could make out of my companions at first were featureless blocky shapes.

Madame Kapoushka called on any presence to reveal itself by tapping on the wooden table twice. At first there was nothing. We waited. We waited some more. Was our visit to be in vain after all? Were there to be no manifestations? The tension grew. My own concern was less spiritual, however, wondering if we could get a refund on our contributions if nothing supernatural occurred.

At last, in response to her repeated query, there resounded two raps, so portentous as to make the table quiver. I confess that even I felt a tremor of excitement, while at the same time recognising how simple it would be to agitate some device under the table to cause the effect.

"Here is somevun from beyond who vants make contact," Madame said in husky tones. "I sense letters.... G... no, J... J...D... Is anyvun here knows dat?"

I felt Mrs. Dixon, next to me, near jump out of her skin.

"Can it be Jonathan?" she exclaimed with strong emotion. "My son Jonathan."

"Is it Jonatan?" the medium then asked of the spirit. "Two taps, please for yes."

The two taps sounded out.

I have to say, I was fairly disgusted and most sorry for my gullible friend. After all, knowing Mrs. Dixon was to be present at the séance, it would have been an easy matter for someone to discover the probability of why, and from that the dead boy's name. What followed did nothing to dispel my revulsion. Jonathan, through Madame Kapoushka, assured his mother in the vaguest terms that he was happy (well for her to believe that, all the same) and walking in the gardens of paradise with his grandfather. To my mind, Madame Kapoushka then fished around, discovering through a series of carefully worded questions that there was no affianced young lady in the picture, though establishing a pet. This was further narrowed from bird to cat and finally to dog. Jonathan then wanted to know if his dog was well and although the medium stumbled over the name, suggesting an R, Mrs. Dixon was ecstatic, stating that it was just like dear Jonathan to be concerned about Flash. Other trivia followed, the while my friend gripping my hand tightly. I could tell she was deeply moved.

All too soon for her, Jonathan retreated back into the shadows. Now we were to be treated to a real display, a materialisation no less, seeming to emanate, in the dim light, from Madame Kapoushka herself (by now in a state of trance), taking the form of a disembodied head, that floated above us, so near indeed, the portrait of the villainous gentleman that I strongly suspected an inflated ball, painted to resemble a face

159

and covered in whiskers, had somehow been pulled from under the chimneypiece.

"Oh," cried Miss Swift, "it has quite the look of my father. Papa, can it be you?"

Apparently, it could, the head bobbing about above us for some moments, though the father faded quite fast (disappearing as the gas leaked out of the head perhaps), and did not have much to say for himself, speaking through the deep throaty tones of the medium, it seemed now without any foreign accent whatsoever. The late Mr. Swift had time only to tell his daughter that she should have nothing more to do with young Benson, since he was a gold-digger and only interested in the small inheritance coming to her soon from an aged aunt.

"Oh, Papa," the maiden sobbed (I imagine from her age and appearance, young Benson's was the only offer she had ever received), but her father was adamant. Instead, he ordered, she should place her trust in new friends who could advise on profitable investments. I wondered if Madame also claimed the gift of prophesy regarding the stock markets.

The psychic, seeming to wake up, pronounced herself pleased and gratified at news of the manifestation, of which she maintained she was unaware. She now sensed another spirit present. They coming thick and fast, we were certainly getting our sovereign's worth at last.

"S..." she hissed and I saw through the murk the silk on her head twist like a snake..."S... and... and H...."

Mrs. Dixon nudged me. S and H indeed. My husband's initials, since, although I always refer to him as Henry, and although that was his preferred nomenclature, his first Christian name was in fact Samuel as Mrs. Dixon knew well. Why my dearest departed would suddenly revert to that unaccustomed first name from beyond the grave was, however, a mystery and I rather preferred to believe that an advance study of my situation by certain personages had revealed me to be, in formal address,

160

Mrs. Samuel Hudson.

That S and H were also the initials of my lodger, Mr. Sherlock Holmes, still at that time considered dead and gone (this being before his amazing resurrection), struck me as an amusing coincidence, though why post mortem he should wish to contact me of all people, I could not imagine. In any case, I was not inclined to make either of these connections known to the group, not wishing the psychic to ask me to assure "Samuel" that his aspidistra was flourishing, or indeed to inform Mr. H that his lost cufflinks had finally turned up at last in the inkwell.

"S H is very very vanting to make contact," the psychic insisted.

Mrs. Dixon nudged me again but again I did not respond. Madame Kapoushka gave in.

"Poor spirit," she said. "Dere is no vun here vanting you..."

It seemed as if a forlorn sigh faded on the air, as if a lost soul had felt itself abandoned.

What happened next changed everything.

Madame started to shake violently and a rattle emerged from her throat. Suddenly in a totally new voice, high-pitched and querulous, she shrieked out, "They have poisoned me, I tell you. They have poisoned me. My name is Letitia and they have poisoned me."

Someone screamed out. There was a thud and the circle of hands split apart as we saw through the gloom how the psychic had collapsed forward on to the table. .

I instantly produced the sal volatile I always carry with me and applied it in the vicinity of the nostrils of the apparently unconscious woman. She immediately leapt as if stung, shaking her head and giving me a most venomous look.

"Qvill," she spat.

This maiden apparently knew what was required, for she stepped forward with a glass of a liquid that looked like water but smelt to me, who was next to her, suspiciously like Holland gin. Madame Kapoushka downed it in one.

"Vot happened?" she asked weakly. "Anozzer manifestation? I remember nutting. Vot is it?"

I looked around at the group. All seemed in shock. The eyes of the villainous gentleman over the mantel seemed more than ever to glint and wink in glee.

Madame Kapoushka then raised a heavy hand to her brow and whispered to her companion.

"She must rest now," Miss Quill informed us. "The spirits have emptied her. You must all go."

"Well," said Mrs. Dixon, as we made our way back to the railways station, on foot this time, the two of us feeling the need for some air. "Whatever do you make of all that, Martha?"

"Most intriguing," I said.

"I told you she had powers."

"You did, indeed."

"And do you not wish now that you had spoken to dear Henry?"

"Belinda," I replied quite tartly. "Do you truly believe that Henry was there in spirit? Why ever would he revert to a name that he loathed?"

"I suppose not," she said. "It must have been someone else."

"Mr. Sherlock Holmes, perhaps," I said to tease her.

"Good heavens!" Mrs. Dixon was discomfited. "Yes indeed. It must have been he. I did not think." She paused. "Yet why did you not wish to talk to him, Martha? It might have been enlightening."

"Mm." I could not bring myself, since the womans words had at least brought her some ease of mind, to tell my friend that I considered our psychic an out and out fake. I then had to listen while she babbled on about the comfort in knowing Jonathan was happy in heaven with his grandfather, and was it

162

not amazing that Miss Swift's father had actually materialised.

"If only I could again see the face of dear Jonathan in the same way," she said, "I would be completely satisfied."

"Maybe if you had left a little more silver in the saucer," I said before I could stop myself, "such a manifestation might have been arranged."

Mrs. Dixon looked so hurt that I quickly added, "I jest, my dear. I am sorry."

She went quiet then and we proceeded on to the station.

It was only later, sitting on the train and staring, as we passed, at the backs of the mean houses of South London, that I suddenly sat up, exclaiming, "Stinking fish!"

Mrs. Dixon stared upon me with astonishment, as if fearing I had suddenly gone mad.

"Martha, my dear," she said. "Whatever made you say that?"

I started to chuckle then, while debating with myself what to tell her. Finally, again for my friend's own peace of mind, I tailored the truth.

"I have just remembered," quoth I, "the person of whom I was reminded when I first saw Madame Kapoushka. It was a Billingsgate woman I used to frequent until she sold me bad fish."

Mrs. Dixon still regarded me with some confusion. "A Cockney, no doubt."

"Oh, no doubt at all about it."

"Then it could hardly be Madame Kapoushka, Martha, for she is Russian."

"Or Polish." I replied and, looking out of the window again, bit my lip.

The more I thought on it, the more convinced I became. Somewhat older, considerably fatter and certainly richer, yet if not one and the same, then the identical twin of the fishmonger I now recalled to be one Flossie Hutch. It seemed that since I last

163

had seen her, the erstwhile purveyor of rotten fish had found a far more lucrative profession.

I considered the matter now to be at an end. If Belinda Dixon wished again to go to Sydenham, she would have to do so without me. That was my firm decision. I could not then have known how soon I would have to change my mind.

A week or so after the events I have described, I happened to observe an item of news in a sheet passed to me by a neighbour. I am not in the habit of going to the expense of purchasing such ephemera myself but I find discarded newspapers most useful for setting fires, cleaning windows, lining the cat box and other household tasks. The piece that caught my eye was headed "Sudden Death of a Psychic." Imagine my astonishment, on reading further, to discover that the deceased was the very medium Mrs. Dixon and I had visited so recently. It seemed that she had died of a heart attack in the very course of a séance. It further stated that Madame Kapoushka was a lady of White Russian extraction who had only lived in London for a short while, but that during that time she had established herself as one of the foremost psychics in the city.

I may, I am afraid, have snorted at this announcement. Still, I was not happy to hear of her passing, any more than I would rejoice at the death of any of God's creatures. I was simply relieved that she had not succumbed during our visit to her. It would have been most disagreeable.

Again, I would have given little more thought to the matter had I not shortly thereafter heard a clatter on the door, which, as it turned out, heralded the arrival of Mrs. Dixon, accompanied by a person whom I was surprised soon to recognise as none other than the medium's assistant, Miss Quill.

We sat us down in the parlour and I called on dear Clara to bring in some fortified wine, since it seemed from the agitation of both visitors that tea would not serve in the present circumstances. Miss Quill, indeed, was in such a state that it was only after some time, and some copious administration of the remains of the Christmas port, that any sense at all could be found in her. When at last she had calmed sufficiently to impart her news, it was indeed a startling tale she had to tell.

Although the doctor had been more than happy to sign a certificate of death due to natural causes, Miss Quill stated herself certain that her employer had been poisoned.

"Why then come to us?" I asked. "Why not go to the police?" "The blue bottles, is it!" Miss Quill spoke bitterly. "As if they would listen to me when the doctor was insistent that Madame's heart had given out. He insulted me, mum, that doctor did. He told me I was a silly hysterical girl and offered to bleed me!"

Her eyes flashed yellow, and I was suddenly reminded of a lynx cat I had once seen in the Zoological gardens in Regent's Park.

"He maintained that it was clear from Madame's condition that her heart had just burst. But it's not true, mum. There was nothing wrong with Madame's heart. As I already told Mrs. Dixon, it was poison for sure."

"Again I have to ask," I repeated, "why come to us? How do you think we can assist you?"

Miss Quill shifted her eyes from mine and I seemed to detect in them a sly look.

"I understand, mum," said she, "that you have been for many years the landlady to a gentleman detective."

"If you mean," I said with dignity, somewhat displeased at the girl's presumption, "Mr. Sherlock Holmes, then I am afraid you are too late. Mr. Holmes, as your erstwhile employer was no doubt only too well aware, has been dead this many months."

"Oh," Quill replied in sugary tones, designed no doubt to appease my bad humour. "I am sorry, mum, if I have upset you. Yes, the passing of Mr. Holmes was a great loss, a great loss. But

I have heard from Mrs. Dixon here that something of your lodger's genius has rubbed off on you and that you have solved cases which have foxed the" (and here that bitter tone again) "blue bottles."

Despite the antipathy I felt for the woman and her late employer, I have to admit that her words struck home. This is not to boast of my abilities in any way. I am sure that it has indeed simply been as a result of quietly observing Mr. H in action that I have sharpened my own wits and thus managed to establish the truth of matters overlooked by the authorities, bringing justice where otherwise there would be none.

It was as I was pursuing this train of thought that Mrs. Dixon suddenly broke in.

"Martha," said she. "It is your Christian duty to help this poor girl as best you can."

I looked at the two of them for a few moments, considering.

"I am willing," I said, for, despite my prejudices, the case interested me, "to examine what evidence I can. Nevertheless, if I establish that the doctor's diagnosis is the correct one, the matter must rest there. Do you agree?" addressing this last query to Miss Quill.

She eagerly concurred, assuring me again of her conviction of a poisoning, even against the word of Dr. Agnew.

"Dr. Agnew," I said, starting up. "Was he not the gentleman present at our séance?"

"The very man, mum," Miss Quill stated. "He was there again when Madame took bad and died."

This information put the whole matter in a new and, possibly, sinister light. I thought back to the earlier evening and its disturbing finale. I now reminded Miss Quill of this and asked if the identity of "Letitia" had ever been established, to which she replied in the negative.

"Now," I said, pouring her another glass of port wine,

"tell me why you think Madame Kapoushka was poisoned."

The story the girl related, while not conclusive in any way, was certainly suggestive. She told how the psychic was partial to sweetmeats and particularly, as I had already observed, to that variety known as Turkish Delight. Indeed, Miss Quill was frequently dispatched to Fortnum and Mason's establishment in Piccadilly to purchase a fresh supply for her mistress. However, on the fateful day in question, a box of the delicacy had been delivered to the house by a messenger boy, with the inscription "Only for You because You Love Them So" and signed merely "A Fervent Admirer".

Miss Quill was about to bring the usual platter to Madame before the séance. However, her mistress stated her intention of sampling her gift, it being under a label not previously known to her.

"Excuse me," I asked. "Did she offer to share the sweets with anyone?"

"No, mum," came the reply. "She was not in the habit of sharing. On this occasion she showed us the note that said "Only for You." "I cannot," she told us, "disobey my fervent admirer" and proceeded to eat a considerable portion of them in front of us, finding them, as she said, superior in every way to the sweets I usually bring her."

It was, as Miss Quill continued, shortly after consuming one Madame pronounced strangely bitter, that she showed signs of distress, choking and jerking about in a most alarming way. At first they all assumed, since similar symptoms had occurred before, that this was the result of a communication with some particularly violent spirit and suspected nothing amiss; but then, in a final terrible paroxysm, she collapsed across the table.

"Dr. Agnew sprang to her assistance and we carried her to an armchair but alas, nothing could be done for the poor lady."

"Hmm," I said, "and what of the sweets, for I assume, from what you have recounted, that you suspect the poison to have been administered by that means?"

"There is another mystery, mum," said Miss Quill, after recovering herself (she had become quite tearful recounting the demise of her mistress). "I could not find the box after, nor the note neither, search everywhere though I did."

"Immediately after?"

No, for it seemed that quite a considerable period of time had elapsed, she busying herself quite naturally with Madame. Indeed, it was only after the doctor declared the psychic dead that Miss Quill thought to recover the box and its accompanying note, only to find that they had disappeared. The maid servant, who had entered the room earlier, summoned by the doctor to bring a cold compress, denied all knowledge of the matter.

"All that I found was a pair of gloves that must belong to Mrs. Cork, who had already gone home," Miss Quill went on. "And a single lump of Turkish delight under the table where it must have fallen from Madame's hand."

She produced a plain linen handkerchief, folded into a tiny bundle, and placed it on the table. Then she unfolded it, revealing a pink cube, powdered with sugar. We all stared at it.

"I have no means," I said at last, "of testing this to see if indeed it is poisoned, and would once more recommend, Miss Quill, that you place the matter in the hands of the police."

"So you too refuse to help me," the girl cried out in angry tones. "Then maybe this will persuade you." And to the utter horror of both Mrs. Dixon and myself, she seized the sweet and put it into her mouth.

What the outcome might have been but for the swift reaction of my friend, I cannot say. Mrs. Dixon immediately sprang to her feet and clapped the girl so hard on the back that the sweet flew out of her mouth. I seized the thing in the handkerchief and kept it by me.

Miss Quill sank back into her chair.

"It was not bitter," she said. "It contained no poison."

I was filled then with pity for a girl who had clearly loved her mistress so very much that she would risk her own life to prove a point, and I relented to the extent of promising to look into the matter, having only the very slightest notion of how to proceed. I questioned her further on the circumstances surrounding Madame Kapoushka's demise and received some revealing details, as a result of which I proposed to pay a visit to Dr. Agnew the very next morning.

Mrs. Dixon not wishing to be left out, insisted on accompanying me back to Sydenham. I was, I admit, happy enough to have her support, for I was by no means convinced of the rightness of Miss Quill's case and was unsure how we would be received by the doctor.

We took the train once more from Victoria station and once more hired a cab, this time to the address furnished us by Miss Quill. A highly polished brass plate on the gatepost indicated that we had arrived at the right place and a most respectable house and one most suited to an eminent doctor it proved to be, set in its own well- maintained grounds. I had made use of a telephone to advise Dr. Agnew of our visit, though not of its purpose, and, we being shown in to his consulting room, the gentleman politely expressed pleasure at meeting us again.

"But I hope," he said, his large hand on the desk in front of him holding a pen in readiness over a pad, "it is not a serious matter that has caused you to come to me."

"That depends," I replied and started to state the case.

"I must interrupt you at once," he said, with some asperity, throwing down the pen. "It is too bad of Miss Quill to involve strangers in this sorry business. As I told her at the time – and I have practised medicine, Mrs. Hudson, for over forty years – there is no reason whatsoever to suspect that Madame Kapoushka's death was anything but natural. You have seen the woman. Her over-indulgent habits were always destined to bring a sudden collapse. No, ladies, you have wasted your time and mine too." He stood as if to show us out. He was an imposing man and I think used to being obeyed.

"And yet," I said softly, keeping my seat and gesturing to Mrs. Dixon to do the same. "It would seem unusual under the circumstances as described to me by Miss Quill not to have examined the body further. Muscular spasms, choking, frothing of the mouth, stiffness of limbs, are these not symptoms of poison? Strychnine, to be exact."

Dr. Agnew stared at me, frowning, and then lowered himself into his chair again. Placing his elbows on the desk and extending his forearms to his face, he joined the tips of his fingers together, all the time considering me or perhaps considering his next words.

"Yes," he said at last. "I congratulate you on your diagnosis, Mrs. Hudson. Those are precisely the symptoms of strychnine poisoning. However, they are not the symptoms I observed in Madame Kapoushka. I fear, deliberately or not, you have been misled by Miss Quill."

Why did I not believe him? Was it those fingers pressed so hard together as to offset a tremor? Was it the flinty look in those grey eyes, fixed as if hypnotically on mine? The sliding away of those eyes as I returned his stare?

I stood.

"Please accept my apologies, doctor," I said. "I see that we will receive no resolution here."

I left the room with Mrs. Dixon hurrying behind me.

"So Miss Quill was mistaken," she murmured as we made our way out of the gate.

"On the contrary, Belinda," I said. "I am now completely convinced she has been telling us the truth."

"Good gracious, Martha. You astonish me. Why should the doctor lie? Oh, such a fine figure of a man, I cannot believe it of him."

"It is most strange indeed," I said. "And yet lying he most certainly was. If we discover the why, then maybe we can get to the bottom of the matter."

I could not but feel that the answer to the conundrum lay partly in the outburst we had witnessed at the séance. It seemed to me imperative to discover the identity of this Letitia who had claimed from beyond the grave to have been poisoned. Since I was certain that Madame Kapoushka was a fake with no psychic powers whatsoever, then she had spoken the words with an ulterior motive of her own. I needed to discover what this could be and turned my feet to go up the hill.

"The station is down that way," said Mrs. Dixon, pointing in the opposite direction.

"We are not going to the station, Belinda," I said. "We are going again to visit Miss Quill."

A little maid opened the door to our bell and called, rather too loudly, for that young woman. She proved anxious indeed to see us and showed us into the same room where the séance had been held. Now bathed in daylight through the open curtains, the heavy tapestries having been taken down, it presented a much less ominous aspect than before, although the gentleman over the mantel continued to regard us all with sardonic mockery. Miss Quill sat us at the séance table, now covered with a heavy, fringed cloth patterned in the Turkish manner, in dark red, green and black. She expressed not an iota of surprise to hear of the way Dr. Agnew had received us.

"Of course, mum," she said. "Of course, he would deny all."

"Please inform us," I asked, "who else was present when Madame collapsed." I had in mind among other things to verify from them the symptoms displayed by the deceased and to find whether these accorded more with the account of Miss Quill or with that of Dr. Agnew.

It was rather surprising then to learn that several of the

171

same persons who had been present at our séance had returned for another session. The doctor was there, but not his wife. Mr. Beckett but not his wife; Miss Swift and Signor Orsini; in addition, an elderly woman named Mrs. Cork. I asked if Miss Quill had any further information regarding these persons. She demurred.

"I really know nothing at all about them," said she, fiddling with a fringe of the tablecloth.

"Come, come, Miss Quill," I said briskly. "This will not do. You must be completely frank with me if you wish me to uncover the truth."

Now she was absorbed in plaiting the fringe.

"Let me make it easier for you," I went on. "Flossie Hutch is not unknown to me."

The girl raised wide eyes to meet mine. "Flossie... who?"

"Miss Quill, I can hardly be expected to have faith in those who claim psychic powers, when they are in fact Cockney fishwives pretending to be White Russians."

The fringe unravelled. Miss Quill gave a great sigh.

"All right," she said. "But, you know, mum, Madame did a lot of good. She brought great comfort to people." She looked at Mrs. Dixon. "To you, mum."

"I don't understand," Mrs. Dixon began, gone pale. "Do you mean she made it all up? She didn't summon Jonathan."

Miss Quill started on that dratted fringe again. "Well, mum, she had powers..."

"She had the power to bamboozle the credulous," I said, perhaps somewhat too harshly.

"But how then," my friend went on, "did she know so many particulars? About grandfather, for instance. About Flash?"

"Such persons," I said, "prepare well in advance, Belinda. After you have made an appointment to visit, I presume they do some thorough homework, possibly by getting the trust of servants, or even by bribing them. Is that not so, Miss Quill?"

The young woman, head down, declined to reply.

"Other details." I continued, "can quite safely be guessed at: it is very likely for instance that at least one grandparent of an adult person will be deceased. As for Flash, Flossie or Kapoushka cleverly elicited the details from you, without you noticing."

"No, no. That would have been impossible."

I placed my hand on my friend's trembling one.

"You wanted so much to believe," I told her, "that you ignored something obvious to me. You wanted to believe, so you did."

I turned back to the sullen girl, her brow twisted in a frown. "Now," I said, "tell me about Madame's clients. Agnew I know is a doctor. What of the Becketts?"

Miss Quill started slowly, then became most forthcoming, the details she provided giving quite some food for thought. Mrs. Beckett it turned out was daughter to Dr. Agnew. Her husband was a pharmacist. Signor Orsini was music teacher to the Becketts' little boy, Benjamin, and played the violin in a small orchestra. Miss Swift was governess to the child. Mrs. Cork was the widow of a grocer and was without any known connection to the group. I made a mental note that perhaps she was the person to contact first.

"And you," I went on. "How did you come to work for Flossie Hutch?"

"Please," Miss Quill begged, "please continue to talk of her as Madame Kapoushka. That is how I think of her. It distresses me to hear the other name."

The tale she told was rambling and punctuated with much wailing and sobbing. I will summarise. Myrtle Quill, it seemed, had started work at age fourteen as kitchen maid to a distinguished family, that of a judge of the high court no less. In due course, being diligent in her duties, she was noticed and

173

raised to the position of chambermaid. It was then that the judge, father of a family and a man most respected in the community, had seduced her, pretending that he loved her, but cruelly casting her out when nature took its usual course and her stomach started to swell. The sordid tale she told was one too often heard, I am afraid, though I very much doubted, looking at the dry and rigid aspect of the girl, that she could ever have been much loved by anyone. The villain had cold-heartedly taken advantage of her youth and innocence simply to satisfy vile lusts. Her subsequent overtures to the police had been to no avail. Indeed, when they heard whom it was that she was accusing, they threatened to throw her into prison for slandering such a pillar. (I understood now her mistrust, nay hatred, of the forces of law and order and her reluctance to approach them.) A sorry future seemed to lay ahead of her. Only for Madame taking her in, she said, she would have ended up selling herself on the streets.

"And what of the child?" asked Mrs. Dixon gently.

"I lost it, mum." Miss Quill turned away and would say no more. I could not help wondering how exactly the child had come to be lost, and if the psychic had had a wicked hand in the matter.

"I owe her everything, mum," the wretched girl concluded. "I owe it to Madame now to find out who killed her."

"Would it be acceptable to you," I asked gently, observing her distress, "if I examined some of Madame's personal effects in the hope that they might throw some light on this case?"

"Oh, I don't know, mum," the girl replied. "Would it be right?"

"My dear," I said. "If your mistress was poisoned, then someone must have had a motive to do such a dark deed. Can you think of anyone?"

"No, mum." Her eyes took on that shifty look again. "Everyone loved her."

"Not everyone, apparently. I assure you, my dear," I continued, "that I will be most discreet. In the meantime, Mrs. Dixon might perhaps order you a cup of hot tea, or something stronger." I added the last because I had observed that Miss Quill was partial to strong spirits. Indeed, from the smell off her breath, I believed that she had already partaken that morning. I was also hoping the drink would distract her, since I very strongly wished to examine her employer's room without having her hang over me.

"There's gin in the cupboard," she said, waving a hand at the heavy press.

I nodded to Mrs. Dixon, indicating she should fetch some, and for myself proceeded up the staircase to the bedroom I soon ascertained had belonged to the departed psychic. It was surprisingly barely furnished apart from a large wardrobe filled with various loose and flowing robes in bright colours, quite unsuited, in my opinion, to a person of Flossie's age and girth. A dressing table stood in front of the window, surmounted by a smudged mirror, and covered with powders and potions, an overflowing jewellery box, as well as a tub of Turkish Delight bearing the imprint of Fortnum and Mason. Not the fatal box, then. A stool and bed completed the meagre furnishings.

I forced myself to overcome my natural reluctance and opened as many drawers as there were, but found in them only undergarments and the like. I felt under the drawers, behind the wardrobe, under the mattress, but found nothing hidden there. I could not think where else to look. Perhaps I was wrong in my suspicions or perhaps whatever there was had been concealed elsewhere in the house. And yet would the woman not wish to keep secret papers as close as she could? I sat on the bed and stared around me, my eyes then alighting on the wooden floor covered in rugs. I pulled these aside and studied the boards. Was there not one by the wall that seemed to rise slightly above its fellows? I pressed down on one end of it and, lo! the other end

175

popped up. Beneath was a recess that I was gratified to discover contained a box. I lifted this out only to find that it was locked and the key not in evidence. No amount of prising and levering could open the thing. In frustration and even though I should have preferred to examine the contents alone, I carried it down to Mrs. Dixon and Miss Quill.

The latter claimed ignorance of the box and the surprise on her face at the sight of it led me to believe her. She then summoned the little maidservant, who, likewise denied ever having seen the box before and had no notion of the whereabouts of a key. However, seeing that we dearly wished to open the thing, she forthwith removed a hairpin out of her bun and fiddled it around inside the lock. After a while, it gave a most satisfying click and the lid opened. The maid smiled as at a job well done and I could not help but suspect that it was not the first time she had opened a lock in such a manner.

Nevertheless, my priority was not to dwell upon the significance of this, but rather to view the contents of the box, which consisted largely of papers. I examined these, careful for my own reasons to conceal my discoveries from the others for the time being. My expectations, however, soon turned to disappointment, they being various receipts and bills which hardly needed to be concealed in such a manner. Under the papers, lay various bits and bobs including several keys, though quite obviously not the one to the box itself, being somewhat larger. I did not mention these to the others.

"Nothing much here," I said with a sigh, closing the lid. "None of the papers I was expecting to find."

Not having been dismissed by Miss Quill and it not being my place to do so, the little maid had stayed in the room all this time. She now spoke up.

"Excuse me, mum, but did you look in the safe?"

"What safe?" I asked.

Miss Quill shook her head.

"Don't tell me you didn't know of the safe," exclaimed the maid merrily. "Lor, Madame didn't think much of you then."

This addressed to Miss Quill, whose yellow face now turned an unpleasant shade of orange. Had the impudent chit been in my employ, she would not have stayed long. However, I did not know anything of the arrangements of the household, especially now that its mistress was no more, so I simply asked, "And where, pray, miss, is this safe?"

"Can't you guess, mum?" the maid continued in the same disrespectful tones. "And you a detective and all."

I laughed at that.

"I am no detective, girl."

"Myrtle says you are."

"Well, I am gratified at the compliment, but I assure you that I am a mere amateur of mysteries. However, if you will not tell me, let me think where the safe might be concealed."

I paused as if in thought, then stood up and walked straight over to the fireplace raising the base of the portrait of the villainous gentleman to peer under it. It was as I had expected: the safe was indeed, set into the wall under the picture.

The others looked suitably impressed with my discovery, as if I had performed some magic trick in front of them. Even the saucy little maid deferred to my apparent powers. However, it was no trick or even lucky guess on my part, since it was she who had, inadvertently, revealed the place to me when, while still challenging me, her eyes had flickered over to the mantel.

She helped Miss Quill lift down the portrait, and they left it face to the wall, which was a relief to me since I hated that mocking face. We then examined the safe which proved, like the box, to be locked fast and this time no amount of probing with a hairpin could open it.

For reasons which will become apparent, dear readers, I did not inform the others that I had a fair notion where its key was located, and sent both Miss Quill and the little maid on a search of the rest of the house. Once they had left the room, I besought Mrs. Dixon to stand guard at the door and to let me know when either of them was returning.

"Why?" she exclaimed.

"Do not ask," I said. "We must work fast."

I swiftly removed the bigger keys from under the papers in the box and tried them one by one. On the third attempt I managed to open the safe.

"Oh!" from my friend.

Within, as expected, was a heap of papers. I scooped these into my reticule, luckily capacious enough, and had just enough time to lock the safe again and secrete the key in my pocket, when Mrs. Dixon whispered that someone was approaching. We sat us down at the table, apparently innocent, though I feared that Mrs. Dixon might give all away by the agitation of her manner.

Miss Quill, for it was she who entered, noticed nothing amiss, being herself distracted.

"How is it," she asked us, in some distress, after stating that she could find no key that fitted such a lock, "Madame confided in Lizzie and not in me?"

"You are shocked," I said. "And yet I doubt very much that Madame Kapoushka confided in anyone. Is it not much more likely that the maid discovered the safe while performing cleaning duties around the room? Cobwebs, you must know, gather behind pictures and need to be brushed away regularly. Moreover, the girl seems of a prying nature and would no doubt take advantage of the absence of her superiors to poke her nose into places where it should not go."

Miss Quill looked gratified with this explanation.

"Truth told, Lizzie was a pickpocket before Madame ever took her in," she said.

A picker of locks too, it seemed. Madame, whatever her motives, was revealed as quite the philanthropist to surround

178

herself with such people.

I was anxious to be gone and examine the papers from the safe as soon as possible, so it was shortly thereafter that we took our leave of Miss Quill, advising that she would probably require the services of a locksmith to open the safe.

"Though she will be most disappointed," I said to Mrs. Dixon as we walked away from the house, "to discover it quite empty."

I had offered Miss Quill to return the lost gloves to Mrs. Cork, the elderly woman who had been part of the fatal séance. She fortuitously lived near the railway station, in rooms over her late husband's shop, so that I could justly claim that it was on our way. The proposal was not of course a purely altruistic one on my part. I wished to discover exactly what that good lady had observed at the time of Madame's seizure.

We were perhaps lucky to find her in, for she had just returned from some errands and, ushering us inside, announced herself mightily pleased to have her good gloves returned to her.

"I have others," she informed us, "but not of such quality. These are doeskin, you know. I could not think where I had mislaid them."

Mrs. Cork was a small woman of sixty and more, with a bustling, chatty manner. I could well imagine her, apron-clad, behind the counter of the grocer's shop. This same premises was now managed by her son, Alfred junior, though, as she hastened to inform us, she kept an interest.

She had invited us into a bright parlour which overlooked the high street of the town, her chair so positioned by the window that she could observe the comings and goings of the busy throng, as she explained to us, and so that she could run down to the shop if she saw an acquaintance or some old regular customer approaching. She shifted the chair now to face us where we sat and kept repeating how delighted she was to have

179

visitors now that Alf senior was gone and her life become so dreary, Alfred junior not always appreciating her offers of help.

"The young, you know," she said. "They have their own ways and don't like to be told."

A girl of about eleven, who turned out to be Alfred's eldest, soon arrived with a tray of tea and almond biscuits, which, as Mrs. Cork informed us, could be purchased in the shop downstairs, where they had proved a most popular item.

"Why cook them, I say, when you can get them ready made and so tasty?" she commented and we agreed, undertaking to purchase some on the way out, even though I have to say I consider my own homemade biscuits far superior to any shop-bought ones, and these were no exception.

"It must have been a great shock to you to be present when Madame Kapoushka took her fatal turn," I ventured in one of the very brief silences that ensued, partly to discourage yet more information about Alfred junior and his ways, of which his father would certainly not have approved, or about his wife (with much head shaking) who did nothing except keep having babies.

"Oh, indeed, it was a shock, Mrs. Hudson," she agreed. "A terrible shock. I was hoping, you know, to have another little chat with Alf. The first time he materialised I got all of a flutter and didn't ask half the things I should have. That last time I brought a list but we never got round to it."

I feared she was about to enumerate exactly what was on the list, so I quickly intervened.

"The jerking movements, the choking, the foaming at the mouth must have been horrible to witness," I offered.

"Indeed, it was, Mrs. Hudson. You have hit the nail right on the head there. Horrible, the very word. Of course, at first we all thought it was part of the show and she had been taken over by some angry spirit, the way she was thrashing about. That was at first, you know. Then, when she went all stiff and her face took on such twists and her eyes rolled back in her head, well, I

180

could see at once it was over for the poor woman. Alf passed so sweetly in comparison. I hope I go the same and not like her." She took another biscuit and consumed it in two bites, shaking her head at the same time. "Terrible it was. Horrible."

Mrs. Dixon and I shook our heads in sympathy.

"She did not mention Letitia at all, did she?" I asked.

"Letitia who?"

"I do not know. The name came up at the séance we attended."

"Letitia..." she thought for a minute. "I wonder do you mean Letitia Beckett."

Mrs. Dixon gasped. I managed more self-control but truth to tell I too was astounded.

"That is the only Letitia I know of," Mrs Cork went on, oblivious to our emotion. "Miserable piece of work she was, even though I know, Mrs. Hudson, Mrs. Dixon, that it is wrong to speak ill of the dead. The young couple must be relieved to be rid of her, though I'm sure they would never admit as much."

"Related then, I presume," I said, trying to keep my voice steady, "to Mr. Beckett the pharmacist."

"Not related really," Mrs. Cork replied, momentarily dashing my hopes. "Well, I suppose in a manner of speaking. In a manner of law. She was his stepmother, do you see. A nasty old witch, if you ask me, two-faced, always complaining about the price of things, the quality, as if we don't stock the very best here. Just ask anyone. Even better, ladies, why not see for yourselves. We at Corks pride ourselves on only selling the best of everything. Well, you can tell from these biscuits." And she took another.

I feared she would go off on a tangent again but she returned to the subject that interested us.

"No," she went on, "That Letitia Morton trapped old Mr. Beckett rightly with her pretence at sweetness, and then, once safely married, terrorised the life out of the poor man, even

181

getting him on his deathbed to make the son solemnly promise to look after her for the rest of her days. Boasted about it, she did, in the shop, in front of me who hardly knew the woman."

Mrs. Dixon and I journeyed home in a state of great excitement. It was almost more than we could do to resist the temptation to examine the papers right there on the train, but we were not alone in our compartment and could not take the risk. After all, my manner of acquiring them was somewhat irregular. Arriving at last at Baker Street, my friend was most regretful that she could not accompany me into my house, it being by now late in the afternoon and she having to return to prepare supper for Mr. Dixon on his return from the office. He would not have tolerated a delay. Meantime, she secured an undertaking from me to keep her informed of any developments. Hurrying in thereafter to No. 221B, I hardly paused to remove my coat before running upstairs to my bedroom, that being the most private place in the house, to go through the haul.

Shocking indeed were the discoveries I made. In her time Flossie Hutch may have dealt in stinking fish, but the stink from those papers far exceeded that of any rotten herring or cod. No psychic she, but a common blackmailer who hardheartedly made use of the information gleaned to extort sums of money from a number of the poor deluded ones who consulted her. These sums were listed in a little book I found among the papers. I must say that she kept excellent records even though her hand was vile and her victims only identified through initials.

I merely glanced through most of the letters and various documents that comprised the grounds for her villainy, not wishing to be privy to the darker secrets of the unfortunates who had fallen into her clutches. I could not help but notice a few, however, some from victims begging for mercy. One particularly chilling message caught my eye, clearly from someone already sucked dry by the blackmailer. It concluded: "I have no more money. I cannot go on." A red X had been drawn through the writing and the scribbled word: "Suicide".

At last I found what I was looking for, a note that bore the imprint of the Beckett pharmacy. This read as follows: "Be content, my dear Grace. Your anguish will soon be at an end and I promise you that L will be gone from our lives forever". It was signed "your loving Charles." I could not doubt but that this was the hold Flossie had over the young couple, by whatever means it had come into her hand. It was hardly conclusive evidence of wrongdoing, nevertheless, and could be open to several interpretations. A closer examination of the document revealed the mark of a pin upon one corner, indicating that another page had once been attached to it. I searched further and soon found a scrawl in that now familiar crabby hand, apparently taken from the testimony of some serving maid or other stating that to her certain knowledge Mr. B had emptied a powder into a drink which he then handed to LB. The maid witnessing his act reflected in a mirror, asserted that Mr. B was acting in a furtive manner, not realising that he was observed by the undersigned, Molly Goggins. Again, by itself, this was by no means damning. Mr. Beckett's action might have been quite innocent. However, putting the two documents together certainly suggested a more sinister reading. I wondered how best to proceed with all this new information, and spent a restless night as a result.

The morning cast no clearer light on the matter, even though the sun came smiling through my window. A hammering on the street door shortly after admitted a telegram which Clara hastened to bring to me as I sat in bed over my breakfast dish of coddled eggs.

The message was from Miss Quill, stating that the house had been broken into in the night and the place ransacked. The safe had been discovered (I wondered had they restored the villainous gentleman to his place of guardianship in front of it) and had been – no surprise to me there – emptied of its contents. "Please come quick," she concluded.

I sighed. These trips to Sydenham were becoming somewhat tedious and I could not see that my presence there would prove of any immediate assistance. Surely the girl must now have overcome her reluctance and called in the local constabulary. I wondered, all the same, what else might have been taken. If silver teaspoons and the like were missing then perhaps it was a simple and coincidental robbery, but if, as I suspected, the motive was solely to find the safe and remove its contents, then the matter became of greater interest to me. I decided not to return precipitously to Sydenham but to take my time to consider all developments. Meanwhile, I buttered another slice of toast, finished my eggs and drank a second dish of tea.

Later that morning yet another telegram arrived, sending my susceptible young kitchen maid, Phoebe, into quite a tizzy. I rather fancy she has her eye on the new messenger boy. The telegram turned out, however, not to be, as I had feared, yet another from Miss Quill but it was rather from Dr. Agnew, requesting my presence in Sydenham that very day and stating that a carriage would fetch me at noon, it now being close to that hour.

The high-handedness of what amounted to an order tempted me to send the carriage back empty. I felt so near a resolution of the matter of the Sydenham psychic, however, that I swiftly changed into my good bombazine and, as an additional touch, put on the pearls that I had inherited from my dear mamma. Let not these people imagine they were dealing with a person of low station, whom they could intimidate. There was no time to contact Mrs. Dixon, and indeed the invitation, if such you could call it, had not been extended to her. I felt somewhat loath all the same, to venture alone into what might prove to be a gang of poisoners. There was nothing to be done, however, for the carriage was already at the door. I gave instruction to Clara to contact Mr. H's old acquaintance, Inspector Lestrade of Scotland Yard, if I had not returned by nightfall, and, in addition, gave the address to which I assumed I was going. She looked at me with wide eyes, but knew her place well enough not to query my directive.

For speed alone, I have to say that I prefer the railway train. Nevertheless, the carriage that arrived for me was well-appointed with good leather upholstery, and the journey, though slow, was comfortable enough. After an hour or so, we arrived at the Agnew residence, which greatly relieved me, since I had apprehension of being removed to some remoter spot, at the mercy of desperate men.

Such fears were almost utterly dispelled when I was shown into the large and most delightful withdrawing room of the house. This reflected, I imagine, the taste of Mrs. Agnew in the modern lightness of the decorations. Indeed, the room resembled, to my eyes, nothing so much as a spring glade, with wallpaper in a pleasing leaf and flower design of pale greens and pinks, colours that were reflected in the furnishings, the light wood of the occasional table and the tallboy, the pretty china ornaments. The persons gathered there, however, seemed to me, with their grave expressions and sombre attire, to cast dark shadows around themselves. All were familiar to me from the séance I had attended, excepting that Miss Quill and Miss Swift were absent. His white hair rising like a plume from his forehead, Dr. Agnew stood tall and imposing in front of a marble fireplace in which I was rather surprised to see an unseasonal blaze flaring up. The Becketts sat together on an ottoman nearby, eyes cast down. Over at the window Signor Orsini leaned negligently on the sill, an unpleasant expression on his swarthy face. My hostess was the only one present with a smile for me as she urged me to be seated.

"We must apologise, Mrs. Hudson," the doctor began, "for bringing you here in such a hasty manner. I hope you have not been too much discommoded."

Reassured by his friendly tone, I replied that I had

certainly been surprised to receive the summons, but that I was happy to attend if, in some way, unknown to me, I could be of assistance to anyone here present.

"You can return the papers you stole from the safe," the Italian cut in, eyes flashing.

"Papers I stole?" I repeated, riled by the accusation. "Whatever are you saying, Signor?"

"Now, now," the doctor interposed. "There is no need for anyone to get on high horses. We are all friends here, I trust. In fact, we have decided, Mrs. Hudson, to take you fully into our confidence in the hope that, as a reasonable woman, you will be able to agree with us on a mutually acceptable course of action."

The maid then entered with a tray of tea and biscuits, the very same almond biscuits, I was somewhat surprised to observe, much admired by the grocer's widow. The doctor saw me looking at them.

"Yes, we have spoken to Mrs. Cork," he said. "She told us, among other things, that you were partial to these biscuits."

"Tea, Mrs. Hudson?" asked his wife.

I accepted but, as a precaution, did not taste mine until I had observed the others drinking the same without ill-effects.

Meanwhile the doctor began to explain the matter to me, some details of which I already knew.

Mr. Beckett had felt bound, by the solemn promise given to his father on his deathbed, a promise sworn on the Bible, to support his stepmother, Letitia, for the rest of her life. She however became the cause of great misery in the household, being given to frequent violent outbursts, and indeed her extreme jealousy of the young Mrs. Grace Beckett gave that lady reason even to fear for her own wellbeing and particularly for that of her beloved son, Benjamin. It was in vain that they tried to persuade Letitia to allow herself to be set up in a separate establishment of her own, a generous settlement even being offered by Grace's father, Dr. Agnew. Her rages on these occasions were terrible to behold and were often followed by physical reprisals on the boy.

"She was quite mad, Mrs. Hudson," Mrs. Beckett put in. "We did not know what she would do next."

It seemed that Mr. Beckett started secretly to administer certain draughts that helped calm his stepmother for a time.

"Please believe me," he said. "We did not poison her. The draughts were harmless. She died of the influenza."

"It is true," the doctor said. "But Letitia's personal maid, a vicious young woman as bad as her mistress, thought differently after, apparently, having witnessed on one occasion Charles administering the powder, and she sold a statement to that effect to Kapoushka, accusing Charles, which you will know already if you have read the document." He studied me but I said neither yea or nay and continued to listen carefully, examining the faces around me to try and judge if what I was hearing were indeed the truth. "This maid also stole a private note from Charles to Grace, which she likewise sold on."

"Where is she now?" I asked.

"The Americas," was the somewhat surprising reply. "We thought it best for her to take her lies far away with her."

They had paid the girl off, then.

"You must know," Mr. Beckett said. "Madame Kapoushka was a woman of the worst kind. She lured us with covert threats to attend the séance at which you yourself were present, and made it known to us there that she had firm evidence of a supposed crime, nothing less than the cruel murder of Letitia Beckett."

"We knew that we were not her only victims," Mrs. Beckett added, in trembling tones. "She boasted as much. She cared not if the evidence were true or contrived as long as she was able to squeeze money out of us."

"Did she succeed?" I asked. "Did you give her money?"

There was a pause.

"At first," Mr. Beckett said, "we thought to purchase

back the papers."

"Even though guiltless," added his wife.

"Against my advice," said the doctor. "If you once start on that road, there is no end to it."

"The woman was a parasite," said Mrs. Agnew in her soft voice.

"She was. And what," her husband added, "do we do with parasites? I'll tell you what, Mrs. Hudson. We squash them." With that, he brought his fist down upon the mantelpiece so hard that a delicate china shepherdess thereon flew off and smashed.

"Harold!" admonished Mrs. Agnew in distress

"No matter," the doctor said, kicking the fragments into a corner. I could feel the force of the man's rage.

"Am I to understand then," I said, "that you are confessing to the murder of Flossie Hutch, otherwise known as the psychic Madame Kapoushka?"

"No," came his reply. "Not at all. No one is confessing to anything." He stared into my eyes and this time his did not flicker. "The woman died of a heart attack as I wrote on her death certificate. However, we should greatly appreciate the return of any letters you may have in your possession that could lead someone else to a false conclusion."

"Why ever do you imagine that I might have them?" I asked.

"We have made our own inquiries," Signor Orsini said. "A little bird suggested it."

Madame's pert maidservant, of course, her sharp eyes everywhere.

"Mrs. Hudson." Grace Beckett now stood and took several steps towards me. She seemed weak and I feared she might collapse. "We have endured hell for so long. It cannot, it must not continue. For God's sake, for the sake of my little boy and the child I am carrying, have pity on us, and, if you have them, I beg you with all my heart to return the papers."

Some movement outside caught my eye. I looked past her, past Signor Orsini and through the window. Miss Swift was playing in the garden with a little boy crowned with dark curls like his father's. Their carefree laughter drifted up to us. I watched them for some moments, considering all things, then reached into my reticule. I drew out the fateful letter and accusatory statement, and handed them to the young woman. She fell upon me in an embrace, whispering, "God bless you!" into my ear. The doctor stepped forward, examined the papers and seemed satisfied. He then cast them upon the fire, where they blazed up briefly and were gone.

I informed Miss Quill in due course that I had found no evidence to indicate that her mistress had been poisoned. She had to accept this, since such was our agreement, but did so with a clear reluctance. The thief who had broken into the house was never apprehended. How could he be when the police had not been summoned? If I were to suspect anyone of that deed, it would perhaps be the wiry Signor Orsini, but suspicions do not amount to evidence. Mrs. Dixon was greatly disappointed when I told her that the papers from the safe contained nothing of any interest. It troubled me to deceive my dear friend but I felt that it was better for all concerned that no one else should know the truth of the business, especially someone like Belinda Dixon who did not always guard her tongue as she should. Those papers I could identify, I returned under seal to the fishwife's victims, the rest I burnt.

I leave it to you, my readers, to decide if my actions were just, but for myself, I have no regrets. No regrets at all.

Mrs. Hudson Goes to Edinburgh

The following adventure took place during that period of time when we all still believed that Mr. H had tragically perished in Switzerland. As a result of this I, as his erstwhile landlady, had fewer domestic duties to occupy me and so, when I received a telegram from Edinburgh in the July of that year informing me that my youngest daughter, Judy, who dwelt there, was about to give birth to her third child, I decided to take the long journey north, to help out as best I could. I admit that I was still in mourning for Mr. H, in spirit as well as in outward apparel, my best bombazine furnishing me with the appropriate garb but one hardly able to contain my deep grief.

The good doctor, who called in to Baker Street from time to time, supported me in my plan. He had once met with my son-in-law, John McPhee, when the young couple was visiting, both men delighted to discover they shared not simply an occupation but also a mutual acquaintance in Dr. Joseph Bell, who had, some years before, taught John at the Royal Infirmary of Edinburgh. Dr. Watson, indeed, gave me a letter of introduction to this august personage, the which I had no occasion to use, however, being caught up in more pressing matters.

Judy and John were by now living in the New Town of Scotland's capital city, in a small but highly respectable house in a side road near the main thoroughfare of Princes Street. No doubt, had John chosen to work exclusively for his wealthy

190

neighbours, he might have afforded a bigger residence. Much of his energies, however, were given to succouring the poor who lived beneath the castle, in the slums of the old town, something which, of course, was most laudable. I feared, all the same, that he might track some atrocious disease into the family home from those pitiful tenements but soon learned to still my tongue on the subject, since John, a most serious fellow of strong Presbyterian leanings, was not one jot pleased when I raised the matter, and silenced me with a look.

In any case, I had much to divert me, particularly in the lively shape of my granddaughter Effie, aged five, whose abundance of spirits had her poor mother, in her advanced condition, quite worn out, especially since there was two-year-old Henry to care for as well. I gladly took it upon myself, therefore, to entertain the little mite and with her to explore the splendours of this so-called "Athens of the North". Since I have been, from my girlhood, a great walker, if the weather suffered it, we would take ourselves off in early morning and spend much of the day rambling away from the smoke of the city, the which had brought upon it another, less noble soubriquet, namely that of "Auld Reekie". On occasion, we would travel by omnibus to one of the pretty little villages along the banks of the Firth of Forth and there I would sit upon the beach, while Effie would fly up and down collecting colourful or strangely shaped shells and stones which she would then present to me for safe-keeping. The quantity of these being so great, I would, I admit, drop a few out of my hand before we set off home again. So long as Effie had three or four to show her mamma on her return, she was content.

On other days we explored the beauties of Holyrood Park and particularly its lochs and ruined chapels. I had read the novels of Sir Walter Scott (puzzling at times over the Scots dialect therein) and was curious to view some of the places mentioned. Above all, I was of course ever conscious of the rock that loomed over Edinburgh, namely Arthur's Seat, and longed to climb it and observe the city from its heights. Whether Effie would be able to manage the climb was a question I was soon able to answer. The child had far more energy than I and could certainly reach the top of any hill with all the agility of a mountain goat. She also was keen to attempt the climb, although I had to promise Judy to keep the two of us away from the treacherous cliffs of Salisbury Crags, from which many a poor soul had fallen to injury and even death.

The morning boded well for our enterprise, being bright and still, since, as John informed us, the winds at the summit could sometimes prove strong and dangerous. I had even seen the place cloaked in mist but that was unlikely to befall us on such a day as this, and we set off light of heart. Once off the road we rejoiced to feel the spring of grasses under our feet and Effie sang a little song, "a wee ditty" as she called it, having a charming Scots turn of phrase, as well as a lilting accent.

On the way, we discussed the forthcoming arrival of a new brother or sister for her to play with, Effie firmly announcing her wish for a sister. But when she asked where the baby would come from, would we be buying her in a shop, I replied, as my mother had told me when I was little, that the child would be found under a gooseberry bush in the garden.

"But Grandmamma," Effie remarked very seriously, "I am not sure that we have a gooseberry bush in our garden."

"Well, then," I replied, somewhat discomforted. "Any fruit bush or shrub will surely serve."

This seemed to satisfy her, in her innocence, and she danced on ahead of me.

The climb, gentle at first, becoming quite steep and, not being as young as I used to be, I had to take my time. Up ahead, the merry little face of dear Effie peeped down at me from behind one boulder after another, I calling upon her to wait, since even this supposedly easy walk was not without its perils and there being few other people around if one or the other of us should fall into difficulties.

What did the little imp care for that, however, and by the time I heaved myself up the last steps to the top of the hill (it, after all, hardly warrants the name of mountain), she was sitting on the rocky summit laughing at me. Once I had got my breath back and grabbed little Effie by the hand, for the wind had risen and threatened to lift my hat from my head despite the jet-tipped pin holding it in place, I was at last able to admire the view. It was indeed truly splendid, from the vista leading up the Royal Mile from Holyrood House, where our Queen was often pleased to stay; past the spire of St. Giles Cathedral, and further on up to the very castle itself (and how minuscule that great pile appeared from this lofty height!); then south to the Pentland hills, purple in the distance; northwards over the Firth of Forth, glittering in the sunlight, speckled with tiny craft, and spanned by the red steel webbing of the mighty railway bridge. It had been opened by the Prince of Wales only a few years before this account, thereby making the Highlands accessible to all. I confess, my heart rose at the magnificent sights around us. Effie, however, was simply taken with the fact, to be relayed to her parents, that she had beaten her old Grandmamma to the top.

I had brought with me some light refreshments – fruits, cheeses and bread – and we looked about us for somewhere to rest ourselves and eat. The summit would not suit and so we descended a way down a grassy slope dotted with boulders. Soon we found a sheltered spot and sat ourselves on the dry grass that formed a comfortable enough cushion. Sitting still would not do for Effie, of course, and she soon danced off again clutching a cut of bread in one hand and an apple in the other.

"Do be careful," I cried after her but the breeze carried my words in the opposite direction.

It seemed almost inevitable. Before I had time to raise myself up and go after the child, she had disappeared from view with a cry. Horrified, I ran after her to the edge of the cliff and peered over, fearing to see her poor little body at the bottom of some chasm. Luckily, this was not to be. The cliff she had tumbled down was sister to the one old blind Gloucester fell from in Mr. Shakespeare's "King Lear". That is to say, not a cliff at all. Effie had merely rolled down a slope and was sitting quite merrily not ten feet below me, beside a gorse bush. My relief was so huge I forgot to scold the child. In any case, I was completely distracted by the sight that met my eye. Effie was clasping in her arms a wicker basket and within the same basket a sleeping baby.

"I have found my new sister," Effie called up, excitedly. "She was beside this bush and I found her."

I clambered down carefully and looked more closely into the basket. A tiny rosy-cheeked infant, surely of no more than a few days old, slept quietly within, soft breaths rising and falling in her tiny chest (although at that time to be sure I did not know the sex of the little creature). I looked around. No sign of another living soul.

"I don't think that this is our baby, Effie," I said. "I expect her mamma will come back for her in a minute."

"But I found her," Effie retorted crossly. "She must be ours."

"Well," I replied. "Let us wait and see for a while if anyone else returns to collect her."

It seemed unimaginable that anyone would leave a baby in this remote spot even for an instant but still we waited. We waited and we waited, Effie peering in the basket constantly, presumably hoping the little creature would wake up and want to play with her. I meanwhile kept casting an eye over the surrounding landscape but saw no persons there except, in the far distance, a shepherd with his dog and flock, and the occasional hikers – in groups or alone – who passed near us sometimes with a nod but no other hint of recognition. No one, it seemed, was coming for the baby. After an hour or more, that was clear and Effie was hopping to be gone. In any case, heavy dark clouds were starting to gather over us and I feared it might rain after all. Nothing to be done then but to take the baby with us, for I could not abandon her to a night on the cold hillside. Where we had landed was fortuitously on one of the main paths that led back down to the city and we hastened home with our basket and its most unusual contents.

Effie burst into the parlour, where her mother sat alone, quietly sewing. It being now past seven of the evening, Henry had already been dispatched to bed by Nanny, and John was away no doubt tending to some needy soul.

"Mamma," Effie cried. "You cannot guess what has happened. I have found our new baby."

I followed with the infant, who was now waking up and starting to fret.

"Good heavens!" Judy exclaimed, peering into the basket and proceeding to regale me with questions which Effie insisted on answering.

"She was under a bush, just like Grandmamma told me she would be."

"The poor little thing," my dear daughter said. "Imagine leaving it there to die."

"I do not think that was the intention," I said. "Whoever had left the baby intended no harm but meant it to be found and quickly." I then explained how the basket had been placed on a path in full view of anyone walking it. Indeed, I went on, I had the feeling, as we descended, that we were being watched from some hiding place, even though my frequent backward glances failed to spot any person, any shadow, any movement.

Judy took the baby from the basket to comfort her, meanwhile sending Effie to fetch Nanny.

"Some desperate woman from the old town," she guessed, "unable to afford another mouth to feed."

195

"I rather think not," I said, examining the contents of the basket. "The baby looks clean and healthy, and the basket is new and softly lined. Above all," I went on, touching the swaddling clothes, "here is fine linen."

Nanny entered with Effie hot on her heels. The kindly old woman likewise expressed amazement at the sight of the baby.

"It's our new baby," Effie informed her.

"No, my dear," said Judy. "Our baby hasn't arrived yet."

"But Grandmamma said babies could be found under bushes and that's where I found her," Effie continued most insistent, and I began greatly to regret my earlier words.

"Well," Judy went on as the baby started to cry louder – and really it always amazes me how much noise such a tiny scrap can emit. "The most important task we have at the moment is to dry baby, for I can feel wet clothes. And then baby must be fed."

Most fortuitously John returned home at that moment and was apprised of the situation. What pleased me most was that even this austere man melted at the sight of the tiny child. I admit that I had uncharitably feared he might away with it to a foundling hospital. Instead, though clearly worn out from the day's endeavours, he immediately took it upon himself to prepare a formula of milk for the baby, the means for this as well as a nursing bottle, he was able to find in his surgery.

Meanwhile, I accompanied Nanny and Effie to the nursery, where Nanny was to clean and change the baby. For my part, I wished to look more closely at the fine linen in which she was wrapped (for now we were able to establish firmly that she was a girl, much to Effie's satisfaction).

"She must have a name," Effie said.

"You are right. But what would be a good name, do you think?" Nanny asked.

"I don't know." Effie's little face scrunched up in thought.

"How about Rose," I suggested, "since she has such rosy cheeks."

Effie nodded gladly, so Rose she became.

Meanwhile, I took the linen wrap and peered at it closely. What I found there was most interesting and enlightening. I descended to the parlour again and showed my discovery to Judy.

"Why, it is just a plain piece of cloth," she said.

"Not quite," I remarked, rather pleased with myself. "If you look in this corner, you will see that stitching has been unpicked. It is, I rather think, a monogram that might give us a clue as to where the baby came from."

Judy looked more carefully at the place I indicated, where tiny pin-pricks indicated a pattern of letters and arabesques.

"Why yes," she said. "I can see it now. Let me take it under the lamp, to view it more closely."

The result was telling. An L and an S on either side of a larger B.

"I cannot think," Judy said, "who might make such a mark but John might know."

That gentleman soon re-entered cradling baby Rose in his arms, she sucking most vigorously from the bottle he was holding to her little mouth.

"LBS," he said thoughtfully. "I really do not know."

"B," I said, "is no doubt the family name, L the initial of the wife and S the husband."

"Good heavens," Judy said. "Can it be Lord and Lady Balhinnie? Is not she Lydia and he Silas?"

John furrowed his brow, while moving little Rose to a more comfortable position. "It most certainly fits," said he. "But why on earth would such people leave a child on Arthur's Seat? I cannot believe it."

"It may not be them," I said. "Just someone with access

to the linen. Someone from the household perhaps."

"Of course," John replied. "Certainly such a family can have no involvement here. I know Lady Balhinnie from her many charitable activities. A most respectable woman, if somewhat lofty of manner."

"But whatever shall be done?" put in Judy. "We can hardly keep the child ourselves and do not want to involve the police for they will surely take the poor little thing to the orphanage where she is like to perish soon after. It is not a place for a new-born infant."

"Such establishments are not as bad as they were," replied John.

"I should be most happy," I said, "to pay a call on Lady Balhinnie tomorrow. She may after all, be able to shed some light on the business."

This was agreed.

"Although I trust," John added, "you will tread circumspectly, Martha. She is after all a very exalted lady indeed."

I was somewhat surprised at this from such a champion of the downtrodden, yet I assured him of my discretion. Secretly I felt that, no matter how exalted, if her ladyship were involved in this sorry case, she must be discovered.

The townhouse of Lord and Lady Balhinnie was very grand indeed set as it was in Charlotte Square, one of the most coveted addresses of the city. I doubted indeed that her ladyship would readily see me and was therefore most surprised to be ushered by the footman who answered the door directly into the presence of Herself.

I regarded my companion with interest. A woman of about my own age, of stately build, dressed most fashionably in a dress of burgundy silk, with a cream lace shawl, her lustrous dark hair, of a shade perhaps not readily found in nature, caught up in a chignon, with little curls at the front and artfully escaping ringlets at the back. A woman designed to impress.

She received me graciously, though with some condescension, addressing me as "Mrs. Herriot." When I corrected her, it transpired that I was mistook for a rector's wife who was expected at that very moment in order to discuss some charitable enterprise. Her ladyship was too well-bred to send me packing at once and enquired after my business with her, clearly anticipating some further request for a donation to a good cause.

I then withdrew from my reticule the linen sheet that had encased baby Rose and asked her ladyship if she recognised it.

"Should I?" she asked. "There is nothing special to see there." I then directed her gaze to the corner of the sheet where the monogram had been unpicked. Did I detect the slightest of hesitations before she stated that again there was nothing to be seen?

"I know it is only pinpricks and difficult to make out," I said. "But this might assist your ladyship." I then produced a drawn rendition of the design, which Judy had made.

"What is this?" Lady Balhinnie rose up angrily. "Who has been copying our monogram and to what purpose?" She glared down at me, although I sensed in that proud gaze something else. Agitation or even fear perhaps. Or perhaps I imagined it.

I then explained how a newly born baby had been discovered by myself on the upper slopes of Arthur's Seat and how it had been wrapped in the accompanying linen sheet. I was about to add that I had only noticed the monogram later last evening, when her ladyship cut in with cold fury.

"Am I to understand," she said, "that you are accusing me of abandoning a baby on a mountain side? Do you understand who I am? Do you understand who my husband is? And who are you, madam, might I ask, to make such a heinous charge against us?"

I thereupon made soothing noises and stated that I merely wished to ascertain if the linen indeed came from the house.

"There are," I said, "scores of ways in which someone, anyone, might have taken the cloth for their own purposes. Far, far be it from me, your ladyship, to impute any guilt whatsoever to yourself or other members of the family." Not quite yet anyway, I added to myself. "My only concern is with the little baby and a mother who must have been truly desperate for her to take such a step."

The lady calmed somewhat at this and betook herself to her chair again.

"Forgive me," she said, though in tones that suggested she at least needed no forgiveness. "Of course it must have been most distressing for you to find a little girl in such circumstances. How terrible! Nevertheless, although it is possible I suppose that the linen came from this house, it is most certain that the baby did not. I can help you, madam, no further in this matter."

At that point, her ladyship rang a bell to indicate that our discussion was at an end.

The footman must have been waiting by the door, for he entered instantly.

"Show Mrs... er..."

"Hudson," I prompted.

"Show Mrs. Hudson out, Fraser," she said, and looked away.

Oh, she was proud.

There was nothing for it then but for me to take my leave. I wished her well and passed back through the hallway, Fraser opening the front door for me with the most imperceptible of bows. There on the doorstep, I encountered, about to ring the bell, an elderly woman of impeccable respectability, no doubt the rector's wife, Mrs. Herriot, come on her mission of mercy. I nodded politely to her as I descended the steps into the square.

When I turned to regard the house, I saw her ladyship standing at the window, looking back out at me. I raised my hand and she, after a pause, did likewise, hoping no doubt never to set eyes on me again. An unlikely ambition, under the circumstances, for I was just then wondering how, since I had particularly avoided mentioning it, did Lady Balhinnie know that the abandoned baby was a girl.

I took my time returning, since a long walk I always find conducive to profitable thought. Traversing the city as far as the park that is called the Meadows, I ambled along a tree-lined path that took me almost back again to Arthur's Seat, and gazed up at its heights as if it could reveal to me the solution to the mystery. That Lady Balhinnie knew something of the matter I had no doubt, but whether she was directly involved in some way, of that I had as yet no notion. Moreover, how to progress my search further without offending propriety, I could not at the moment imagine. Then of course there was Rose herself. Failing to track down her parents, whatever was to be done about her, for certain it was that, despite Effie's insistence that Rose was her new sister, Judy and John would not keep her, and I unquestionably could not.

I sighed and turned my steps back to Edinburgh, passing over the high bridges that look down into the misery and squalor that is the old city. It was like looking down into hell. Rose would not under any circumstances be consigned to a fate there, of that I was determined.

It so happened that several days later, during which time no amount of discreet enquiries elicited any progress in the search for Rose's origins, a reception was to be held to raise money for the poor of the city, my son-in-law John being one of the chief organisers on the committee. Because the nine months wait for Judy's confinement was already past, John would not let her attend the event and so she suggested I might go in her place. I was not sure how John felt about this, but he was far too polite a gentleman to demur. For my part, I was happy to attend, not, you may be sure, in order to mix with the upper ranks of Edinburgh society or to partake of the banquet provided – though I wondered that money should be spent on feeding the already well-fed when the poor were the ones in need of meat with their bread and tea. No, I was anticipating that Lady Balhinnie, that well-known philanthropist, would be present so that I might regard her more closely, along with her husband whom I had as yet to meet. It also occurred to me that I might perhaps be able to make discreet enquiries about them among the other guests. Of course, I revealed nothing of this to my son-in-law, who would no doubt have been shocked at my plan and who might therefore have refused to take me. I should say in addition that John had been making his own enquiries, although these were rather different from mine, namely to try to find a suitable family in which to place the poor little foundling. Meantimes, I had been turning a notion over in my head on this same topic, of which more anon.

My black bombazine served well enough for the purposes of the evening once Judy had lent me a pretty black lace capelet ornamented with jet beads to wear over it. Although I say so myself, by the time I had brushed my hair up into a neat chignon, I looked very well and quite the lady philanthropist myself. I was somewhat astonished to see John arrive down in full Highland dress, wearing a tartan kilt of the McPhee clan (as he proudly informed me) of red, green and black with a fold of plaid flung across his shoulder, secured with a handsome silver pin in the form of a thistle, the national emblem of Scotland. His jacket and waistcoat were of black velvet with white trimmings. His legs were bare but for patterned stockings to his knees and he wore heavy boots. Most amazing and eye-catching of all was something I now understand to be termed a sporran that was suspended from his belt. It was a large pouch of some sort of animal fur, embellished with heavy tassels that hung from a silver mount, likewise in the form of a thistle. Judy, observing my surprise, explained that at formal functions such as this, all the gentleman would be similarly clad and I was not to raise my eyebrows at the sight.

John and I took a cab the short distance to the hall where the reception was to take place. As one of the organisers, he had to arrive early, before the event, and thus the place was empty of all but the few persons setting out chairs and tables. Because I had no official function, I seated myself near the door, to observe those entering, and true it was that the gentlemen outshone the ladies in the splendour of their Scots regalia. Tartans of all patterns and shades were in evidence, each no doubt indicating the clan or tribe of the wearer. It was all most bewildering and unlike anything you would see in London. Most glad was I when another lady sat beside me, the spouse, as she informed me, of another of the organisers. I was most lucky, too, that this lady, a Scotswoman named Mrs. McKechnie, was of a garrulous, not to say gossipy bent, happy to explain to me – a Sassenach, as she called me, smiling the while in case I should think it an insult – what was going on and, more to the point, who was present. As the guests started to enter, she regaled me with all sorts of tittle-tattle regarding them, in which I pretended interest, not by nature being one who revels in the scandals of others. However, when finally Lady Balhinnie arrived in the company of an elderly gentleman of distinguished investiture who had to be her husband, it was most useful for my purposes that Mrs. McKechnie needed no prompting at all to expound upon the couple. His lordship, by the by, was wearing a tartan predominantly of a bottle green with stripes of an egg-yolk yellow, not to my mind the most attractive of combinations, his wife in the same green also, a striking gown in the latest style, with a high neck and wide sleeves, no bustle but featuring fine pleats down the back.

"She appears so superior, does she no, Mrs. Hudson," Mrs. McKechnie was saying with a sneer. "Looking down her nose at the rest of us mere mortals. But I've heard a thing or two about that grand lady, to be sure. Or rather, about him... You'd think to look at him wouldn't you, Mrs. Hudson, now that's a most respectable old gentleman. Not a bit of it. The number of housemaids who have had to fight him off, if you get my meaning. Or the number who gave in..."

She pursed her lips and nodded at me with all the self-righteousness of a fanatic follower of John Knox, while secretly, I felt, revelling in the unseemly rumours.

While I usually abhor such scurrilous talk, in this case it served me well and I looked more closely at Lord Balhinnie following this revelation, reviewing my initially favourable impression, for, as my dear Henry was used to say, "fine feathers do not always make fine birds". His lordship was a somewhat hunchbacked, grey- haired man of sixty and more, clean-shaven but for immense pepper- and-salt side-whiskers, of florid countenance, with thick red lips that he constantly licked, and small fat hands with fingers that wiggled like little maggots. I should not like him or his hands, I thought, to be near either of my daughters and wondered if he it was had fathered baby Rose, abandoning her mother along with the child. I could well believe it. Behind them slouched a lanky boy of sixteen or thereabouts clad in the same tartan.

"Their son Hugh," whispered Mrs. McKechnie. "Poor lad."

"Why poor?"

"Just look at the laddie. A right dunderheed, and no mistake. A sore disappointment to his father, so I've heard. And him the only heir."

At that moment, as if knowing they were being discussed, mother and son both looked across directly at me. I nodded to her ladyship, but she turned away instantly, declining the acknowledgement. The boy, however, regarded me so keenly that I felt a trifle discommoded. Mrs. McKechnie noticed nothing, thank heavens, intent as she was in spreading gossip concerning the next set of people to enter the hall.

Had it not been for my particular interest in the Balhinnies, the evening would have been most dreary for me. I knew nobody but John who was too occupied to bother much with me and, Mrs. McKechnie having been swept away by ladies of her acquaintance, I sat where I was, almost invisible. Not entirely, however, for I was aware from time to time of Lady Balhinnie's dark eyes boring into me, and wondered if she would bring herself to cross over and speak to me at last. She did not.

We soon adjourned into the banqueting hall, where I was sat next to John, introduced as his mother-in-law and thereafter politely ignored since I could not join in the local news. On the other side of me sat an elderly deaf minister of the church with whom, it is true, I tried to conduct a sporadic and hard-earned conversation. Since, however, I knew nothing of his parish of Leith, the only subject in which he seemed interested, I finally gave up and concentrated on my meats, fish, blancmanges, ices and other delights, which I have to admit were of the finest quality, particularly the roast venison. Again I could not help but wonder what the poor of Edinburgh would make of such a feast in their honour and whether the leavings were to be distributed among them. I was fain to ask this of John, but he was too engrossed to bother with me.

There were speeches and more speeches, some in such powerful Scots dialect that I almost wondered if a foreign language were being uttered. I soon gave up any attempt to follow what was being said until my son-in-law, John, rose to speak. He gave an impassioned address on the parlous state of the medical services provided for the indigent of the old town, which would have impressed me more had I not observed him eating and drinking as heartily as the rest of us. But perhaps I am unfair. He is a good man, I am sure, does good work and provides adequately for his family.

There was some milling about after the meal and pledges of donations. I saw Lady Balhinnie approach John and engage him in earnest conversation possibly about the cause, although both glanced across at me at one point. I rose to join them, but before I could, Her Ladyship disappeared off into the crowd.

"You have made an impression, Martha," John said to me. "There was Lady Balhinnie no less enquiring after you."

"In what regard?" I asked.

"She had not known of your connection to me and furthermore was most surprised when I told her the name of your erstwhile lodger." Meaning, of course, Mr. H, whose fame had evidently spread far north.

I have noticed before how my connection with the eminent detective often seems to have the unwarranted effect of transferring some of his distinction on to my unworthy self. No wonder Lady Balhinnie, if guilty in any way regarding Rose, had rushed away at my approach. To be fair, however, her haste might have been inspired by something else altogether. His Lordship, as I had noticed, having partaken excessively of Burgundy with his supper and thereafter glasses of port wine and brandy, by now had a complexion even more empurpled than before. He was at that very moment discoursing with a buxom young lady who displayed a rather too deep décolletage for modesty, his lordship leaning close over her, a wet smile on his thick lips. Lady Balhinnie, a deep frown furrowing her brow, had to whisper several times in his ear, before managing to seize his arm and lead him away, he stumbling somewhat. I caught Mrs. McKechnie's eye at that moment and she nodded at me knowingly, evidently having been keeping an eye on His Lordship for her own gossipy purposes. The son Hugh still stared across at me from time to time and I wondered did he wish to

206

speak to me on some topic. There was something about him that seemed familiar, although I could not imagine where I might have seen him before. Certainly not at the house on Charlotte Square. However, the evening was over before this could be discovered and we were all swept away to our various parts of the city and beyond.

The next day, at breakfast, I came upon John and Judy in deep conversation, him stating that it was not possible for Rose to stay longer in our household, particularly in view of the impending birth of his own child.

"I have found a respectable farming couple who, for a fee, would be willing to take her in."

"Oh, John," Judy said. "But will they be good to her? I fear for her so much."

Here I cut in, my having anticipated such an ultimatum, to express a thought that had been taking root in my mind.

"I should like first," I said, "to write to a family of my acquaintance that would, if they are willing to take her, provide a happy and secure home for little Rose."

I had in mind the Reverend Felix and Mary Goodhart, whom I had got to know in the course of another sad case that had come my way. The couple had now three sons they adored but to my knowledge dearly wished for a daughter, Mary, however, having been told it would be dangerous for her to bear another child. They lived in Hampshire, to be sure far distant from Edinburgh, but, if the true parents had no interest in the child, then that would be of no great matter. John agreed to give me time to write to the Goodharts and to wait until we heard back from them before removing Rose from our household. And to be sure, the little thing was no trouble, sleeping well at night, according to Nanny, and thriving despite her lack of mother's milk.

I forthwith took up my pen and wrote to Mary explaining the circumstances of our discovery of the babe on the mountainside, knowing this would stir her motherly heart, but making no mention of the possible involvement of the Balhinnies. The very next day I received a letter back from my friend expressing the joyful willingness of herself and Felix to take in the poor foundling and suggesting that I bring the child down with all speed. This however was not convenient, since Judy's time was come and the baby due to be born at any moment. I wrote back explaining the situation in the hope that perhaps Mary or Felix would themselves take the long trip up to Edinburgh.

After many hours of travail, Judy finally gave birth to a healthy little boy on the eve of July 15th. Effie, woken by the commotion, must have started, I am afraid, to understand that babies are not after all found under gooseberry bushes but that they come from somewhere else altogether. At that moment, however, she was too delighted with the arrival of brother Alistair (even a brother!) that such questions did not enter her head.

We finally all retired to bed late that night, with great relief that mother and baby were well, not imagining – and how could we? – the terrible drama that was about to unfold. For some time in the early hours, when we were all dead to the world, an intruder broke into the house.

I was awakened toward dawn by great cries and wails and left my room to find what was the matter. It could not be worse news. Baby Alistair had been plucked from his crib beside his mother and carried off. No one had heard a thing, not Judy or John, not Nanny or any of the servants, not even I who pride myself on being a light sleeper. The household was in the highest panic, as can well be imagined. The police were informed and a search set in train at once. But who could have done such a thing and why? Nothing else had been taken, so robbery it was not. Distressed though I was, I put my mind to the problem and finally came up with an explanation that might fit the business.

Leaving Judy in the capable hands of Nanny, though without saying a word as to my true intent except to remark that I could not stay home doing nothing and would search the neighbourhood for clues, I set off through the city again to Charlotte Square. There I found almost equal consternation. It seemed that the boy Hugh had also disappeared that night and no one knew where he could be. Lady Balhinnie at first shrank at the sight of me, then became incensed to the extent that I thought she was going to strike me, as if I had some responsibility in the matter.

"Calm yourself, Your Ladyship, and perhaps tell me the truth at last," I said.

That proud gaze was cast upon me again as if to say who was I to make such a demand.

"Let me surmise," I went on. "The foundling on the mountain was Hugh's daughter."

She looked at me then aghast as if I was possessed of soothsaying powers, but in fact the truth had come to me in a flash of recognition as I sat beside my weeping daughter, reliving the events of the past few days to try and make sense of them. I had suddenly remembered where I had seen lanky Hugh and his shambling gait before: on that day on Arthur's Seat, in the garb of a hiker, passing myself, Effie and baby Rose as if with indifference. And if, as I was now convinced, it was indeed he, then why should he have been there if not to check what had happened to the baby, and why again if not because he himself was most closely and desperately involved.

At last Her Ladyship collapsed, her pride giving way to concern for her son. We withdrew for discretion to her private chamber and the words started to pour out of her. It seemed that Hugh, who for some reason (Her Ladyship stated with disdain) preferred the company of servants to that of his peers, had fallen in love with the daughter of the gardener on their country estate in the highlands. This girl, Isla, a mere child of fourteen, had actually arrived at Charlotte Square several days before great with child (her ladyship freezing with horror at the memory), having been turned out, for shame from the family home. In front of Lord and Lady Balhinnie, she had claimed the child to be Hugh's and he, freely admitting the same, now wished to marry her at once. This, of course, (Lady Balhinnie stated) was out of the question, the wretched girl being utterly unsuited to be the wife of a future laird. Besides which, she added, the two of them were mere children. A terrible row ensued in the course of which the girl was struck to the ground by Lord Balhinnie, who then dragged Hugh off and locked him in his room. While (and here Her Ladyship lowered her voice and averted her eyes.) the girl was confined to a cellar until the next morning when she was discovered dead with her new-born baby in her arms.

"Dear Lord," I exclaimed, more shocked than I could say.

"I assure you," Lady Balhinnie put her hand on her heart (if heart she had), "it was a terrible accident, Mrs. Hudson. No such outcome was dreamt of, even less intended. Not by me at least."

I merely stared at her. No words coming to me. What sort of people were these!

She continued her account in trembling tones. His Lordship in his rage was for leaving the child where it was, for nature to take its inevitable and horrible course, but Lady Balhinnie pleaded with him for mercy. ("I am not a bad woman, Mrs. Hudson," said she, "despite what you might think"). He then proposed to send the infant immediately the foundling hospital but (and here Lady Balhinnie shed one or two tears) she demurred, having visited such grim establishments in the course of her charitable duties. Some discussion took place then as to whether the gardener would after all be prepared to take his grandchild in. The same man, being of rigid religious convictions, and having been heard to describe children born out of wedlock as spawn of the devil, this course of action was not considered likely to succeed, even if a handsome sum of money should be offered to him. As to involving the authorities, it would cause the most terrible scandal for the circumstances of Isla's death to become known. Worse still, His Lordship might be accused of manslaughter. (Or even of murder, I thought).

"And the girl?" I asked. "What happened to her?" Lady Balhinnie looked at me uncomprehending.

"What should happen?" she asked. "I told you she was dead."

"Did you arrange," I asked, "for a Christian burial at least?"

"Of course," she replied, though failing to catch my eye.

I feared she lied or at least knew nothing of the circumstances. She rushed on with her account.

Hugh, it seemed, had become hysterical when apprised of Isla's death.

"We had tried to keep the full tragic circumstances from him, telling him she had gone away somewhere safe," Lady Balhinnie said.

Then, reading my expression, added, "to protect him, Mrs. Hudson, to protect my son." Unfortunately, the servant who had discovered the girl's body, had revealed the truth to him and even showed him the child. In his desperation and grief, he then made off with her to places unknown.

"Unknown that is," Her Ladyship stated with a curl of her lip, "until you, Mrs. Hudson turned up on our doorstep."

Again, the fault seemed in her eyes to be mine, as if, the baby disappearing, that should have been the end of the matter.

"And now," she concluded, "Hugh has vanished and with him, most probably, your daughter's new baby. Though why he should take it, I have no idea, unless he has gone completely mad."

Here she broke down again, though I am afraid I felt no

211

pity for her, only horror and disgust. However, when I spoke to her, it was gently and kindly – for it was of the most urgent necessity to find baby Alistair as soon as possible.

"Have you any notion at all where he might have gone?" I asked.

She shook her head. "To friends, maybe."

"I do not know who his friends are. As I said, he rejects his own and prefers the company of the lower classes. Oh, Mrs. Hudson," she cried out. "Hugh has been such a worry to us. He shows no interest in the pursuits appropriate to a gentleman of his standing. He is to be Laird one day but tells us all he wants to do is paint pictures. Imagine what my husband thinks of that!"

"May I see his room," I asked. "It may furnish us with a clue." She was evidently surprised at the request but agreed, calling Fraser to show me the way.

As I climbed the stairs behind the footman, I wondered that Her Ladyship had not asked after the health or fate of baby Rose, her own granddaughter after all. It seemed she had a heart as hard, for different reasons, as poor Isla's own father. I suspected, too, that her anxiety at the disappearance of her son had less to do with the safety of the boy himself and more with any scandal he might engender.

Hugh's room displayed his artistic bent, containing a table covered with sketches and others pinned to the walls. To my admittedly untutored eye, they demonstrated a sensitivity and skill. One in particular caught my attention, that of a smiling young maiden in a frame placed next to his bedhead, presumably a likeness of his beloved.

I leafed through more of the sketches, under the coldly watchful eye of Fraser, in case, I suppose, that I might think of pocketing something. The subject matter of the pictures I found particularly interesting, as they were nearly all studies of slum dwellers or views of wretched streets and houses. But there were others, too.

I then asked Fraser if I might be shown the kitchen and he, taken aback as I could tell, nevertheless bowed and led me down to the back of the house, to a scullery where several women were busy over steaming pots and pans or engaged in other domestic chores. I instantly felt more at home there than in the cold parlour upstairs.

"You may go now, Fraser," I said in a firm voice, for I did not want him present while I talked to the women. "I am sure Her Ladyship requires your services elsewhere."

Again he seemed taken aback but, after giving the slightest of bows, withdrew.

One of the women turned to me with a grin. "That's telling him, the bawbag."

I did not know what the word meant, but could tell from her tone that Fraser was not a favourite below stairs.

I introduced myself and requested permission to ask a few questions of them, to which they readily agreed.

"It's about Master Hugh," I said and noticed how they glanced at one another, almost as if in warning. "I think," I went on, "he was fond of you all and knew you well." Adding, "I have seen his drawings. Many are of this kitchen and of you ladies. He's a fine artist."

They laughed at my use of the word "ladies" and there was a palpable softening of atmosphere, together with cries of "Indaid, he is," "A grand wee laddie, to be sure" and other such expressions of affection.

"It is most important that he be found as soon as possible," I said, explaining about Alistair.

"You think he has your wee bairn?" asked the cook, a Mrs. Campbell. "Ah no. Sure, there's no wickedness in him. He wouldnae take a wean."

"I think he came to us last night intending to recover baby Rose, but in the dark mistook the infant. Alistair is new born and, while I am sure Hugh intends him no harm, he is not able to give the baby the care he needs and I fear..." my voice breaking at this point, "I fear for the baby's very life."

The women looked at me in silence.

"If you have any notion at all where he might be – you all being his friends – I beg you to take me to him. He will be in no trouble, I assure you. I understand that he is acting under extreme distress, but we must, we must restore baby Alistair to his parents."

Mrs. Campbell caught my hand.

"Lord and Lady Balhinnie, God forgive me for speaking ill of them, but they are wicked people. That boy of theirs is ten thousand times better than they are. You cannae know the evil they have done."

"I think I do, Mrs. Campbell, for Lady Balhinnie just confessed all. They as good as murdered the mother of Hugh's child." It was no time to mince my words.

The kindly soul gave me a hug.

"Then you know all about it," she said and turned to the youngest there present, a chit of a girl, the scullery maid.

"Fiona," she said. "You know where to take Mrs. Hudson.

With all speed, hen."

"We'll go by cab," I said.

"No cab will take you where you need to go," the cook replied, "but near enough."

We went out through the servants' door. I did not feel it necessary or desirable to take my leave of Lady Balhinnie.

Fiona was so clearly excited to travel in the cab that I suspected the bare-foot girl had never entered such a conveyance before in her life. Throughout the whole journey, she looked around and about herself and out of the window at the city with wide eyes. The cab trundled up the cobbled streets toward the castle though that was not to be our destination. We had to alight by one of the closes, a dark alleyway with steep steps leading down between high tenements. I seemed to recognise it and its wretched denizens from Hugh's drawings. We followed the close down a way before Fiona stopped at one of the buildings, beckoning me through a stinking doorway and up several flights of stairs awash with all manner of detritus that I was glad I could not clearly see, the flickering gaslight providing only the meanest of glimpses. She at last reached the door she sought and tapped on it in a queer rhythm. It opened after a moment and I was able to make out through the gloom a poor but neat enough room. Hugh was sitting by a narrow window that admitted only weak light, a crowd of small children playing around his feet, while, by a small fireplace, I could just make out the form of a woman.

"Mamma," said Fiona, "here is Mrs. Hudson come for the bairn."

The woman turned to me and I saw that she was nursing a baby at her breast. It was Alistair himself for I recognised him by the little garments that I myself had sewn.

With a cry of joy, I rushed forward. At the same time Hugh, in terror, made for the door as if to flee, but Fiona halted him.

"You need fear no harm, maister," she said. "Mrs. Hudson promised."

"Best let the bairn finish his feed," Fiona's mother said to me gently. "Would ye be pleased to sit doon for a wee while, ma'am."

While Alistair guzzled happily at the breast, I spoke to Hugh, assuring him again that he would not be punished for his actions.

"My father is the one should rot in prison," he said bitterly. "But of course he will not. Even if all is revealed, no judge here would sentence him. They are all his friends."

He explained how, in terror that evil would befall his baby ("For Mrs. Hudson, you must know my father is capable of every abomination"), he had rushed off with her to Arthur's Seat,

215

there waiting in secret to see if some respectable person would save the child from harm. A guileless, childish response to a problem, as I understood. Seeing us take the baby, he had followed at a distance to see where would go, and was reassured at first. But then, having confessed to Mrs. Campbell, he had second thoughts and wished to retrieve the child, thereafter breaking into our house at night without realising that there was not now one baby but two, and in the dark not seeing the difference. He had fled with the child in his arms to the only place where he felt safe, vouchsafing his secret to the servants who loved him and who promised to honour it.

"I do not mind," he said, "that they told you, Mrs. Hudson. To be sure I was meaning to bring your baby back to you tonight, under cover of darkness."

He looked so desolate I could not but try to reassure him that all must now be well.

"How can that be?" he asked, raising tearful eyes to mine. "With Isla dead and me not able to care for the bairn."

I explained how a good family, friends of mine, were willing to rear his baby until he was able to look after her himself.

"Only, of course, if you are agreeable to that, Hugh," I said. I explained who they were and where they lived ("Hampshire!" exclaimed the boy as if I were planning to send the baby to darkest Africa).

"But I cannot stay here," he said. "I cannot live with my parents any more. I want to go to Paris and learn to paint properly. Paris, you know," he added eagerly, "is the centre for all the artists these days."

"Well, it may be," I answered somewhat sternly. "And yet as I have heard many of those same artists are starving in garrets. If you are intent on art as a career, might I suggest you apply to a school in London. That way you would not be so very far from your daughter and could visit her regularly. In addition,

216

the school would teach you how to earn a decent living by your art, something by no means easy, I assure you."

"The lady speaks good sense, maister," said Fiona's mother. "You can make your father pay for your studies."

"He will not," Hugh cried in despair. "He hates the notion."

"If I speak to him," I said. "I think perhaps His Lordship might see sense. To you I may appear only as an anxious grandmother, Hugh, but I have certain most eminent connections both in the police force and with the newspapers" (thinking of my other son-in-law, Mathew, who writes for The Times of London). "Lord Balhinnie would not, I am sure, wish for his name to be spread over the broadsheets."

"So will he not be punished for murder then?" exclaimed Fiona.

I shook my head.

"It would," I replied, "be hard to prove that murder was intended. Indeed, I hope and pray it was not. Other charges might be brought of violence and neglect but with a clever advocate His Lordship would most likely be found innocent of all but a father's understandably rash action."

"So we will blackmail him into acceding to my demands," said Hugh with some relish.

"Let us not call it that," I replied. "Gentle persuasion, rather."

To conclude my account rapidly, I can add that everything turned out well enough in the end, excepting of course the horrible death of poor Isla. Alistair was reunited with Judy and John, and no worse for his adventure thanks to the kindness of Fiona and her mother, the which I must add was amply rewarded, Fiona even being given a place in the McPhee household. Mary and Felix took in baby Isla Rose, as she was now known, sad not to have the full adoption they had been hoping for but glad to foster her,

Hugh becoming a familiar and welcome guest at the vicarage. That young man has gone on to show great promise as a genre painter, during his course of study at the Royal College of Art in London, specialising in scenes of urban life. One of his paintings of Edinburgh's old town, indeed, hangs on my wall in Baker Street, a constant reminder of the events described here. As for Lord and Lady Balhinnie, following a brief but pointed conversation I had with them both, they withdrew from society to take up permanent residence in the Scottish Highlands. For all I know, they are there still.

Also from MX Publishing

MX Publishing is the world's largest specialist Sherlock Holmes publisher, with over a hundred titles and fifty authors creating the latest in Sherlock Holmes fiction and non-fiction.

From traditional short stories and novels to travel guides and quiz books, MX Publishing cater for all Holmes fans.

The collection includes leading titles such as *Benedict Cumberbatch In Transition* and *The Norwood Author* which won the 2011 Howlett Award (Sherlock Holmes Book of the Year).

MX Publishing also has one of the largest communities of Holmes fans on Facebook with regular contributions from dozens of authors.

https://www.facebook.com/BooksSherlockHolmes/

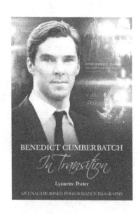

www.mxpublishing.com

CPSIA information can be obtained
at www.ICGtesting.com
Printed in the USA
LVHW031938171019
634538LV00010B/840/P